THE BIG BOOK OF BONDAGE

Also by Alison Tyler

A Is for Amour
Afternoon Delight
B Is for Bondage
Best Bondage Erotica
Best Bondage Erotica, Volume 2
C Is for Coeds
Caught Looking (with Rachel Kramer Bussel)
D Is for Dress-Up
E Is for Exotic
Exposed
F Is for Fetish
Frenzy
G Is for Games
Got a Minute?
H Is for Hardcore
The Happy Birthday Book of Erotica
Heat Wave
Hide and Seek (with Rachel Kramer Bussel)
Hurts So Good
I Is for Indecent
J Is for Jealousy
K Is for Kinky
L Is for Leather
Love at First Sting
Luscious
The Merry XXXmas Book of Erotica
Morning, Noon and Night
Naughty or Nice
Never Have the Same Sex Twice
Open for Business
Playing with Fire
Pleasure Bound
Red Hot Erotica
Slave to Love
Three-Way

THE BIG BOOK OF BONDAGE

SEXY TALES OF EROTIC RESTRAINT

EDITED BY
ALISON TYLER

Published in the United States by Cleis Press, Inc., 2246 Sixth Street, Berkeley, California 94710.

Cover design: Scott Idleman/Blink
Cover photograph: Malek Chamoun/Getty Images
Text design: Frank Wiedemann

First Edition.
10 9 8 7 6 5 4 3 2 1

Trade paper ISBN: 978-1-57344-907-6
E-book ISBN: 978-1-57344-917-5

"We cannot be more sensitive to pleasure
without being more sensitive to pain."

—Alan Watts

Contents

INTRODUCTION

". . . And I guess that's why I like bondage so much," I announced loudly in line at a coffee shop last week. My best friend and I were chatting while waiting for our drinks, and the machine in front of us whirred away at a busy clip. Of course, my sentence was spoken at a higher decibel at the moment when the shop seemed to go unnaturally silent. After all of these years of being a shy pornographer, you'd think I'd learn. Based on the way people turned to look in my direction, I realize that *bondage* remains a buzzword right up there with *fuck* and *anal*. (Try saying *anal* in a public space and see the reactions you get.)

Ah, but you want to know the first part of the conversation, right? The part that led up to me saying "...that's why I like bondage..." right? Well, the answer hasn't changed, not even after having edited anthology upon anthology on the subject. I am fascinated with the sensation of giving up, giving in, of putting one's pleasure (and pain) into the hands of another. To me, bondage means "I trust you to keep me safe," and yet BDSM can also mean "I trust you to hurt me." Ooh, did you get a naughty little shiver from the base of your spine right up to the nape of your neck? I know I did. Because the most important part of bondage, of dominance, of all the slippery ways one can play with those concepts is trust.

But in the BDSM realm, trust involves crops, whips, blindfolds, handcuffs, paddles, belts, gags, and toys.

How deliciously, devilishly twisted is that?

For *The Big Book of Bondage*, I desired stories that delved into what bondage means to different couples. Sure, these couples are fictional, but their fragile emotions, their darkest desires, are as real as any off-the-page lovers you'll find at your favorite club—or even at the coffee shop.

Which isn't the worst place to discuss my favorite kind of kink.

I'll be the silver-streaked girl in the corner, quietly drinking her shot in the dark and wearing the handcuff key on a string around her neck.

XXX,

Alison Tyler

COMMUTER TRAINING

Teresa Noelle Roberts

Daniel sends the texts to her at the same time each workday, right around the time Aileen is shutting down her computer and wrapping things up at the office. All of the messages are fully spelled out, no demeaning the language with abbreviations or numbers substituting for words, typical of Daniel, although unlike the emails he will send her when they're apart for more than the hours of the work day, the texts are utilitarian. No room for flights of the linguistic magic her poet-professor lover can weave. Most of them say the same thing: *See you at the station. I love you.* After three years together, the simple words still make her smile and fill her with warmth, even with heat.

Once or twice a week, though, Daniel adds a command.

Most often it's the simple one: *The usual.*

He sends that text only on days he knows she wore a skirt to work. Because of Daniel, though, she wears skirts often. If it's too cold to go bare-legged, which it often is in Boston, she wears either stockings or tall socks and boots. On *The usual* days, she slips her panties off in the restroom and tucks them into her purse, positioning them, as she knows Daniel wants, so they might spill out or be visible in their pink lace or leopard-spotted satin glory when the conductor checks her commuter rail ticket. It would be easy enough to put her pass in her jacket pocket or on a clip around her neck like many people do, but she doesn't. Instead she's always intentionally clumsy opening her bag. The conductor's never said a word, but a few times she's caught a funny look that suggested the panties were noticed, and got a little thrill, hoping it led the conductor to pleasant, sexy thoughts while riding the Littleton/Fitchburg route for the fifth time that day. She likes to think of it, as Daniel has taught her, as a public service she accidentally-on-purpose provides.

If Boston ever puts pass readers on the commuter lines like they have on the T and busses, this game won't be quite as fun. Still, Aileen would be just as aware of her hidden nakedness, how she is doing Daniel's bidding by secretly baring herself. The odds of flashing through a careless movement are actually small; she doesn't wear very short skirts that might easily reveal her shaved mound and many piercings to unsuspecting seatmates.

Still, the chance is there, and even when she's wearing a calf-length skirt and boots, almost as modest as jeans, some stray draft will remind her she's shed her panties for Daniel.

Sometimes the closing-time text, instead of *The usual*, says *Skirt up*. Those nights, Aileen sits, in a careful simulacrum of carelessness, with her skirt tucked up behind her, her bare ass and thighs against the aged vinyl, which, winter or summer, is cool yet sticky. It's much harder not to reveal herself on those days, hard not to flash her seatmates or the people across the aisle. It's harder yet to conceal her growing lust, the need Daniel's instilled in her from a distance. Sometimes, when Daniel orders her to sit this way, she leaves a slick of moisture on the seat, a trail betraying the whereabouts of an aroused woman.

And then there are the unexpected days. She never knows exactly what Daniel will demand when he's struck by a whimsy of desire, but over the years, they've worked out a set of options that she can easily pull off in the restroom at the office before getting on the train. By now Aileen keeps a hidden arsenal in her prodigious purse.

Today, the text comes in just when she expects it. Its contents are a surprise, but not entirely. *Nipple clips and balls. I love you.*

Aileen's coworkers think she's a pack rat, that she carries paperbacks and snacks and a makeup kit worthy of Hollywood in her voluminous red purse. It's partly true, though she's long since switched to a Kindle instead of the three or four books she used to carry in case of train breakdowns and other emergencies. The bag that looks like a makeup kit, however, contains mascara and one lonely red lipstick.

The rest of its secret contents, the things she takes care not to spill out when she actually puts on lipstick and mascara in the women's room, are supplies for Daniel's closing-time texts. A clit clip with decorative beads. Crotchless panties, ridiculous when she so often goes without panties anyway, but Daniel occasionally likes the look, and the fact that they're slightly uncomfortable, rubbing on her pussy lips in a way that both irritates and, as a constant reminder of Daniel, arouses. A remote-control vibrating egg for her to bury deep in a cunt wet with knowing it's under command. The remote function doesn't have much range, so she knows Daniel will pick her up at the train station and probably take her out somewhere where he can delight and torment and embarrass her by bringing her to the verge of orgasm in public. Another vibe, this one with batteries, to use on herself before she leaves the office restroom. A garter belt, to go with the fishnets, both black and red, and outrageous black stockings with a rhinestone seam and Cuban heels—any of those might mean he'll be taking her out to dinner, or simply that he'll be taking her, as soon as she sets her purse down and is stripped to nothing but the garter belt and stockings. Bunny ears— that's one of Daniel's more unusual kinks, and one she finds secretly giggle-inducing. Still, his reaction when she walks in the door wearing them is well worth the odd looks she gets on the train. She might not understand the fascination, but she can certainly appreciate that he's fascinated.

The items she seeks this afternoon in the cramped white stall are silvery tweezer clips connected by a chain, and silicone ben wa balls.

Her breath catches as she takes the toys out, sets them on top of the toilet paper holder.

Her clit is already throbbing.

This set of toys is tricky. She'll have to work fast to catch the train because she can't leave her desk too soon no matter how complex Daniel's instructions are, and if she misses the 5:45 she'll have to wait at North Station with her nipples on fire and her cunt constantly teased for forty minutes before the next train home. The train ride's long enough to be exquisite torture with the toys in place, bur that additional wait turns it to torture pure and simple.

Acting fast, Aileen strips her sweater half-off, leaving it around her neck. She shucks her red bra and shoves it into the depths of her purse.

The restroom is warm enough that the women in the office joke about saunas and cut-rate tropical vacations when they head there, but Aileen's nipples stiffen as if the air is icy.

No, they stiffen as if Daniel is watching her undress, as if Daniel's long-fingered hands with the sprinkling of freckles are picking up the clips, as if Daniel, not Aileen, is pinching those pink nipples to make them even harder and more prominent.

Desire shoots through her, cuttingly sharp yet melting. Her hands want to linger on the softness of her own breasts. The temptation to draw out the caressing, to feel that surge of lust, is almost impossible to resist. Her already stiff nipples harden some more. She started getting wet as soon as she read the text and started imagining carrying out the instructions. Now, actually doing so, she's flooding, the damp pressure of her red cotton hipsters, which she hadn't noticed all day, suddenly an erotic torture. Aileen twists her nipples, telling herself it's just to make sure she's ready for the clips, and stifles a soft moan at the pleasure-pain.

No. Time presses, the commuter rail doesn't wait for distracted perverts, and she's lucky no one's waiting yet for the occupied stall. Everyone wants to use the bathroom at this time of day, before getting on the T or commuter rail or beginning a walk to home.

She puts the right clip on and slides it to just the right degree of tightness, enough that she can feel it pressing snug and safe, but not so much that it will turn to agony before she gets home. Then the left. She's biting her lip now, letting that small pain help her think through the delicious pain in her nipples. She lets the chain go then, hisses at the shock of its coolness against her heated skin. Too good. There's no way she's going to make it home this time without coming. One jounce of the train might finish her, and she doesn't even have the ben wa balls in yet.

God, the ben wa balls! She has to take care of those quickly. Aileen pulls her sweater down carefully over the clips, aware as she wasn't before how the silk-cotton blend is both soft and ever so slightly abrasive. Then she eases her panties down.

Maybe she should have taken care of the ben wa balls first. The chain between the clips sways as she moves, tormenting her further. By the time she actually gets the panties into her hand, she has to use them to blot cunt juices from her upper thighs, shuddering with need as she does.

It's easier to throw the panties out than stow the sodden bit of fabric in her purse.

Aileen smiles. She'll have to tell Daniel about how she wished she'd carried out his commands in a different order because she was making herself even more crazy, how she'd thrown out a perfectly good pair of panties because they were too wet to carry home in her bag without making her wallet smell like rut. Daniel loves to know he can make her lose her mind even when he's not with her, drive her wild with desire when he's miles away teaching or working on his book or making dinner. Hearing it will make him even harder than he'll be from knowing she's wearing nipple clips and filled with a toy for him.

She'll send him a text on the train to tell him, she decides.

Her hands are unsteady as she opens the little brocade-covered box that holds the ben wa balls. She puts one foot up on the toilet seat, even though there's someone going into the other stall who might glance down and wonder what she's doing.

The ben wa balls aren't very large in her hand, but they feel surprisingly huge inside her, much bigger than she remembers them. She's that swollen, she figures, that full of need and desire.

She wants to stay in that stall a few stolen moments, swaying back and forth to feel the balls' subtle pressure, maybe playing with herself. Instead, she pulls her skirt down, zips her leather jacket, and heads off to the train.

Her preparations have taken long enough that she has to break into a jog to make it to the train on time. Each step tugs the clips on her delightfully tender nipples, sways the cool chain against her rib cage, shifts the ben wa balls so they tease places deep inside her. Each step reminds her, as if she could forget, how wet she is and how sensitive and swollen her clit has become. Each step reminds her how Daniel will have his hands under her clothes while they're still at the station. She'll probably have her first orgasm before they're out of the line of traffic waiting to leave the parking lot. Ten minutes later they'll be home, and ten minutes after that—or less if they just fall on each other in the foyer—he'll be inside her.

She's one of the last people to make it onto the train before they shut the doors. She must look wild eyed, maybe feverish, because the conductor, a short, tired gray-haired man with a face like a rumpled sock, asks her if she's all right. "Just ran for the train," she says, and since it's true as far as it goes, and she's a little out of breath, he nods and waves her on.

She squeezes into a seat more than half-occupied by a large man in hospital scrubs, pale with exhaustion. He sprawls into sleep before the train reaches Porter Square in Cambridge, only minutes from North Station. Like a cat, her seatmate seems to expand as he relaxes. Even the heat of the stranger's not terribly attractive body, the heat of his flesh pressing against her thigh and side, adds to Aileen's spiraling arousal.

One hour. It takes one hour and ten stops to get home, where Daniel will meet her at the station.

At the fourth stop, she sends him a text: *Balls before clips next time. You owe me new red panties. Agent Provocateur?*

The panties were actually from Kohl's, cute but inexpensive. She figures Daniel knows she wouldn't throw out any of her few bits of high-end lingerie, but it's worth a try. If nothing else, they'll enjoy an afternoon in Boston browsing through the elegantly naughty store.

Predictably, she gets a text back: *Provocateur? Name the date!*

She responds, simply: *After payday.* She knows how budget-be-damned they get around great lingerie.

The track needs work, and there are places where the ride is rough, making her even more aware of the balls inside her, of Daniel's orders, of the way she obeys him because it brings them both wild joy. Each time the train stops or starts—and there are inevitably extra, unscheduled stops and starts tonight between stations—the nipple clips sway and the balls shift subtly, and Aileen feels it as a gift both from Daniel and for him.

At the ninth stop, the one before she'll be safe in the car with Daniel, the train lurches and grinds into the station, jolting the clips painfully/blissfully. Aileen's body can't take any more. Her stomach muscles flutter, her cunt contracts, and the top of her head seems to dissolve as sensation overwhelms her. She has to fake a coughing spasm to cover the real spasms of her orgasm.

As she leans back on the seat, red-faced and trembling with the aftermath, Aileen curses Daniel and blesses him at the same time. He's insane, expecting her to do this kind of thing for him, and she's just as insane to go along with it. But she wouldn't wish for either of them to be cured of this madness.

SMALL MERCIES

Rita Winchester

T ake them off. Please," I whispered.

"Nope. I won't."

"Why not?" I twisted in the wind, basically. Not that I was outside; I was in our bedroom tied to the shelf in our walk-in closet. My arms sang with stiffness and I shifted again, my pussy so wet that I was barely thinking straight.

Twin nipple clamps bit into the tender flesh. They looked like little black steampunk alligators. Jaws designed to cause a good amount of pain but inflict very little damage. Any damage they produced would fade in minutes to hours. But at the moment, my pulse was pounding away, a savage drumbeat, between my thighs.

"Say your word," Jack said.

I sighed. "Red?"

"Is that a question?" he asked, smirking.

"Um…" Damn, damn, damn; my mind raced. I could *never* remember my safeword. Jack's theory was that if I truly wanted things to stop, I'd remember.

My eyes roamed the room. He always left a reminder of the word somewhere. The problem was we traveled a lot, and every room in our home was packed full of art and trinkets and…stuff.

"I'm waiting. And I'm getting annoyed," Jack said. He touched my clit with the grip end of his nasty black crop.

I had that terror to deal with, but in the back of my mind I pondered what would come *after the crop*… Could I do it?

"It's *red*," I said, nodding. My eyes had settled on a red batik wall hanging.

"Wrong," he said, nudging the nipple clamps with the grip of the crop. The pressure caused a biting pain to shoot through my nipples. Between my legs, the wet flex of my sex became even more distracting.

Jack took his time walking around me. He prodded my rib with the crop tip and I jumped. Then he slid the business end down the ladder of my spine, slipping it between my asscheeks before dragging it lower down the backs of my thighs. Every time he slowed or paused, I braced myself for the blow…and then he moved on. He reached my calves, stroking me with the slender crop, and just when I sagged a little, wondering if he was *ever* going to do this thing, he delivered. The blow fell along the meat of my right asscheek.

"Jesus fucking Christ on a hobby horse!" I hissed.

"Silence, Virginia, unless perhaps you want to say your word?"

"It's not *red*?" I blurted.

Another sharp snap of the crop, this time across the left cheek. A few tears slipped free of my blinking eyes, but my pussy was wetter than I could remember.

"If you wanted this to end, dear, you'd remember your damn word," he said, pressing his lips to the back of my neck. The pressure right at the nape made the fine hair along my scalp bristle. A shiver shook me from top to toe.

"I…"

"You what?"

"I'm sorry?" I said. After all, it was my stupidity that had me in this bind. It was I who'd told his boss he didn't leave work early on Wednesdays to go to physical therapy anymore but to hit a bucket of balls and unwind. I was the one who, at a dinner party, had informed the boss that Jack's shoulder injury had been rectified *months ago*.

"Is that a question?" he asked for the second time today. Then he laid the crop down right across the flesh of my ass, spanning both cheeks and the crack. I jumped and sobbed simultaneously. I could feel that skin rise up like a candy cane stripe of flesh. The red would accent nicely to my lily-white ass, I knew. I could picture it, and after all was said and done—after the fucking, the soothing and more apologies on my part, he'd take me into the hallway, give me a mirror and show me his handiwork. And it would get me wet and then...he'd fuck me again.

I was eager to get to that part. However...you had to walk through the fire to get to the other side. Or something like that.

"I'm sorry!" I really did feel like a shit for telling on him. I should have realized that he was simply carving out some time for himself alone. That it was a small white lie and he'd eventually stop doing it. My god. Why hadn't I just kept my big mouth shut?

I twisted in the cuffs that loop through the overhead shelf and hoped, as I always do, that I wouldn't manage to bring six hundred pounds of handbags, belts and sweaters down on my head.

Jack made his way around me and stared me down. Big dark eyes—almost black—flashed with annoyance but yes, also, arousal. His cock was hard in his trousers, and I could see his pulse jumping like a small fish trapped under his skin.

He wanted to fuck me. I just needed to remember that.

"Say it again, Virginia."

"I'm sorry. I'm so, so, so sorry," I babbled. My eyes darted around the room, though. Just in case I needed my word. I really had pissed him off this time. So much so that he'd delayed this punishment because Jack believes you never do this bondage thing—that's what he calls it—truly angry. So at least I knew he wasn't truly angry…anymore.

"Good." He gave a nod. "I forgive you, little girl." He nudged the nipple clamps again with the grip of the crop and I gasped. I had almost forgotten those horrible things. The sting in my ass had distracted me. But he'd provoked them, and they seemed to be biting into my skin ten times harder than before.

"Please," I moaned.

He reached out and unclipped one single clamp. First he ran the tip of the crop over my nipple, and when I sighed at the pleasantly painful feel of restored blood flow, he leaned in to lick the flushed tip. "Small mercies, Virginia. That was one."

He left the other clamp and circled me again.

I squawked, I'm embarrassed to admit, like a chicken. Horny, irate and truly sorry. Couldn't he see that in me?

"Like I said, small mercies, take them when you can. I took that clamp off, but you still owe me seven blows. I wanted ten, you only gave me three."

"I…you…" I stammered frantically. My eyes were leaking tears I didn't want to shed.

"Hush," he said. And then the crop bit me on the ass, laying a new line of red flesh over a parcel that was just starting to calm down from his last blow.

"What was that?" Jack asked.

"Four," I whispered, my voice hitching.

Five was hard and six was a bit less. By seven, eight and nine, I could tell he had backed off some, but my ass still throbbed like a giant heartbeat. Between my legs I was beyond wet. I was slippery, to be honest. I could feel the slide of fluid at the top of my thighs. The full and urgent feeling of a pussy that needed to be filled.

He pushed himself up against me. His cock was out and hard, pressing to the seam of my ass. He'd take me this way so that every thrust would brush my tender flesh and remind me.

"Yes," I whispered, beyond ready. "Yes, yes, please…"

His lips brushed over my neck and shoulders and he speared me with three fingers, feeling how wet I was, *tsking* like he was ashamed of me when secretly he was thrilled.

He gripped my hips and moved me just so and then he drove into me, shaking my handcuffs and making me sob for other reasons this time. Good ones. I came almost immediately, my pussy gripping his thrusting cock and capturing each bit of friction he offered.

He wouldn't last long, I could tell by the way he was breathing. By the grunts and the sighs and the restless whisper of his fingers on the meat of my hips. And then he reached around and took the end of the clamp in his fingers, tugged without releasing me. Stretching my fragile flesh and making pain slither under my skin.

Jack whispered "Small mercies" and thrust hard and high. He opened the jaws and set my nipple free. I came when he gently stroked my skin. He thrust once more, getting himself deep enough to lift me up off my feet a little.

His lips on the back of my neck, my body humming with the aftermath of orgasm. Small spasms of joy deep inside me. He kissed me once more and moved to uncuff me.

"So what *is* my safeword?" I asked.

Jack chuckled as he released my arms. "You chose it, Virginia." He shook his head. "But I stand by my theory. If you ever need it, you'll remember."

THE NAUGHTY CHAIR

Donna George Storey

The naughty chair was one of the most unremarkable pieces of furniture Jillian had ever seen. It was made of oak, square and squat with two wooden slats across the back and a worn upholstered seat of a blue material that resembled burlap. Zach had inherited his dining set from the apartment's last tenant. Three of the chairs were of a matching black plastic minimalist design from IKEA, making the naughty chair, despite its homeliness, the most comfortable of the lot. This was why Zach insisted she enjoy its comforts when he hosted her for meals. And this was why she was sitting on the chair the very day it earned its name.

Zach was fully dressed because he'd just run down to the corner café for bagels and lattes. Jillian was naked under his terrycloth bathrobe, which she'd purposely tied to show some cleavage. Fresh from Sunday morning wake-up sex, their glowing eyes and knowing smiles suggested round two was soon to follow. Jillian turned her chair toward Zach and lounged back, extending one bare foot to rest on his blue-jeaned thigh. He squeezed her toes in his large, warm hand, but she couldn't help but notice how uncomfortable he looked in that rigid, straight-backed Scandinavian chair.

"Do you want to finish eating in bed?" she suggested.

"Well, I was planning to finish by eating *you* in bed." Zach wiggled his eyebrows.

"Why wait?" Jillian replied. She envisioned an immediate shift from the dining room to a picnic on his futon, but Zach interpreted her words differently. He nudged her foot from his leg and fell to his knees before her. Looping his hands under her thighs, he opened her legs, tugged at her belt and let the robe fall open around her.

Giggling in surprise, Jillian glanced guiltily toward the dining room window. The faded lace curtains would probably hide them from all but the most prying eyes, but the very *thought* that someone might see made her blush.

"Not here, Zach."

Smiling mischievously, he bent over and planted a kiss on her brown curls, right above her clit.

She let out a squeal and tried to get up off the chair. While the idea of someone watching made her belly clench with dark pleasure, she'd never been as bold in her actions as in her fantasies.

"Give me two minutes, Jillian. If you don't want me to continue after that, I'll stop."

She nodded, not wanting to seem prudish so early on in a promising relationship. Yet no sooner had he lavished one long, slow lick along her cleft than she instinctively put her hands on his shoulders and pushed him away. Zach sat back on his heels and narrowed his eyes.

"Naughty girl. This time I want you to hold on to the edges of the chair. Tightly. So you won't sabotage my efforts."

To her own surprise, Jillian obeyed, curling her fingers around the cool, oaken edges of the chair seat. Oddly, the sensation of the sturdy wood soothed her, making her feel grounded and safe.

Zach made no move to continue. He seemed to be enjoying the view. *If he only has two minutes, why is he just staring?* Then it struck her that there was no clock in the room, nor were either of them wearing a watch.

"Look, you're so excited, you've already made my robe damp," he murmured.

She let out a soft "oh" of embarrassment as her right hand reflexively moved to cover herself.

Clicking his tongue, Zach grabbed her wrist and moved her hand back to the edge of the chair. "One more slipup and I'm going out to my car to get some rope to tie your hands to this damned chair."

Jillian's body jerked as if she'd been slapped. Yet the image of Josh marching back into the apartment with a coil of golden rope made her cheeks flame and her vagina flutter.

"But you won't make me do that, will you, Jillian? You're going to be a very good girl and cooperate. Because you know you want this."

Jillian squirmed, but she dutifully kept her hands clenched around the edges of the chair. She wasn't quite sure how he got the idea she wanted him to eat her pussy in front of the window, but his game was arousing her intensely. Her breasts were flushed, her belly churned with lust and her clit was impossibly stiff, as if it were preening before his gaze like a tiny cock.

"You do want it, don't you, Jillian?"

She whimpered and bit her lip.

"Tell me you want me to lick your tasty twat right here on my dining room chair until you come so hard you scream."

Zach had whispered dirty things to her in bed before, but this was different. His bold words seemed to slither up inside her, hot and hard and nasty.

"Say it, darling. Say you want this." His voice was softer now, almost pleading.

He was right, she *did* want it. She opened her mouth to speak. "I..." She tried again. "I want..." Her throat closed up around the shameful confession.

"I understand," Zach said. "It's hard for a woman to admit these desires out loud. But as long as you hold on tight to the chair, I'll know I should keep going. As soon as you let go, I'll stop. The power is in your hands."

Her fingers clutched the chair tighter. She closed her eyes. It was as if she were at the crest of a roller coaster, waiting for the bottom to drop out.

Hot breath tickled her thighs. Then a gentle hiss of air caressed her vulva.

"Good girl. You're showing them you want it. All the people looking in at us through the window with their binoculars. Now, if I did tie you to the chair, they might think I was forcing you. But this is voluntary bondage. One woman's struggle between her desire and her inhibition. It's really something to watch. I wonder which side will win?"

His low, insinuating voice made sweat rise all over Jillian's body. Strange how these words alone could inflame her desire, creating an obscene picture of voyeuristic neighbors across the alley—a gray-templed man in a Hawaiian shirt, a housewife still glowing from her weekend morning yoga class—studying her wanton sexual display through big, sporty binoculars, their own hands creeping between their legs.

Zach started in again, flicking her clit with lazy, catlike motions. At first, she was still able to worry— faintly—that someone could actually see them. As he picked up the tempo, pleasure overtook caution. The pressure on her hands set her arms tingling with the strain. Gradually the sensation moved into her chest, her torso, swirling down to meet the thrumming pleasure of his mouth on her sweet spot. With each breath the feeling grew, until her whole body was like a buzzing clit. She felt the telltale pressure of an orgasm deep in her core, but she didn't want to come yet. This taut, raw feeling was too delicious.

Still, it took all the willpower she had to pry her hand from the chair and touch his shoulder.

He pulled back, smacking his lips. "Had enough?"

"No, I didn't mean stop…" She faltered.

"But you just asked me to stop. Those were the rules."

She opened her eyes and gazed straight into his. Then she deliberately curled her fingers around the edge of the chair again.

"Ho, ho, it's not as easy as that. You have to pay a forfeit." He wasn't smiling, but his eyes danced with amusement.

"What kind of forfeit?"

He paused.

"Tell me you want it, Jillian."

Why was this so difficult? After all, it was just a few simple words. She'd already *done* worse, exposing herself to any stranger with a view of the window. "I want it," she said softly.

"Even with the whole neighborhood watching?" he teased.

Jillian's throat tightened. This was still the shame for her—and the thrill.

"I…want them to see me come," she choked out.

"Right, then. Let's give them a good show."

His tongue slipped into the magic groove to the right

of her clitoral hood while his hands slid up over her belly to take her nipples between his fingers. Using the chair as an anchor, Jillian pushed her breasts forward provocatively as if she were a stripper performing the headliner show. She closed her eyes again.

There behind her eyelids she could see *them*. Her audience. Watching her. Watching her body twist and tremble with their desperate, hungry stares. She pressed her fingers into the chair with such force, she was sure she would leave a permanent mark on the wood.

Just then Zach pinched her nipples hard, tipping her over the edge.

She bellowed as she came, her thighs jerking, her hands milking the edge of the chair in time with her contractions.

Zach pulled her to the carpet and wrapped her in his arms. "Oh, my god, you are so hot. I'm taking you to bed right now to make you come again on my cock."

"Why not here?" she asked with a playful frown. "Don't *you* have the nerve to perform for your neighbors?"

He grinned back. "The couple in the next house over are on vacation. I saw them get into an airport van yesterday."

She had to laugh as he led her back to the bedroom. He might have told her a little lie for fun, but he did keep his promise to make her come again—twice—before the afternoon was over.

* * *

Jillian didn't visit Zach's apartment again for several days. He stayed over at her condo a few times that week instead. Although her place was more upscale—Zach worked at a new-age pharmacy and was studying for his acupuncture license—Jillian actually preferred the Bohemian charm of his Noe Valley fourplex. On Friday night, they finally went back to his apartment after hanging out at a club downtown. Zach retreated to his galley kitchen to get them both glasses of cold water to take the edge off of the martinis.

This left Jillian alone in the darkened dining room with the chair.

There it is—the naughty chair.

A pang of lust shot through her. She and Zach had already decided to sleep off the liquor and make love in the morning, but suddenly Jillian wanted it *now*. On that chair. She crossed her arms over her tingling nipples. Of course, she was being ridiculous. It was just a chair. A perfectly plain, old, boring chair. Not in the least naughty—why had she just given it that name? If it were fitted out with black leather straps and fixtures to attach self-twirling dildos and vibrating butt plugs, maybe her arousal would be justified. She must be drunker than she thought to react so strongly. Giving the chair a dismissive scowl, she followed Zach to bed.

The next morning Jillian awoke to the smell of coffee and fresh oranges.

"You were sleeping so soundly, I thought I'd make us

breakfast first to fuel up," Zach said cheerfully. Another advantage of staying over with him was that he always insisted on playing the proper host.

Rubbing her eyes, Jillian wandered into the dining room to find a place set out for her in front of the naughty chair. Her pulse leaped. *This is absolutely ridiculous. A chair can't make me do anything I don't want to do.* Defiantly she settled herself on the burlap seat. It felt oddly warm against her buttocks, and softer than she remembered—as if she were sitting on a cushion of flesh.

Over Zach's eggs and toast and fruit salad, Jillian managed to fake her way through a discussion of the jazz combo they'd heard the night before. But she still couldn't stop thinking about the chair. The way she screamed and thrashed as she climaxed on Zach's mouth. Her own wrists, bound with a rope that snaked under the chair to keep her in place, so that she was forced to endure more indignities at his pleasure. Then she pictured Zach kneeling between her legs, this time to slide his cock in and out of her until his pubic hair was frothy with her juices.

The seat of the chair began to pulse beneath her.

"Something the matter?" Zach asked with concern.

"Ah, well, I was just remembering our breakfast last Sunday."

He smiled.

"It's weird, though. It's like this chair remembers it, too."

Zach didn't laugh as she feared he might. "Maybe it does. It was pretty memorable."

"Speaking of last week…"

"Yes?"

Jillian swallowed. Then again, Zach did say he liked it when she talked about sex. "Do you really have rope in your car?"

The flicker in his eyes made her stomach do a little flip.

"No, I made that up. It felt right at the time. I hope you don't mind."

"Oh, no. I was just wondering if…if you'd ever tied anyone up for real."

To her surprise, he blushed. "I've dabbled in it. Panty-hose, scarves. Once I buckled my belt around a woman's knees, and then I… Well, as I said, I messed around a bit, but I'm no expert."

"Oh, that's fine," she said, a bit too quickly. Silence settled over the table. She shifted in her seat. "Okay, Zach, I have to ask you something else."

"Shoot."

"Will *you* sit on this chair for a while? I swear there's some energy happening here. Or else I'm still messed up from last night and totally hallucinating."

"Sure, let's switch. I'll give you my professional opinion. Energy flow is my specialty."

This was yet another advantage of dating a new-age guy—you got the inside scoop on auras and meridians and things like that. Yet when the exchange of chairs was done, she felt a bit silly sitting in his rigid, unexpressive chair while he sat in hers, his head tilted and lips pursed as if he really were making a diagnosis.

"I don't feel anything yet," he said, "but let's give it some time. Since we're on the topic, may I ask you if you've had experience with bondage?"

"Just pictures and a couple of articles. And, well, last week with you, although that might not count. You didn't actually tie me up."

"Oh, that definitely counts. Bondage is more about the head space than the actual ropes." He took a sip of coffee, as if they were discussing the weather.

His nonchalance made her bold. "Have you ever been…tied up by a woman?"

Zach shrugged. "Officially, yes, but there wasn't much psychological punch. It's not easy to top, especially for beginners."

"Maybe that's why it's a profession? I read in a magazine that lots of powerful men pay a dominatrix to tie them up and 'torture' them because they're tired of bossing everyone around and want a rest."

He frowned. "That strikes me as a little too easy an explanation. Masters of the universe are as trapped by their positions in society as the little guy. I worked on a fair number when I was a masseur at an overpriced spa a few years ago—their bodies are a wreck."

"Because of all those sessions in dungeons?"

He snorted. "They'd be more relaxed if they were having that much fun. I have a different theory. I think

BDSM isn't only about reversing roles. Sometimes it intensifies conflicts that are already there. Being rich and powerful is a kind of prison, but they can't admit that, even to themselves. It's the pure honesty of the scene that gets them off."

"But why was it so effective for me? I'm not a powerful man."

"You're pretty important at work, aren't you?" Zach lifted an eyebrow. "Actually I have another theory about you."

"Do you now, Doctor?"

"Women are told they're sluts if they express sexual desire outside of marriage and the missionary position. Only a total slut would give a cunnilingus show to the neighbors, right? I pushed you a little—to enjoy yourself. Apparently you did."

She couldn't exactly argue with him there. "And what about you?"

Zach glanced down at his lap. Jillian recognized his "I'm getting a boner" smirk. "Well, I think you might be right about this chair."

"Good, it's not just me," she said.

"Or it could be that talking about bondage and domination with a smart, beautiful woman is simply a total turn-on for me."

"It's the chair, I'm telling you. I never came so hard in my life. Maybe just sitting on it isn't enough? Maybe you have to have an orgasm there to feel a real connection?"

Zach's broad grin suggested he agreed.

Jillian's eyes wandered down to the oaken edge of the chair seat peeping coyly out around his thighs. Taunting her. Challenging her.

Without a word, she rose, closed the curtains and went to get her pantyhose from the bedroom.

"May I tie your hands to the chair?" she asked, keeping her tone as even as she could.

He nodded, a cool smile playing over his lips. "All right."

"Hold the edges tight."

Zach did as he was told. Jillian wrapped one leg of the pantyhose around his thick wrist and tied it in a square knot. "Not too tight?"

"Oh, no." He still seemed perfectly at ease.

She pulled the pantyhose underneath the seat of the chair and secured his other wrist using the other leg.

"Let's pull down your pants," she said. "I want to watch your cock get hard."

Only then did a flush creep over his cheeks. Jillian was surprised at the surge of pleasure in her belly. Maybe she *could* be as wild in her actions as in her fantasies? Before she could lose her nerve, she knelt before him and loosened the tie of his pajama pants. He obligingly lifted his hips and she pulled them down to his ankles. He was already erect, of course, but she knew he could get harder. Indeed, before her eyes, his penis twitched higher, like a gentleman rising in the presence of a lady.

She stood and gave him a leisurely once-over. She was enjoying this side of it more than she expected. She fixed her eyes on his cock.

"We both know it's hard for a woman to express her sexuality honestly, but I can see it's sometimes so very, very hard to be a man, too."

Zach glanced down at his hard-on with amusement, but seemed to know it was not his place to reply.

"You poor men. You're surrounded by attractive women, strangers you'll never touch, but oh, how they taunt you with their pretty faces and their full breasts straining against their blouses and sweaters. As if they're just begging to be cupped and caressed and kissed by your hungry lips. These women look so innocent, so unaware, but they know what they're doing. They plan it out in their bedrooms—the low-cut tops that show off the shadowy valley between their tits, the tight skirts that hug their full, round, fuckable asses. They do it all on purpose to see the helpless look of longing in your eyes. They do it just to make you hard."

Zach sighed and shifted in the chair. The veins in his cock seemed to throb, and the head was now swollen to a shiny, purplish-red hue.

"Am I right, Zach? Do you get turned on by attractive women? Do you imagine them naked and get stiff in your pants?"

He nodded and looked away.

"Don't you want to see me naked?"

His eyes darted back to her face. The eagerness in his

expression was answer enough. Jillian inched the collar of the bathrobe down over her shoulders. Her breasts tumbled free. She cradled them and flicked the nipples with her thumbs.

His face was deeply flushed now, and his fingers tightened around the chair.

"Girls aren't supposed to touch themselves, but they do," she cooed. "I'm a very naughty girl. After our first date, remember? You were so *respectful* that you didn't even kiss me good night. But I was bad. I was so hot for you, I went to bed and masturbated. I said your name over and over when I came."

"Oh, god, Jillian."

"Do you want to see what I did that night? Should I reenact the scene right here in front of you? You know how much I like to be watched."

Zach made a funny sound in his throat.

She smiled and let the robe fall to the floor. His eyes glinted with a silvery light as they traveled up and down her body.

"How am I doing for my first time? Is there enough *punch*?"

"Actually, you're doing very well," he whispered.

"Thanks. But maybe I'll save the self-love exhibition for next time. Because today I want to make you come in the naughty chair. I could give you a blow job, but I'm a selfish girl. I want to come, too."

Jillian stepped in front of the chair and turned her back to him. Straddling his thighs, she took his shaft in her hand and guided the knob to her entrance. Then she lowered herself onto him as if she were merely sitting in his lap.

Zach let out a groan.

"Don't have too much fun yet. You aren't allowed to come until I'm satisfied. That's what a gentleman does, right? So just hold tight to the chair and let it happen. Feel the energy."

She rested her left elbow on the table to support herself, then dipped her right hand between her legs.

"I'm using you for my pleasure, just like a horny, sex-crazed man uses a woman. I'm *using* your body," she chanted.

"Yes," he whispered. "*Use* me."

"Remember, all you can do is sit there and stay hard."

"I will," he breathed.

Jillian tweaked her nipple with her free hand and strummed her clit faster, rocking back and forth on Zach's lap. He was part of the chair now, a tool for her pleasure. His cock felt harder and thicker than ever, pushing into soft, new places inside her, like her own custom-ordered sex toy. She tightened her walls around him, raising herself, then sliding back down again and again.

Soon she felt the orgasm rising, up from the fleshy seat of his thighs, fanning out through her belly. She grunted and cupped her mons as her body shuddered around his cock. He grunted, too, and began thrusting into her, his hands still firmly riveted to the chair. She braced herself against the table, letting him use her in return. She smiled as he came with a long, low howl.

They rested there together for a moment, enjoying the glow.

"Okay, I definitely felt something," he said lazily.

"See, isn't the naughty chair amazing?" she asked over her shoulder, still perched on top of him.

He planted a kiss on her back. "I can't deny it, but I have to point out this was just a plain old chair until you came along. I think there's something special going on between you two."

"Are you jealous?"

"A little, but I'm glad you're bringing out the best in each other. Just don't do anything too wild without me."

A few months later, when his lease came up, Jillian invited Zach to move in with her. The very first thing he unloaded from his hatchback was the naughty chair.

It didn't exactly fit with her Mission dining room suite, but she immediately placed it at the head of the table.

Homely as it is, it's still her favorite place to sit to this day.

ELEVEN O'CLOCK DEADLINE

Thomas S. Roche

Karen didn't freak out when she heard the door to the office open and close. She often worked this late; she knew the cleaning guys were still in the building. She also knew that if Chad came by to pick her up and found parking, he might sneak in through the back entrance—which the cleaning guys always left propped open—and come up to get her in person.

So when the door went *click-hiss-ker-chunk*, she didn't even look up from the copying she was doing—documents for Phoenix, almost done and still with an hour to make the eleven P.M. West Coast FedEx deadline.

Karen was starting to relax—the stress melting out of her, helped along appreciably by the half-drunk beer on the cutting table next to her. The beer, like the other thirty or forty beers stuffed into the overflow refrigerator in the utility room, was left over from the holiday party. It was actually not the half a beer that helped Karen relax so much as the two that had gone before it, however; their bottles were now meticulously rinsed out and placed in the office recycling bin. Between the beers and the sheer exhaustion, she was feeling pretty loose and ready to be done with this terrible day. But she was eager to finish her copying before Chad buzzed her cell phone to tell her he was downstairs on the street. She was so busy, in fact, that she didn't even bother to look over her shoulder to see who was in the office with her.

So when she felt one big heavy hand in her hair and another grabbing her wrist, she might have freaked out a little bit. She screamed.

Then she heard Chad's hot, familiar growl in her ear. It was his *bad* voice, equal parts red wine and dark chocolate…and the scream died in her throat.

He told her, "Don't move a muscle. Don't fight. Don't struggle, and don't you *dare* scream again, lady. Do exactly what I tell you to, or you'll be sorry."

The scream turned into a moan, then a whine.

Karen said, "Chad, what are you doing? The cleaning guys are still here! They could come in…"

Chad growled: "I'm counting on it. Think they'd like to see me fuck you? Or do you think they'd like a piece? If you're a good girl, I'll think about giving them one…"

Karen's body rippled with sensation. Her knees felt weak. She was helpless.

Chad moved like lightning. He acted like he had done this a thousand times, or planned it extensively in his head. Maybe both. His hand came out of her hair and seized her other wrist. Pinning both of her wrists together in the small of her back was easy for a man with such big hands. In fact, all of this was easy—Karen was 5'3" and Chad 6'2". He had a big, broad, bulky muscled form, and she had the lithe shape of an athlete who went for speed. He power-lifted; she ran. But she wasn't running now—she couldn't. Wouldn't have wanted to if she could, except for the voice in her head that said, "No, this is wrong! Not at the office..."

...And the voice in her pussy, far more seductive, that said, *No, don't, Sir, don't hurt me, Sir, I'll do everything you tell me to.* That voice didn't want her to run, either...it wanted her to *spread.*

Chad made that part easy, the way he practically picked her up by her wrist and her hair and manhandled her over to the cutting table. It hadn't been a cutting table for as long as Karen had worked here; most documents had gone virtual, so the cutter was on its side, tucked between the copier and the wall. The table was naked except for a few reams of paper she'd set there in case the copier ran dry.

The cutting table had very sturdy legs.

Chad kicked her feet to the base of them, forcibly spreading her. She tried to squirm and struggle;

he responded by slapping her ass, hard, right through her straight wool skirt. She gasped and squirmed some more. He spanked her again, pinning her to the table.

She purred out, "I'll scream for help," and he spanked her harder, bringing a sudden flush of heat up and down her legs.

"I wouldn't advise that," said Chad, and spanked her again, harder than ever.

She squealed. She squirmed and tried to close her legs; he kicked them apart again with his big black boots and pinned her to the table with his knee so he could control her while his big hands circled her wrists with rope.

He tied her wrists quick, and very tight. She struggled, her pussy going wet as she felt how securely she was bound. When Chad was done securing her wrists, he grabbed her hair again, pulling her head back roughly.

His other hand came around with a ball gag.

"I'll scream," she purred.

He forced her mouth open easily and shoved the ball gag in. He buckled it tightly behind her cascade of long blond hair.

"Now you won't," he said roughly, still holding her hair. His hand disappeared and came back with a blindfold; seeing it, Karen grunted and squealed behind the gag, but it was too late for her to put up more than a cursory struggle. How Chad learned to put a blindfold on a girl one-handed with such incredible fluency, Karen would never know—but an instant later, she was blindfolded and bent over with her ass in the air and a ball gag in her mouth.

It took slightly longer for Chad to secure Karen's ankles to the table legs. She felt the ropes circling her bare ankles, going tight as Chad knotted them. She tried to struggle, found herself instead stuck halfway between squirming and writhing. Her hips were practically humping the table, she was so turned on. She was dripping.

As she struggled, Chad would reach up and spank her on the ass, snarling, "I told you to stop struggling!"

Karen would whimper and wiggle her butt, and he'd spank her cheeks again through the short blue skirt.

When he was done tying Karen's ankles to the table, Chad stood and yanked up her skirt.

A navy blue garment of quality wool, it was straight in contour but too short to be entirely businesslike. It wasn't quite a mini, but it was short enough that it got lots of looks from the guys in the office, though not a one of them complained to management about it.

Chad pulled the skirt to her hips and tucked it hem-into-waistband.

He shoved his hand between Karen's legs and started feeling her up.

"That's a nice short slutty skirt," he gloated. "And you're not wearing anything underneath. I guess you've been expecting me. You're good and wet, you horny little office slut."

His fingers caressed her bare, smooth slit, stroking

from her wet entrance to her clit. The volume of Karen's moans mounted as she squirmed.

Her pussy was bare—as were her legs—because she'd taken off her pantyhose after the second beer. She was shaved because she *always* shaved for Chad; he liked her that way, and what Chad wanted, Chad got—especially when he asked so nicely.

As for being "good and wet," she was more than that—she was dripping. Had she been when he entered, or was it the struggle that got her all wet and dripping? She often fantasized at work, but she'd been way too busy with the Phoenix account today. She'd probably been bone dry when he'd grabbed her.

She could feel Chad's fingers gliding in and out of her pussy, stroking her channel and her entrance and her clit, wetness smeared everywhere. She could feel rivulets of it running down her naked thighs.

He shoved his fingers in—two, it felt like, with intentional roughness, enough to make her moan behind the gag. Karen could feel—as could Chad—that she was far wetter on the inside than on the outside. That was a sure sign that her arousal had been sudden and powerful.

One of Chad's favorite things was feeling her go from dry to wet as he touched her. Karen hadn't always liked it at first, but Chad's eagerness converted her. Now nothing turned her on more than thinking about how Chad could start her sexual response cycle from zero to sixty in no time flat.

Like he'd done by taking her in the conference room.

Chad unzipped his pants and took his cock out. Karen moaned as she felt the head of it rubbing her slit. He alternated teasing her entrance and her clit with the head and fingering her with two or three fingers.

"You want this?" he growled as he rubbed his cock against her. "You want my cock up inside you, slut?"

Karen played the unwilling victim. She shook her head against the cold hard surface of the cutting table. She wiggled her ass. She struggled and squirmed. As she fought against her imminent ravishment, she felt her arousal mounting—ironically making it harder and harder to keep acting like she didn't want it. Her hips were already grinding in a shameless burlesque of getting fucked. Her nipples felt hard against the table. Her mouth was wet and drooling around the gag. She wanted his cock in her mouth.

But she kept shaking her head—and Chad got the message.

His belt buckle made a rattling sound; the belt itself a harsh, acrid hissing as he whipped it from his belt loops.

Karen squealed and squirmed. She wiggled her ass so hard she shook the table. She made so much noise that when she thought of the cleaning guys, she got scared and excited at once—but she still couldn't stop herself. She was going to be whipped.

"Let's see if this changes your mind," said Chad, stepping back far enough to get him some swing space.

The belt hissed down with elegant violence. A hot slash of pain caressed her naked cheek. The muffled sound that erupted from Karen's mouth with the first blow was as much moan as shriek. But as the afterburn set in, the sound escalated almost to a scream. The ball gag silenced her effectively and Karen felt the heat of catharsis as she realized she could scream as loud as she wanted—no one would save her.

The belt snapped down again and again. Karen fought against the bonds as the streaks of pain mounted across her naked ass and thighs. She was helpless. Chad gave her ten or twelve strokes, then reached under her and grabbed her blouse. He didn't unbutton it; he just *pulled*. Buttons went flying. It was an expensive blouse, but Karen was well beyond caring. He shoved his hand up under her and undid her front-clasp bra like an expert. Her tits exposed, the blindfolded Karen didn't know what was coming—until she felt the first hot hard pinch on one nipple, the pain mounting as she waited for the other to get the same treatment.

Binder clips.

With Karen's arms tied behind her back, Chad couldn't strip her blouse off without ripping it to shreds. Which would have been fine with Karen at that point, but Chad let prudence be his guide. He left the filmy silk garment spread open across her back, pulled down to expose her shoulders. With both of her tits clamped, Karen could feel sensation coursing from her pussy to her nipples to her clit. She bit into the gag as Chad took his position, rubbing his cock against her entrance.

He spoke slowly and distinctly.

"Do you want my cock inside you?" he asked her. "Do you want to be fucked?"

Karen did; she could barely think straight with her delirious craving for it. But she forced herself to shake her head, craving the other thing more—the hot lances of pain across her backside.

With a grim snarl of fury, Chad gave that to her. He stepped back and strapped her with a vengeance, laying stripe after stripe of hot red against Karen's bare ass.

When he swung that thing he moved like a god, she thought, the oiled leather of his belt as supple and smooth as Karen herself had made it just that Sunday evening, kneeling on a pillow before the newspaper-covered coffee table, nude and collared—and impossibly turned on. Did she imagine that he'd use it for something like this? That the big boots she'd also mink-oiled that night would, on Wednesday, kick her high-heeled red pumps wide apart, and the ropes she'd obediently washed and looped into six-foot lengths would circle her ankles and wrists? That she'd be at the office when she smelled the mink oil she'd used on the strap of the ball gag and the soft, supple leather blindfold?

She'd been counting on it.

Chad gave it to her *hard*, as hard as she could take it. He knew exactly when to stop, too—the moment she broke, not because the pain was too much but because her hunger for him had mounted to the point where she couldn't say no. Not even just to pretend.

He pulled her hair and leaned down, his weight atop

her, pinning her bound body more firmly to the table. He spoke into her ear.

"Do you want to be fucked?"

Karen couldn't say no, so she didn't say anything. She couldn't make herself shake her head because she wanted it so bad she thought she'd fucking die if he wasn't inside her within the minute. But not being able to ask for it felt deliciously and horribly like the state she occupied so much of the time: mute in her desire, and waiting for male lust to take over.

It did, this time. Chad took her against her will.

He made a point of it, too, his lips up close at the back of her neck.

When his cock was positioned at her opening and her vaginal lips spread wide by his fingers, he leaned down and told her:

"I guess you really *don't* want it. Good thing for you, I don't care."

He entered her quickly, in one savage thrust, his cock going as deep as it could go. She surged beneath him and bucked and swayed as he started to fuck her. She moaned into the ball gag. Muffled sounds escaped her. Her eyes rolled back behind the blindfold, but there was no one there to see it. She started fucking her body back onto Chad, meeting the thrust of his cock with great shuddering strokes.

She came before he did. Chad never knew it. By the time she came, she was moaning so hard and uncontrollably that the barely noticeable rise in volume didn't tip him off—and he was thrusting too hard and too fast to detect the powerful contractions of her cunt.

An instant later, she felt wetness flood her. Chad's groans echoed above her, bestial and male. She felt him inside her, slicking her up with his seed.

He pulled out, untied her and picked her up in his arms.

She murmured into his sweaty neck: "Eleven o'clock...FedEx...deadline..."

He said, "Don't worry. We've still got half an hour. Where's the package?"

"Shelf...above...the copier," she moaned softly.

"Where's it going?"

"Phoenix."

"What needs to go in?"

"Just the last batch of shit in the copier," she murmured.

He carried her down the hall to the couch in her office. She caressed the rope marks on her wrists as Chad loaded up the package, sealed it and got Karen's coat. She had to button it to make herself decent, since her blouse no longer fastened properly. It was ten forty-five—plenty of time to get there.

Someone was pounding on the dead-bolted door to the office just as Chad and Karen opened it.

The cleaning guys hadn't heard a thing, which left Karen only mildly disappointed.

PREY

Madeline Elayne

She was hungry, and she wanted to play.

The email was short and to the point, but the implied message was pretty damn clear.

When and where?—Jia.

I could feel my chest tighten, both with fear and arousal, at the thought of it—Jia. She only used that name once in a blue moon, when she really wanted to play hard, to hunt me and take me down for it. Fuck, the last time I played with Jia, I had to take two sick days in a row afterward to recover. And this time, she wanted me to set the time and place.

Telling me to set the time, that was a tease. She knew how much these nights terrified me just like she knew how much they turned me on. I wanted to put it off, to give myself time to prepare for the game, but I knew the way she thought. The longer I waited, the more pent-up aggression she'd have waiting for me. What she really wanted was for me to seduce her with my choices of time and venue, to make myself irresistible prey for her to chase down and devour. What I wanted was to run and hide. No, not really. (Well, maybe a little.) What I *really* wanted was not to disappoint her—to make this night, this game, the biggest turn-on of her life. Fuck. Jia.

I pulled up the message so that it filled the whole screen, and kicked my chair away from the desk. My cock, already rock-hard when I unzipped my jeans and pulled it free, left a dribble of precum on my hand. I couldn't be bothered with any niceties like lube right now, I just needed to be mind-numbingly turned on while I thought. I let the words fill my whole vision; the sensation of my hand frantically driving up and down the length of my dick was secondary to the image of Jia toying with me, tracking me and finally fucking me silly. "When, where?"

I closed my eyes and focused on the tiny snippets of scenes that were swarming in my imagination; struggled to put them into a setting that would bring out the predator in her. The more I fleshed out the scenario, the more frantically I jacked off, and it wasn't long before my cock exploded in a wet, sticky mess up the front of my shirt. Note to self: Even when skipping lube, a Kleenex is still useful. Of course, more importantly (and the biggest reason for the gooey mess) was that I knew the perfect place. I grabbed a wet wipe and cleaned up as best I could, then scooted back to the keyboard and started typing my equally economical response:

Molly's café. Friday at 8. Wear leather.

It was Monday when I sent it, and it was sure to be a very, very, long week.

Strangely enough, the week flew by. I spent all my free time making plans for Friday, and so horny I thought that I would explode. I had promised myself that I wouldn't get off again until we met, and my balls were constantly full and fucking sore as hell. Imagining the ways the night would play out occupied most of my waking (and dreaming) thoughts, and even though my productivity at work was practically zilch, still the workdays seemed to pass in an instant.

Friday night, though, *crawled*. I took off work early, and when it was pretty clear that I'd be the only one home for the night, I popped a frozen dinner in the microwave. I was dressed and ready to go out the door by 5:30. Damn, it was going to be a long wait. I stood up, then sat right back down at least ten times in as many minutes. I paced the front room in a circle, then went upstairs to check that the bedroom was the way I'd left it.

The wall hangings and rugs that disguised the room were all neatly rolled away and stored so that the dozens of anchor rings embedded in the wall, floor and ceiling shone silvery and magical in the dim light. I flicked the switch to make sure the strobe was still working and checked the stereo for the fifth time, making sure the right songs were cued up. Yes, the playroom was still perfectly ready, just like it was when I finished setting it up an hour ago, and when I checked a half hour after that. I switched back to the regular lighting and checked myself out in the mirror.

The leather jeans were nothing special; they were my oldest pair, and well worn because I was sure they'd be at the least scuffed and stained by morning. I liked what they did to my ass, though. The black T-shirt was plain enough, too, but I hoped she'd find the boots with the built-in quick-links and the not-too-obvious (but still functional) cuffs and choker complete with D-rings were a temptation to tie me down somewhere good and securely. I took another look at the jungle of anchor points in the room and grinned.

I normally couldn't care less about my appearance over and above being clean and tidy, but I checked my hair yet again to make sure the spiky 'do—so different from the very little I normally do to my hair—was still up the way the guy had left it in the salon. He'd been right, it did take several years off my age, and I was hoping it would give Jia a bit of extra fun, chasing down some young and perky leatherboy tonight.

Double-checking took all of ten minutes, and then I went back to the pacing. I tried to get myself to sit down and read a book, but trying to sit still was an exercise in futility. At seven, I gave in and went to the café early.

She came in during my fifth coffee. From quarter to eight on, I'd had my eyes glued to the door watching for her, but when the goddess in the black trench coat strode in at eight on the dot, my mind took a full count of three to recognize her as Jia. The signature black knee-height Dr. Martens stompin' boots I recognized, and the leather jeans and halter top, but the rest of the outfit—the part I'd never seen before—was what really did it for me. It seemed like there wasn't an inch of her that didn't glint with the shine of new steel, a chain or a cuff or one of the row of links on her belt. Even better, I was sure that most of it would be functional, too. It wasn't just her outfit that was a surprise, though. Her normally shoulder-length brown hair was dyed jet black and trimmed to a sexy bob just shy of chin length, and it was offset with streaks of deep purple that framed her face. Lips stained the same color as the highlights in her hair turned into a quirky smile when she saw me and took the only other chair at my little table.

I'd made sure there was already a tea and a slice of coffee cake waiting for her when she got here (the more reasons I gave her to linger, the longer it would take her to catch up to me), and she cradled the cup in both hands to take a sip, checking me out with an appraising eye over the rim. Meanwhile, I was trying to find a way to surreptitiously inch my chair closer to the table to keep the rest of the café from being exposed to the painfully obvious hard-on trying its best to force its way through the front of my jeans.

"Seems a little public...and quiet for the kind of night I was looking forward to, doesn't it?" She arched a brow and tilted her head to point out the two very nice-looking middle-aged men in the corner playing a game of chess.

I chuckled. "Do you expect me to believe that you'd be here if you thought this was our final destination of the night?"

She conceded the point with a shrug and posed the obligatory reply: if we weren't going to stay here, where exactly were we going? I tossed a couple of twenties on the table and pushed my chair back to stand up. The erection was still there, and still miraculously contained by my jeans, but I was in the moment now and couldn't have cared less.

"I guess you'll have to catch me to find out. A sporting person might even give me a bit of a head start."

My pulse was pounding so hard and fast that it rang in my ears as I turned my back and walked away from the table, but I forced myself to move slowly and deliberately. It was all part of the tease—let her catch an eyeful of my ass behind the leather, and (hopefully) she'd be hungry for more. I didn't pick up my pace until I was out the door and around the corner. I was caught in the adrenaline rush; my heart was beating a staccato rhythm that my feet couldn't even begin to catch up with. Besides, it was bar night in what passed for our little city's downtown, and the streets were packed. Even though I wanted to sprint, I had to settle for a jog.

The nightclub I'd chosen was only three blocks away, and I got there well ahead of Jia. It was still early enough for it to be relatively empty, but it *was* bar hours so the lights were dimmed, the smoke machines were already cooking and the strobes danced off everything enthusiastically enough to give an epileptic nightmares. It was retro night, and this was a place to dance, so the music—an endless stream of techno and synth-pop—was playing so loud you could feel the pulsing rhythm through the soles of your boots. It would be easy to stake out a place where I could see her before she saw me when she came in, especially since her eyes would need a minute to get used to the light change, and it wasn't as if any noise I made would give me away.

I was leaning against the back wall of the dance floor, doing my best to look the cool, casual bar hopper—arms crossed and one foot planted up on the wall behind me. She came to the door and my heart skipped a beat. She was every inch the hunter as she scanned the inside of the bar, not seeing much because of the flashing strobes but taking in all she could. She prowled up to the bartender and showed him a picture. I had imagined her like the lone predator; the thought that she'd get help finding me hadn't even crossed my mind. The guy pointed in my direction and I met Jia's eyes. Hungry, she was so hungry. Was that the way I looked to her, so raw and desperate? I wrenched myself away from her gaze and turned toward the back, where the bathrooms were, and rushed as fast as I could without looking like I was running.

I raced past both sets of doors to the johns. When I was here on Wednesday, the hallway ended in a door to a storage room and through it one to the outside, a favorite place for staff and patrons alike to grab a quick smoke. Neither had been locked from the inside then, and I prayed they weren't today and that it was early enough for the alley to be deserted. When I got out into the cool air of the empty alley, I let out a breath I hadn't known that I was holding. I turned around the corner and leaned against the brick wall to rest a minute. I hadn't really exerted myself, but the endorphin rush was making my breath come so quick and hard I thought I might pass out. Besides, she would assume I went into one of the bathrooms, wouldn't she? That would buy me a minute.

I rubbed my palm against the leather covering the rigid fixture in the front of my jeans and my cock twitched, making me shudder. I was contemplating the wisdom of pulling it out for a quick tease when a sound from around the corner brought me back down to earth in a wonderfully scared-out-of-your-pants kind of way. I pressed myself against the wall and peeked around the corner, my heart in my throat. *Nothing.* Must have been my imagination.

The hand that grabbed my wrist and wrenched my arm behind my back till I was on the tips of my toes came out of nowhere, seriously. I let out an incredibly un-macho squeak, and there she was, her hot little body pressed tightly against my back, shoving me roughly into the cold brick. She smelled like jasmine. Not tall enough for her lips to reach my ear, she settled for growling into my shoulder:

"I'm disappointed, you know, I really had hoped that you'd make this much, much harder."

She gave my arm another wrench, and I yelped, sure she was going to pop my shoulder out of joint. Somehow, I managed to find my voice, breathless as it was.

"Oh, honey. Don't be disappointed...yet!"

I stomped down hard on her left instep, and her grip loosened enough that I was able to pull my arm free. I looked to see her partly doubled over from the surprise pain in her foot. If I were fighting someone else, the obvious next move would be to smash an elbow into that unguarded face. Post-feminist egalitarianism hadn't gotten us that far yet, though. It might be acceptable, in some cases like this one, to fight back, but if you ever wanted to be in a woman's good books again you never, *ever* touched the face. I settled for the slower and less elegant solution of going into a deep crouch and landing a shoulder in her gut on the way up and past. It wouldn't slow her up for long, though, and this time a jog wouldn't do it. I broke into a flat-out run. A low, pained chuckle followed me down the street.

"Oh, you are *so* going to pay for that!"

I sure as hell hoped so.

Fortunately, in a city this size, downtown was fairly small, and on a Friday night it was pretty much foot traffic only. That meant I could as good as ignore the traffic lights as I hopped from alleyway to parking lot toward my next destination. When I'd outrun her by a corner, I popped behind a Dumpster in the back lot of a Subway, and waited till she kept on past me before making a dash perpendicular to her direction—high-tailing it straight for the park. I knew she'd see me, of course, but hopefully I'd at least gained a few paces. Jia was faster than I was in an out-and-out speed footrace, but I had more stamina, so if I could start to get her tired I might outrun her yet.

Technically, the park closed to visitors at sundown each night, but the arboretum trail—the place I was desperately sprinting for—had tiny paths worn through the forest floor toward it from every few feet of the park's perimeter. One of those was right ahead of me. A quick look over my shoulder told me she was only a few steps behind me, but the only light in the park came from those little solar lamps every few meters along the trail. Plenty dark enough for me to hide and buy some time.

Then again, the best laid plans of mice and men, as they say... I was barely a few dozen paces into the woods when my boot caught a protruding root and I went down, landing on my knees and scraping them and my palms into a lovely bleeding mess. The shock through my shoulders, especially the newly sore one, was enough to make me yell out.

"Fuck, fuck, *fuck*!"

Another crunch of footsteps through the brush and

she was behind me. I cringed, and braced myself for whatever she had planned for me. This wasn't what I had in mind at all, one clumsy move and I'd ruined it all!

Instead of a punch or a kick or a fist in my hair, though, she asked me if I was all right. I was stunned silent for a minute; I mean, I was far more all right than if she'd started in on me, wasn't I? But of course, *she* didn't know that, and it just wasn't the same if she wasn't the one deliberately making me scream.

"Yeah, nothing injured...nothing but my pride."

I swear to god she cackled.

"Good."

That was when my world exploded in the pain I'd been expecting heartbeats earlier. Her boot connected with my tailbone so hard I could have sworn she'd taken a running leap to land on me. I went down on my face, and it felt like I was bruised right through the bone and halfway up my spine. She couldn't have jumped on me, though, because that was what she did next, landing knees-first onto the small of my back and knocking what little air I had left out of my lungs. I was still so stunned from the impact that I couldn't even feel what she was doing to my wrists—in fact, I heard the click before I noticed anything at all. She'd fastened them together (using the cuffs and rings I was so gracious to have provided) and anchored them to another one of those evil loops of root just like the one I'd tripped on, high above my head.

Jia let up the pressure on my back to roll me over. I

didn't resist—I was looking for a respite that she wasn't ready to give me yet. As soon as I was on my back, she bore her full weight down on me again. This time, those wicked, bony knees landed one each onto the sensitive inner part of my upper thighs, forcing them further apart. I grunted and tried to shake away the tears of pain that had sprung to the corner of my eyes.

If I craned my neck enough I could see what she was doing to my legs, not that it mattered much since I didn't have the leverage I needed to fight her off. Once for each ankle, she clipped a length of chain off her belt and snapped the loop shut through the ring in my boot and yet another of those roots. Damn, I hated those things! Once I was secured enough for her satisfaction, she lifted her weight off my legs and turned to face me, ultimately ending up straddling me on her knees, positioned so that sitting back just a little bit more would seat her right on my cock, which was still very strongly protesting its incarceration in my jeans. I groaned and thrust my hips up at her, but I was stretched out pretty far; there really wasn't much farther I could go.

"So..." She was breathless as she talked, and I wished that there was more light so I could see the flush I was sure was in her cheeks.

"The woods at night, huh? I mean, it's a bit clichéd, but I guess I can work with it."

She reached down and undid my jeans, and having my cock and balls free again felt so fucking good I wasn't sure that I hadn't come right then and there.

When she wrapped her hot, tiny hand around my shaft and started pumping, my whole world contracted until nothing existed except that sensation. God, I wanted this, I wanted it so much! She started to jerk me off faster and I moaned. The pain in my back, my shoulder, my ass—they all disappeared. There was nothing but the blissful sensation of her, bringing me so close to coming that I wasn't going to be able to hold out much more… well, nothing but that and the nagging thought that this wasn't supposed to be how the night ended.

"Jia, please." It was barely a whisper, so quiet that even *I* wasn't sure I had actually said it. She squeezed my cock and I groaned again.

"No, wait…please, Jia. Please stop."

Much to my disappointment, she did. When her hand left my cock, so close to getting me off, I missed it so strongly it felt like grief. She let out a derisive grunt.

"Let me get this straight. You've been running from me all night—haven't stopped even once to make sure I was keeping up—until you fell on your ass here, and you want me to stop for you now? Why should I?"

She stood up and paced over to lean against a nearby tree, and my moan when she left me sounded to my own ears like a cry of bereavement. At least I had fewer distractions while I tried to explain. I said I'd made some special arrangements for her tonight, and that though the run through the park was part of my design, being caught wasn't. That was the design of the stupid roots and nothing else. I'm not proud to say it, but I begged for her to let me go now, and take her where I was planning on taking her all along. Eventually, she agreed, but only on two conditions.

"Anything," I said, flooded with relief.

She chuckled. "Okay, I'll take that for condition number one. The second one is that I'm done with the running. The chase was fun, don't get me wrong, but I'm getting tired and we haven't even played yet. Tell me where we're going and I'll meet you there."

I was disappointed, sure. The way I'd pictured it she was chasing me the whole way back, but it was a concession I was more than happy to make at that point. Eventually we agreed that she'd me meet me at the house in a half hour—we really were pretty damn close already.

She bent over me and took a long, slow lick around the outside of my ear. I shuddered. Then I heard a click and she stood up and walked away. If I twisted just right I could see that my wrists were being held together with a padlock. She'd put the key in the lock and turned it, then left me there to figure out how to get free. I figured it really shouldn't be getting me this hot, but apparently no one told my body that.

It took a serious amount of squirming and a good ten minutes for me to get myself loose and ready to head home, and even after all that it was a chore to force my dick back into the tight leather jeans. I marveled, not for the first time, that the little brain in my pants really did have less than zero common sense.

All told, there were fewer than ten minutes before Jia

was due to arrive by the time I got inside. Just enough time to wash the worst of the grime out of the abrasions in my hands and knees and get my jeans back on. The boots were a sacrifice that had to be made—they took ten minutes to lace all by themselves. Besides, maybe she had sinister intentions toward my feet that me being bootless might encourage.

I had scarcely made it up to the bedroom and shut the door behind me when I heard the front door open. Round about the time I imagined her finding the orchid vase and note beckoning her upstairs on the table, I turned on the stereo and hit the lights. I leaned against the back wall of the room and listened for her steps up the stairs. They were loud, meaning she'd obviously kept *her* boots on. The thought made me grin.

The steps stopped in front of the door, but she didn't open it. Good, that meant she'd seen the note on the front of the door and was reading it. I hoped she'd be willing to play along. Fact was that if we wanted to do anything really fun in public, we'd probably finish up the night by getting arrested. Here, though—here, we could do anything. This is what was on the second note:

You chase me through most of downtown. When you finally catch me, I've led you back into that first night-club. The music is loud, and everyone on the dance floor is worked up and sweaty, so at first no one notices us. By the time you get me to my knees, though, the crowd has parted to watch us. Someone leaves, maybe just because they don't want to see, or maybe because they want to call the cops, but we don't care. We have the dance floor to ourselves, and you have me at your mercy.

The door opened and my heart skipped a beat. She was looking right at me, on my knees in the middle of the room as advertised. There was violence and passion in her eyes, and as hackneyed as it might sound, I was hypnotized by it. I could hear a strange rumbling noise over the din of the music, and it took me a moment to realize that Jia was growling.

"Hell of a long way to lead me on a chase only to end up all the way back where we started, isn't it?"

She quirked a bemused smile and took in the rest of the room. I had covered the walls on either side of her with a photo panorama of the nightclub on a crowded Friday night. (Technically, they were taken on a Wednesday, but the idea was the same.)

"Huh. I've never done it with an audience before, but... I guess I can work with that, too."

She'd paused just long enough to plant a vicious, hold-nothing-back kick in my diaphragm. As a result, by the time she was done talking I was on my side, curled into a ball on the floor at her feet. A nudge with her boot was all it took to roll me onto a half curl on my stomach, and a knee in the lower back flattened me out all the way.

She reached for my right wrist, but I wasn't letting her get me pinned so quickly, not this time. I'd gotten my breath back—finally—and I echoed her growl, yanked my hand back when she made to immobilize it. I might not be able to get out from underneath her, but I still had more upper-body strength than her by far. I'd gotten my arm away from her three times before she decided to do something about it.

Sharp, crushing pain stabbed into both sides of the back of my neck—she'd clamped her jaws down on me like a lioness felling a steer. I panicked and bucked her off my back, but her teeth held firm, digging deeper into muscle. It wasn't like any kind of pain I'd ever felt. It felt like my neck was white-hot, and it shrank my world to the single feeling of that one point of blazing pain. Then the strangest thing happened. The pain didn't go away, but all of a sudden it was mixed with a kind of euphoria. She hadn't done anything different, she was still pinning me to the floor with nothing but her teeth, but... I can't explain it except to say that I was okay with that. My whole body relaxed, and all I wanted to do was bathe in the sensation. If the reason the antelope on the nature channel went all limp when the tiger caught it just like this was anything close to my current crazy blissed-out sexual high, I had developed a whole new appreciation for natural selection. Wow.

"Mmm...I like it when you behave for me." She purred the words right next to my ear, but they sounded a million miles away.

I was vaguely aware that she was doing something to secure my ankles and forearms to the floor, but I didn't put up the least bit of resistance. I was worried that if I moved at all, it would break the spell of this new high.

"In fact, I like it so much, I think I'm going to make sure you're very, very still for me tonight. You're okay with that, right, pet?"

She bit down hard on my earlobe and I came reluctantly down to Earth.

"Ow!"

I tried to pull away from those sharp teeth that all of a sudden I didn't like nearly as much, and in doing so pulled at the bonds holding my wrists. Ouch, fuck! They were sharp! I looked over and my arm was tied down, about two inches up from my wrist, to the ring in the floor with *picture-hanging wire*, of all things. If I struggled at all, I could very well cut myself quite handsomely. A trickle of fear ran down my spine and I shuddered. She chuckled. I guess she saw that I'd figured out my predicament.

Something metal, sharp and very, very cold traced a painful line down my back, and I heard the sound of stitches ripping. She flashed the knife where I could see it before she put it away with a mischievous grin. It didn't look bloodied; at least that was something. When she stepped out in front of me, I craned my neck to see her. She was still fully (and magnificently) dressed, but she had strapped a thick, veiny dildo the same color of her lipstick to the front of her jeans.

"I want that lovely ass that you've been teasing me with all night. And since you offered me *anything*, I think

I'll take it without any of that inconvenient lube."

She brushed the tatters of my pants off my back and parted my cheeks, pressing the tip of the purple cock against my hole. Her first thrust made me scream, and somehow I knew I'd be hoarse by the end of the night. Of course, I also knew I didn't want it any other way.

IN CHARGE

ADR Forte

Carter's as cold as a December night in Wisconsin. Colder. But he's smart and efficient. He can "walk the talk," as they say. So I respect him, even if I don't like him. And I don't like him.

I miss our old boss. His witticisms and wispy gray hair and those heavenly cookies his wife sent by the dozens over the years. A glaring contrast to Carter with his power suit and Franklin planner, his icy smiles and gel-slicked hair.

Don't get me wrong, I'll give credit where credit's due. Carter gets things done. He creates order and he inspires following. But just as there are no soft edges to his starched jacket, there are no soft edges to his psyche.

He can dazzle like the morning light caught by icicles

on a winter-stripped branch, and he's just as desolate. I've tried to like him, but I can't.

The one good thing about Carter's reign has been the fact he's based out of headquarters and only flies up here once or twice a month. We work together just fine long-distance.

The downside to that is I'm his right-hand girl. So like it or not, when the annual summit comes around I'll be getting packed off to headquarters for a week to provide representation. With him. I think I'd rather be shot in the foot.

Then, two days before I'm due to leave, Tina stops by my desk, tells me she's going, too. I think there's got to be a god after all.

"That's awesome," I say, grinning at her.

She wrinkles her nose and smiles back. "Glad you don't mind me tagging along. Although I can think of a lotta things I'd rather be doin' than going to that summit."

"I'm with ya," I say. She has no idea.

My elation lasts all the way to the West Coast, right up until the point where we're getting settled into our temporary cubicles.

"Tina, Alexa. How was your trip?"

Le sigh. I look up and force a smile and then let Tina answer him. I stay busy trying to hook up my computer and figure out why he makes me so uncomfortable. I find myself wishing I hadn't worn this sweater and jeans to travel. I feel frumpy.

God, it's not that I want him to notice me as a sexpot or anything. I just wish I'd worn something a little more feminine. *Why do you want feminine?* the little reasonable voice in my head argues back. *Do you want Carter to look at you that way? Like a nice, delectable piece of ass?*

No and no.

Crap, I don't know why I'm obsessing about this. I don't know why my face is flushed. I don't know what Tina and Carter are talking about and I have no idea how to respond to Tina's "That work for you, 'Lexa?"

I look up and blink like your average deer caught in headlights. "Um, sorry. What?"

Carter's lips twitch and I want to slap him.

"Carter's asked us over for dinner tonight. Does seven work for you?"

Shit!

"Yeah, yeah. Um, seven works great."

I look over at him and manage to hold eye contact for all of the five seconds it takes to say, "Thanks for the invite," and him to reply, "No problem. See you then."

After he walks away I lean back in my chair and rub my eyes and swear.

"Just freakin' great," I tell Tina.

She swivels her chair and leans around the partition between our cubes.

"Oh, it won't be so bad. I hear he can cook." She

ponders that for a second. "Hmm. He's hot, he's got a good job and he can cook. Not a bad catch, huh?" She winks at me.

I roll my eyes at her. "Go for it. I'm sure Glen won't mind."

She snorts and pokes me in the arm. "For *you*. Carter's about thirty years too young for me, sweetie."

My face burns but I only shrug. "And he's about too much of an alpha for me."

Tina frowns and I see my golden opportunity to get on my soapbox and refute the idea of Carter once and for all. I fold my arms and put on my wisest expression.

"Let me tell you about guys like our dear leader. They're all a bunch of control freaks. They like to be in charge and tell everybody what to do because, you know, they're smarter and stronger and better than everybody. Especially us girls. But of course, they can't *say* that. Oh no! They're sooo smooth and chivalrous and effing PC about it that nobody can accuse them of being the Neanderthals they really are!"

I'm flushed and out of breath from the effort of getting it all out and still keeping my voice low enough for nobody to overhear. While I fume, Tina looks at me for a few seconds and then shakes her head.

"Guess I belong to a different generation," she says with a shrug. "I don't mind my man taking charge." Her smile is placid, as if admitting such a thing, saying it out loud is no big deal at all.

I belong to a different generation, and even the merest hint of him being in charge is so, so not okay.

It's after six, and I'm in the hotel lobby waiting on Tina and waiting on the valet to bring the car up. I'm also regretting my decision to wear a dress, even if it does come down to my knees. It's black with a retro cherry print. What the hell kind of message does that send? I wish I knew.

My phone rings and I grab it, glad of something to take my mind off myself.

"'Lexa? I'm sorry, hon, but you saw that email about the server outage...?"

Oh crap. I feel my stomach go very, very cold.

"Yeah, I did."

"Well, I've got to get on a call in ten minutes. I'm going to have to cancel tonight."

Tina, you can't do this to me!

"Oh no. Well, do you need me on too? I can give Carter a call and..."

"No, no! There's no need to ruin everybody's night over this. Go ahead. You all have a couple extra cocktails for me."

As if the whole world is in on the conspiracy, I see the valet pull up with the rental car, dashing my last fervent hope to weasel out of this. Cursing everyone in I.T. who might even remotely have had responsibility for that server, I hang up with Tina and get behind the wheel.

At least John from mobilization will be there. He's

about as much fun as a wake, but at least when he leaves I can too. Maybe this evening will be mercifully short. I head out of the city as the sun goes down in a glorious burst of color, and I turn up the radio, open the moon roof. I smile. Maybe it won't be so bad after all.

After I ring the bell I wait for a minute or two, admiring the remodeled ranch-style single-story with its wrought-iron fence and perfect flower beds. It must have cost a fortune out here, but trust Carter to buy a house worthy of bragging rights. I start to think that maybe he isn't there and I take my phone out, ready to call him, but the door opens.

His hair is wet and slick with water, not gel, and he's hastily buttoning his shirt cuffs. I can feel the damp heat of his skin and smell his body wash. I sniff even though I don't mean to. It's that trendy stuff, with those commercials where some muscled scruffy guy is getting chased by a bevy of panting girls. I'm surprised Carter uses it.

"I'm sorry. I'm running late," he says with a smile as he lets me in. I shake my head and smile back, say it's no big deal.

I have to walk right by him to enter, and there's just an inch of space between our bodies. Damn, he smells good. But he's Carter, I remind myself. And I don't like him.

I follow him into the kitchen and lean against the wall as far away from him as I can get without making it obvious. I notice he isn't wearing shoes or socks, just slippers. He has long toes, like his fingers. Why that should matter, I honestly don't have a clue.

"Tina had to cancel. She got stuck on a call over that server issue."

He nods as he gets out a bottle of wine and starts to open it. "She messaged to let me know. You'd think if they were taking a piece of something out they'd know where to put it back, but..." He rolls his eyes and shrugs. "Fucking I.T."

I laugh, I can't help it. I had every intention of being an unfriendly bitch, but the kitchen smells wonderful and the windows are open to the warm night and hell... I just can't.

"My sentiments exactly," I say as I take the glass from him and smile.

"John canceled too," he says. "Had to get his kids tonight, so I guess it's just us."

I look up. He's joking, got to be.

"I'll try to make it as painless as possible," he says with a crooked smile. "Besides, Tina said you love garlic mashed potatoes."

Before I can reply, he disappears in the direction of the dining room and reappears with plates and silverware in one hand and his laptop in the other.

"I figure since it *is* just us we can eat in here and then go over the presentation for Tuesday. I'd like your input to the last set of changes I made."

Now we're back on familiar ground. This is the Carter I know and love to hate.

Happy again, I help him set the kitchen table. He spoons an extra-large helping of potatoes onto my plate and I protest that I shouldn't be eating that many carbs.

"So what? Indulge. You can afford to."

He says it offhand, typical Carter, but to my shame I blush.

This can't be. I'm not attracted to this man in any way. But as he comes to sit at my elbow, still smelling of sexy body wash, reaching for the meatloaf that I have to admit is better than my mother's... I'm not so sure.

By the time we're through with eating and he puts the laptop between us, moving his chair around so that we can both see the screen, I realize my nipples are hard. Have been all through dinner. Over Carter.

I push my wineglass away. The last thing I need is alcohol. My judgment is already obviously impaired. Even so, when he asks me a question, I fumble over the answer. I wish now I'd worn something other than this cotton dress. I'm terrified he'll pick up on my arousal the same way I'm picking up on his maleness, his nearness.

The desire that's always been there no matter how much I've denied it.

"Are you okay?"

I glance at him, only making eye contact for a second before looking away.

"Sure. I'm fine."

"Do you need a glass of water?"

I shake my head. "No, I'm really okay, Carter. Thanks."

He shrugs and we go back to working, but I can't concentrate.

I keep staring at his lips when he talks. I want them on my clit, which is now painfully aroused and tingling with anticipation. I bite my knuckle and stare at the papers, mumbling vague "mmm-hmms" in response. Trying to remind myself he's an arrogant asshole. Finally he shuts up.

"Alexa, you're not paying attention."

I sigh. "I know. I'm just not focused. Can we take a break and look at it again tomorrow?"

"Of course."

He lapses into silence, but I'm still avoiding eye contact with him. I nod and stand.

"I guess I should go. It's after nine," I say.

"No. I don't think so."

My head comes up and I stare at him, trying to gauge the tone in his voice. He rises slowly to his feet, looking me up and down.

"Sorry...what?"

My heart is beating too fast. He looms over me and I'm suddenly a little scared of the look in those green eyes.

"I have some other items I want to cover with you," he says.

He takes a step closer and instinctively I back up.

"What items?" I ask.

He laughs. I've seldom heard Carter laugh, but it's a great sound. I feel it in the tips of my toes. He laughs as he reaches for me and grabs my arms. Spinning me around, he crushes my back to his chest and runs a hand down my chest to my breasts. Squeezes hard, and I gasp.

"No." The word comes out automatically, but I feel his grip tighten in response.

"No? You don't say *no* to me, Alexa."

His hand moves down to my crotch and he begins stroking one finger between my thighs, through my skirt. His aim is just a little off and the tease of his touch almost on my clit is maddening. At first I think I'm going to shift, move my hips to guide his touch to the right place, but instead I decide I want to see what will happen if I remain unwilling.

I decide I like this hot, cruel Carter.

"Let me go," I say, wriggling in a genuine effort to get away, but I realize with a tinge of real nervousness that he isn't going to release me.

"I don't think so, darling."

His hand moves to my thigh, slides up under the skirt. "You know what I think?"

He forces his hand between my legs, which I'm squeezing together as tightly as I can. Rubs lace against wet flesh.

"I think you want me to fuck you, but good."

"No!"

I jerk away, but his grip only halfway loosens. He grabs my arms and we crash against the table, scattering silverware every which way. I make the effort to twist and struggle, but his hands are a vise on my arms. Well, not entirely. If I had true fear-fueled adrenaline pumping through me, if I really tried, I could break free.

But I don't. He folds my arms behind me and then flips me over, moving between my legs. He's flushed and gorgeous and so, so dangerous.

Does he know the game I'm playing? Or does he think my resistance is genuine? And I don't know which turns me on more. I don't really care. I just want this.

My arms really do hurt and so my eyes are watering just a little. I squirm and whimper.

"Carter, please."

I see him hesitate just a split second and I bite my lips, worried I've playacted too far, but after nerve-wracking seconds where it seems like eons pass while he studies my face, he smiles and shakes his head. That's the moment I know. That's the moment *he* knows. It's the moment we cross the line and begin to play in earnest.

"You've been a hot little tease for the last time. This time there is no getting away."

He lifts my skirt again. With one simple yank, he rips my panties off. Granted, they were lace and not of the sturdiest variety. Granted, I wore them on purpose, just so that *I* would know I had them on, not because I expected him to ever have reason to know. But he tore them with one try.

He drops the ruined cloth on the floor and I manage a sob. Maybe it's even convincing.

"I'm sorry if I came across the wrong way. Please don't do this."

He laughs again and kisses my neck, soft kisses. He nibbles the skin.

"Don't? That's not what your body's telling me, 'Lexa."

He's never shortened my name, even though everyone else in the office does. Never. My little sob of excitement-disguised-as-fear sounds really genuine this time.

"It's just a physical response," I whisper. "I don't want you like this."

He lifts his head. Raises one eyebrow at me. With one hand, he grabs the neckline of my dress and rips. Shit, he's strong. I'm tearing up again, a little bit with pain, a little bit with nerves. There is no going back now.

He pushes my bra down, baring my breasts with their hard nipples, elevated by my arms tucked under my back.

"I think you do, 'Lexa," he says, stroking my nipple with one lazy finger, and my clit tightens and throbs, longing for that same touch. He pinches the nipple and I suck my breath in. Then he pinches the other nipple.

"I think you want me rough." He pauses and smiles, still playing with my exposed breasts and making my wet cunt thrum with pleasure. "Maybe some part of you really doesn't. But right now," his voice gets soft and husky, "I think she's sold you out."

I shake my head, but he sees my gaze stray to his crotch. He smiles and reaches for his fly.

"Bad girl, 'Lexa."

His weight presses me into the desk as his cock pushes

at the lips of my cunt. I wriggle and beg, begging for him even though I'm hoping it sounds like resistance. I want to play all the way. I want to play it right.

My gasp of shock when he pushes into me isn't feigned at all. It's been a while—okay, longer than I care to admit. And his cock is a burning, aching invasion. I writhe against it as he begins fucking me, and I feel my juices slick between our grinding flesh.

"Carter, please."

"Don't beg. You'll make me come," he whispers.

So I resort to soft whimpers against his shoulder. I can't lie still under him. Even if I could bring myself to, my cunt would still tighten around him with every thrust.

"You're enjoying this," he says, his lips hovering over mine, brushing my nose and my cheeks as he moves in me.

I shake my head.

"No?"

"No."

His thrusts slow down. Still driving the entire length of his cock into my cunt, but slower. Slower. Excruciatingly slow.

"You don't want this?" he whispers.

"No." *No, don't slow down. Don't stop.* I want to urge him, plead with him to keep fucking me, but that's not how this goes.

"What? I didn't quite hear that."

"No!"

He starts to laugh. He laughs and kisses my cheek

and then in one, sudden, devastating motion, pulls out of me. He stands back, erect cock glistening as he contemplates my exposed, aroused state.

"I don't know what to do with you, 'Lexa. You're defiant *and* you're lying to me."

I stare at him, thinking I've never seen him this disheveled, rumpled. Hair mussed, fly undone. Both of us way over boundaries we didn't even acknowledge existed before. I wonder just how far this is going to go. I don't think I care.

I struggle to push myself up. My wrists and elbows protest the efforts to force them out of their cramped misery and make them work as they should again, but I get to my feet. I stand before him and somehow manage to push the remnants of my dress and bra off with fingers that shake like leaves in a September wind.

He nods approval. My guess was right. But then, I know him. I've always been able to manage upward, I guess.

"Good girl," he says. "But you know you need to be punished?"

I nod. I figured as much. I have a request of my own, however.

"Carter?"

"Yes?"

I bite my lip. What if asking is the wrong thing? What if I anger him? What if I ruin it all? God, I don't know the rules and I shouldn't be here!

"I...I want to take your shirt off." I can't look at his

eyes, so I drop my gaze to the offending shirt. Swallow hard. "Please."

He laughs. I feel his fingers stroking my cheek, my neck.

"Would that please you, 'Lexa?"

"Yes." It's just a whisper.

"All right. You may take my shirt off."

Deep breath. Relief so immense it hurts. I unbutton his shirt, letting his cock rub against my stomach all the while, and he sighs.

"God, you're so soft."

I smile at his praise and, suddenly inspired, I kiss each of his wrists as I undo his shirt cuffs. I slide the shirt off his shoulders and then lift his T-shirt over his head. I press my lips to his chest, kissing downward to his navel as I sink to my knees, but when I reach his cock, I feel my hair being yanked backward. He looks down and smiles, shaking his head.

"No."

He pulls me to my feet and leads me to the kitchen window, turns me to face the screen and the cool night air blowing in. After the heat of the kitchen, it feels cold on my naked body.

"Hands up."

I put my hands on the window frame and stand trembling, knowing that anyone looking in can see me like this. And I can't see them.

He leans close to me, warm chest against my skin, lips against my earlobe.

"If you cry out, the sound's gonna carry for miles. This is a pretty tame neighborhood. Normally."

I hear the laughter in his voice. He's loving this. My clit tingles at the thought.

It only gets better when he slaps my bare ass, tightening and tingling at the ripples of impact from each blow. At least for the first dozen, and then the pain kicks in. Stinging pain, making me twist and pull away. But he pulls me back, one hand cupping my belly to hold me in place as he spanks me with the other.

I scream silently, lips parted so that I can suck in gasps of precious air between each slap, and my cunt is tight with need that builds and builds and never finds release. His punishment is just harsh enough to bring me misery and just slow enough to get me aroused like I've never been before. And every now and then he lets his hard cock brush my sore ass, reminding me. Tormenting.

God, isn't his hand hurting by now? Isn't it ever going to end? I'm sobbing now, trying not to be loud. Trying to keep myself upright even though my arms keep buckling and making me sway forward. Every time I do, my nipples brush the rough netting of the screen and my cunt clenches, adding to my torment. I think I'm going to die, I need to come so bad.

I can't feel my legs. I'm dizzy. I hear myself whisper "Carter" and then my strength gives out, my hands slip from the frame and my legs buckle. But I never hit the ground, not even close. He pulls me to his chest, supporting my weight as he turns me around and props my back against the wall.

Panting, I look at him as he leans into me. He's flushed from his exertion, tiny beads of sweat on his upper lip that I long to taste. I want him to kiss me, and after a few moments of looking at me with a concerned little frown, making sure I'm really okay, he does. Wet and hungry and lips crushed into mine until we have to stop and breathe.

"Tell me the truth, 'Lexa."

I can feel the hair of his chest soft against my nipples, skin damp with perspiration, just as mine is. I can feel the tip of his cock pushing at the wetness of my cunt, but not inside. And I need him inside. I need him like this.

"I want you."

"I know *that*. What else?" He pushes a little more, lifting my legs as I clutch at his neck and shoulders for leverage. My ass is in exquisite pain and my clit hurts from arousal. His pants fall down around his ankles.

"I don't know," I sob. "I want this. Please."

"Do you want to submit?" I hear the urgency in his voice. Rough. Demanding.

But he's the one in control.

Isn't he?

"Yes. Yes, Carter. Please fuck me. Please."

Then he does. Gloriously. He fucks me while I arch, head against the kitchen wall, legs around his waist. Sticky, sweating thighs and cock and cunt. The lusty smell of sex and his body wash and my perfume. I feel I'm floating. Floating and floating but for the explosive pleasure in my clit, the pain as my abused muscles clench tight. And his male hardness invading me, male strength holding me tight.

He releases all the pent-up need I've had for him all along and it runs down my bruised ass and drips on his kitchen floor. His cum and mine. Intimate in a way it's never been with any other man, because I've never given this much to any other man. Never given this part of myself with such utter abandon. Or such trust.

My legs slide down his and my toes touch the ground again. I find my balance and then rest my head on his shoulder, wrap my arms around his neck, listening to his breath as he holds me, treasuring the warm weight of his soft cock pressed to my belly. He kisses my shoulder. A simple action that says volumes, says more than the hundred words he could spend trying to explain. I don't need him to explain.

I don't worry about what happens next either, about what to say or about the morning after. Don't get me wrong, there's plenty to worry about like discretion and conflict of interest. There's plenty of practical shit to think about. Later.

Here, alone with him, I don't have to be practical. I don't have to belong to my do-it-all, never-surrender generation. I only have to be his. And I like it.

I like him being in charge.

TOO STRONG
TO BREAK

Sophia Valenti

Did you ever have an affair whose memory you couldn't shake? Not so much because of what the two of you had, but because of what the relationship could have been. That's how I felt about me and Duncan. We'd met back when we were undergrads and had clicked instantly. From that first moment, there was an undeniable sexual attraction, and over the course of the next year, we had a lot of fun sex. Fairly vanilla sex, but it was fun nonetheless. Our relationship was always laid-back and never complicated, but we couldn't say the same for our lives.

As our college years faded into the background and our future plans took center stage, there seemed to be less time for the sort of casual fun that we'd enjoyed for so long. We drifted apart, and I didn't entirely mind. I wasn't ready to think about forever; I was more interested in the right now. But every so often I'd think of him—especially when some other guy had disappointed me or broken my heart. I think that's because Duncan had never done either of those things.

But Duncan's demeanor wasn't the only part of our relationship that stayed in my thoughts. There were also memories of our last few nights together: of Duncan tugging my hair so firmly that my pussy ached and of him holding my wrists against the mattress as he drove his cock into me. At the time, I'd surrendered to the thrilling sensations he caused without thinking about what they meant. But those glimmers of dominance had awakened all sorts of kinky desires in me, ones that only seemed to grow.

And it was those decadent desires that would color my dreams. In my head, I'd replay those tempting episodes with Duncan, but in my fantasy world, he would take things further. Rather than holding down my wrists as he fucked me, he'd bind me tight with cuffs and chains, and once I was his captive, he would do all sorts of deliciously dirty things to me.

It was during nights like that I'd find myself longing for what could have been. That is, if Duncan and I had dared to follow where our lust seemed to be pointing us.

As the years went by and I dated a steady stream of sexually boring guys, I realized I had to start looking for other options. While I'd spend my days in the office discussing legal briefs with the partners, I'd spend my nights transfixed by online personal ads from leather-clad men who seemed to be looking for a girl just like me. Their photos and dangerous promises were titillating, but I couldn't make myself answer even one of those ads. Confessing the sort of feelings I was having via an Internet connection seemed too distant and impersonal to me. I wanted to find someone special and whisper those secrets in the dark, to close my eyes and get swept away.

I suppose I'm a romantic after all.

While I'd never hooked up with anyone whose profile I perusued online, I did start chatting with some local people on one of those sites and finally decided to attend an outing for novice kinksters. After talking over coffee, we were to visit a nearby BDSM club. I'd always wanted to go to a sex club, but I'd never been brave enough to go on my own. It seemed like the perfect opportunity to experience something new.

I was as nervous as all get-out, but I felt this was something I needed to do. Sitting home alone wasn't getting me any closer to realizing the dreams that continued to taunt me. But while these were serious concerns, I was getting ahead of myself. My more immediate problem was what to wear.

At first glance, my workaday wardrobe didn't seem to lend itself to a night out at a kink club. But once I started looking at items piece by piece, it all came together. My white silk blouse was demure and appropriate for court, but it became sensual and seductive with a few buttons undone to reveal cleavage enhanced by a black push-up bra and a belt to cinch the waist and highlight my curves. A garter belt and black seamed stockings complemented my shortest pencil skirt, and when I stepped into four-inch stilettos, I felt more bawdy than businesslike. As I walked across my living room to grab my purse, I felt the satin lining of my skirt slipping and sliding against my bare ass in a sensual caress.

Before I headed out the door, I glanced in the mirror and ran a hand through my untamable black curls, then slicked some ruby-red gloss on my lips. My dark eyes were shining with excitement. I wasn't sure what the night held, but I felt like I was ready for anything. But the anything that awaited me was beyond my sexiest dreams.

When I got to the café, there were ten people sitting around the table, including Melissa, the friendly organizer of the outing. I was given a warm welcome by everyone in the group and immediately felt at ease. We spent some time talking with each other about our experiences, and I was happy to learn that almost everyone was a curious beginner like me.

Before long, the coffee had grown cold and it was close to midnight, which meant it was time to leave for the club. My heart began to race the slightest bit as we headed toward the unknown, but now it wasn't only nerves that I felt—it was nerves mixed with palpable excitement.

I was glad we had a guide with us because I never

would have found the place on my own. A side door off a parking lot with no visible address, it didn't even look like an open business, much less one that would be open for all manner of sinful adventures.

Once past the front door, I parted the thick curtains that guarded the entrance before stepping into the dimly lit foyer. Gradually, my eyes adjusted to the club's lighting, and I saw many people were relaxing on couches that lined the walls, some looking intimately engaged while others seemed to be enjoying the company of friends. A broad-shouldered man clad in a fishnet shirt and leather pants passed in front of me. I noticed that in his hand was a leash that connected to the collar worn by a stunning redhead, who trailed behind him. She was wearing only a thong and high heels. My eyes lingered on her flawless alabaster skin, but when she passed me by I noticed the red stripes that marked her behind. I felt a little ache of arousal deep inside when I saw those marks, as well as jealousy that she had a masterful lover so willing to bestow them upon her.

As my naughty mind began to concoct the scenario that had resulted in those scarlet stripes, Melissa interrupted my thoughts by saying, "Oh, good. One of the owners is already here. When he's free, I'll bring him over and introduce you to him."

I followed the line of her hand to see a man across the room. His back was toward us as he stood onstage under a spotlight. Next to him was a leather-covered sawhorse, over which a lithesome blonde was draped.

The naked girl's wrists and ankles were wrapped in cuffs that were attached to the horse. Each time the tall, dark-haired man slapped her bare bottom, her body would jolt and she'd rattle her chains. The pair must have been at this for quite some time, because her ass was already blushing red. As she squirmed I got a glimpse of her sex, which was shining with the wetness of her arousal. The man turned slightly, but the glare from the overhead lights kept his face hidden from me, so I instead admired his tight ass and how it filled his snug jeans. He wasn't wearing a shirt, and each time he reached around to spank the girl, the muscles in his back and arm would tense in a way that conveyed his strength. After delivering a set of intense swats, the man leaned down to whisper in the blonde's ear, running his hand along her body as she arched her back as much as her bonds would allow. She seemed to be in his thrall, craving his touch, whether it was gentle or harsh.

The man stroked her affectionately, but not in an entirely sexual way, which confused me until he released her from the cuffs, kissed the top of her head and led her over to an older gentleman. It was clear that they were the couple, and the silver-haired man cradled the blonde in his lap as their kisses went from soft to passionate in no time. I felt like I was spying on a private moment, but they were out in the open. Enthralled, I watched the man slip his hand between the blonde's thighs. From the motions of his arm, it seemed he was fingering her. Moments later, she tossed her head back and cried out, shivering in his arms as she appeared to climax.

I was still staring at the couple as Melissa tugged on my sleeve.

"Eve," she began as I turned toward her, "I want you to meet—"

"Duncan!"

That built, masterful man I'd been admiring onstage was Duncan. My Duncan. I felt like I'd tumbled into one of my illicit fantasies. Except this was real, and Duncan was standing in front of me, looking older but breathtakingly handsome—and having just finished spanking a woman in bondage in front of a club full of people. I wasn't sure I could speak.

"Eve," he said softly before taking me in his arms. I could hear the affection in his voice, could feel it in his touch. We held each other for a long while, not in any rush to part.

"Oh," said Melissa, her shock coming through clearly in her voice. "I'll leave you two…"

I have no idea where she disappeared, but that didn't concern me at that moment. Duncan pulled back from me slightly, holding me at arm's length to look me up and down. I felt a little thrill when I saw how his gaze lingered at my exposed cleavage before jumping back up to my face.

"One of the owners, huh?" I finally asked, looking around the club once again. This time I took in my surroundings with new eyes, now knowing that this place was Duncan's doing. I wanted to take in every detail and lose myself in his world.

"Yeah," he answered somewhat sheepishly. "A couple friends and I opened this place a few years back. I've always liked mixing pleasure with my business." Duncan grinned, and I couldn't help but laugh with him. I was glad to see he still seemed to have the same easy-going sense of humor.

"This is a lousy place to talk. Let's head back to my office."

I nodded, and Duncan took me by the hand, leading me to the back of the club. Once inside his office, he closed the door behind us, and I settled onto his couch.

This time it was my eyes that wandered, lingering over his naked torso. His body was broader and more muscular than I'd remembered, but it was a look that suited him. My mind was trying to come to terms with the fact that Duncan had become the very sort of man I craved with the deepest part of my soul.

"So, you're a dom?" The words tumbled out before I'd even realized it, and I know I blushed. I could feel the heat in my cheeks, and I cast my eyes downward.

"Yes, I am," he said, stroking my chin and raising my face, forcing me to meet his gaze. "It took me some time to realize it, but once I did, I started living a more truthful life—and a more fulfilling one." His unblinking green eyes radiated with an intensity that made me shiver. "And what about you, Eve? What's your truth? What do you want?"

Duncan's voice was deep and demanding, and it tripped a switch inside me. I found myself wanting to confess all of the feelings I'd kept inside for too long.

"I want to be bound," I whispered. "I want to wear your cuffs—I want to be yours."

Duncan stared into my eyes, his face betraying his feelings, which were a potent mixture of affection and lust.

He reached into his pocket and pulled out a set of steel handcuffs. "The cuffs are only part of it, baby," he said, locking one around my wrist. I gasped as the metal lock snicked shut. Without waiting a beat, he clicked the second cuff around my other wrist, and then tugged on the chain that connected them, urging me to stand. I did, and Duncan turned me toward the wall, resting my cuffed hands above my head.

"When you wear my cuffs, I own every part of you. You're mine to do with as I please," he whispered hotly in my ear.

Waves of excitement flooded my body, and I nodded wordlessly, wondering what would happen next. I got my answer when he slipped a blindfold over my eyes, plunging me into darkness.

Duncan's hands slowly slid up my legs, tracing the seams along the backs of my stockings and gliding over my thighs before one of his palms settled on my ass. Flashes of my fantasies streamed through my mind, his touch awakening my primal desires.

"Tell me more, Eve. Have you been a bad girl? Did you

come here looking for someone who'd punish you?"

"Y-yes," I stuttered in a barely audible whisper.

"I know all about bad girls like you. I know what you need," Duncan responded, his hand slapping my ass harshly and making me moan. My skirt dulled the blow, but beneath it my flesh still tingled. I didn't move; I stayed in position as he began spanking me slow and hard through the thin layer of fabric. The ache in my sex grew as the burn in my bottom increased. The heat seemed to spread throughout my lower half, making me desperately aroused.

When Duncan finally stopped, I was breathless. He was standing behind me so closely that I could feel the heat from his bare chest through the delicate silk of my blouse. He tangled his fingers in my hair and tilted my head to the side so he could kiss my cheek.

"I've dreamed of having you like this, Eve. All these years, I'd wondered what it would be like to have you bound. To spank you and fuck you while you were cuffed and helpless."

His confession made my pussy even wetter than it was already.

I wriggled against Duncan's body, feeling his erection nestled beneath his jeans. God, I wanted him inside me, but I wanted what he did next even more.

Duncan pulled away from my writhing body and then reached for the waistband of my skirt. Slowly, he pulled down the zipper, revealing my bare ass, which was framed by the black lace of my garter belt.

"Beautiful," he murmured, stroking me lovingly for a moment before planting a gentle kiss on each cheek and sliding my skirt down my legs. I stepped out of the garment and kicked it aside, and seconds later Duncan gently slapped my thigh.

"Legs apart and arch your back. Stick out that sweet ass for me," he demanded, spanking one cheek and then the other. I rushed to obey, sucking in air between my teeth as I absorbed the sweet pain. I swayed my ass from side to side as Duncan's hand spanked me in a decadent rhythm. I felt myself anticipating the next strike and then moaning when his hand made contact with my flesh. It was as hypnotizing as it was arousing, and I got lost in the sensations, in the heady mix of pleasure and pain that raced through my body.

Duncan's hand gradually slowed until he was no longer spanking me but stroking me. But his gentle touches were sparking trails of heat along my flesh. He then gripped my cheeks in his hands and eased them apart so he could slide his tongue down my crack to tease my asshole. As he lapped at my back hole, I nearly sobbed. It felt good, but dirty to be exposed and pleasured so intimately. He released one of my cheeks to slide his fingers up my slit and tease my clit. The way he feathered his tongue and flicked his fingers made it feel like I was being tongued front and back, and it was nearly impossible to keep quiet. My soft moans grew louder as my arousal gradually increased.

I was so very close to coming when Duncan pulled

away. Seconds later, I heard rustling behind me as he seemed to unzip his pants. He stepped closer, wrapping his arms around me, and I felt his erection, hot and hard, nudging my ass as he ripped my blouse open and reached into my bra. He cupped my breasts and then pinched my nipples hard. My cuffs rattled as my body jerked.

"Please, Duncan," I whispered desperately. He squeezed my nipples again, and I felt a rush of honey seep from my slit.

"Please, what? You want me to fuck you? What makes you think you deserve my cock?"

I nearly sobbed when he said those words. The idea that he could deny me what I most wanted seemed utterly cruel. But thankfully, Duncan was only playing. He released my breasts, and then I felt his dick sliding along my wet slit. He kept it there, poised at the entrance of my pussy for a long moment, teasing me with the promise of penetration. I arched my back and begged him with my body.

"You deserve every bit of it," he murmured soothingly as he rocked his hips and slipped his dick inside me. "I want to take care of you, Eve, to give you all of the pain and pleasure you crave."

Duncan moved his hand around my body, sliding down my stomach and over my mound to find my clit nestled within the slippery flesh below. He pressed his fingertips against my button, rubbing in small circles as he continued pumping his shaft in and out of me. I was lost in bliss as he increased the pace of his bucking hips, slapping his pelvis against my well-spanked cheeks and making them burn anew. He continued fucking and stroking me until my climax broke, and I pounded my fists against the wall as the pleasure filled me and years of dreams exploded into bursts of color in my mind. I rode those rhythmic waves as Duncan gripped my hips and pounded into me furiously, groaning as the spasms of my orgasm massaged him and induced his own release.

Seconds later, Duncan slipped off my blindfold and unfastened my cuffs, kissing my wrists where the metal had chafed my flesh. "It's still there," Duncan said, his voice filled with breathless awe. "That connection between you and me. But it's even better now."

I settled against his chest, feeling protected and possessed by his embrace as I answered, "Some bonds are just too strong to break."

FILTHY RICH

Shanna Germain

'm face down on the bed, my wrists and ankles wrapped in the softest fleece and leather cuffs. A sharp-toothed clamp is attached to each of my nipples, sending soft shoots of pain through me each time I shift on the silk sheets. TJ is lightly whipping my back and the curves of my ass with my favorite flogger, a velvety leather toy we bought on our last trip to Paris. I'm wet inside my lace panties—I always am when TJ whips me—but my mind is elsewhere. Where? I'm not sure. It's not the kind of good, mindless elsewhere that being bound and spanked usually takes me to. This is a turning and churning, my brain going round and round so much that I almost forget I'm being tortured by a man that I love and lust after and who loves and wants me in return. My skin feels the floggings, the pain, the pricks of pleasure, but somehow, the sensations are not making it all the way to my brain.

After a few minutes, the flogging stops, and the next thing I feel is TJ, lowering his body onto mine. He's still dressed, and the buckle of his leather belt presses into my ass. His teeth find my ear and nip lightly along its curve.

"Feeling bored, aren't you, baby?" TJ asks.

I don't know how to say yes, even though as soon as he asks it, I know it's the truth. I *am* bored. We have all of these gorgeous toys, a custom-built bondage bed with hooks and chains, and all the time in the world to play. I have a man who still lusts after me after all this time together, a gorgeous, tall man with dark hair and green eyes like the dark parts of an ancient forest, a man who gets me, who spanks me and ties me up and pulls my hair. And despite it all, I'm bored, bored, bored.

I know, it makes me sound like an asshole, doesn't it? Which is why I don't know how to answer TJ. It's why I lie there silent underneath him, my breath hardly even catching, not half as wet as I should be.

TJ and I are rich now, but it was mostly accidental—TJ's in a band, and he sold one of his songs to a car company. Every time they use it in their commercial, he gets a royalty for it. And they use it a lot.

But before that, we were poor for a long time. I mean, poorer than dirt-poor. So poor that we scrubbed mold from our apartment bathroom. So poor that we got past-expiration-date groceries and dented cans from the bargain store in the bad part of town. We worked hard, at dead-end jobs, and we had each other and we got by.

We were wicked then too, though. Or TJ was. I was mostly an innocent, wide-eyed and untouched, with a brain full of fantasies that I didn't dare speak aloud. Still, TJ knew what they were, what was on my brain, and he made them come true as best as he could.

"You want to be bound in those, baby?" he asked once after we'd walked by some fetish store, beautiful black leather cuffs and a red collar on the model in the window. I did, but I didn't know how to say so and I knew we couldn't afford those things anyway. So I just shook my head and pulled in closer to TJ.

TJ always knew, though. I don't know how. I still don't know how he knows what I'm thinking, what I'm lusting after. A few days later, he came home from work with a plastic bag and one of his signature sadist smiles.

I'd had a shit day of waiting on college students for ten hours. My feet were tired, I hadn't been able to wash the stink of fryer grease out of my hair and I'd made a ton less money than I'd hoped—and still that smile of his made me perk up just a little.

"What's that for?" I asked, the question more about the smile than whatever was in the bag.

"Later," he said. And for four days, that was the end of it. I knew where he kept our "toys"—which then consisted of an old belt that had a broken buckle, some well-used clothesline that I'd washed at the Laundromat so it wouldn't scratch, a couple of clothespins that had been sprung open a little so they didn't squeeze so tight, and a ten-dollar vibrator I'd had since college—but I didn't want to ruin the surprise. Even then, I was a good girl. Or at least a good girl for TJ.

He finally opened the bag on Sunday, our one day off together, the day we'd spend in our cheap futon on the floor, feeling luxurious for getting to sleep late. Feeling like royalty. He'd been teasing my nipples with his fingernails—such great fingernails, he had, kept longer and sharper on his right hand for guitar playing—and my body was already responding in that lazy morning roll and buck, hips tilting up to beg for his hand. His ready cock nudged my thigh, the moisture already wetting my skin. I wanted his fingers against me, making me damp, and then his cock in me. I wanted his hands to fall like rain and thunder against the curves of my ass as he fucked me. I wanted so much then. Everything and then some.

I buried my face against his neck, covered his skin with soft kisses. "Touch, please," I mumbled, still surprisingly shy about asking for what I wanted.

"Soon," he said. "Close your eyes."

His touch told me everything I needed to know. The way his fingers moved my hair away from my face, brought the leather around the circle of my neck, how they fastened the buckle tight behind me. And the feel of the leather on my skin, oh, god, I'd never felt anything like that. So rich, so soft, like being draped in the world's most expensive butter. I was a queen, a goddess, a million ages of what women are meant to be. I was afraid to open my eyes, to see the real world come back, the graying bedspread, the peeling walls. I wanted to be here, bound in the arms of my man for a bit longer.

"Oh, TJ, Jesus, we can't afford—"

His kiss hushed me, his fingers sliding between my legs brought my voice back into the room. "You deserve this, this and more," he said. "Someday."

I could only reach up and feel the leather about my neck, let my fingertips slide over its softness.

"Do you know what this means?" he asked.

"No," I said. But I did, even before he said it.

"It means you're mine," he said as his fingers found the leather around my neck, tugged me and turned me until my ass was in the air. One hand was curled around the collar, holding my neck up, curving my back. The other dipped between my thighs, stroked me until I was wet and panting.

"Mine," TJ said as he entered me, filling me, blotting out all the poorness of our lives with his hard, slow strokes.

"Yours," I said.

We got married years later, in a public ceremony, but we both knew that moment was really the one that mattered, the one that had bound us forever and ever.

* * *

As TJ is pressing his weight down on me, I have a sudden memory of that collar, the first one he ever bought for me, the first one I ever wore. I wonder where it is. I know now that it was cheap, but at the time it was the most gorgeous thing I'd ever owned. I wonder if it's a bad sign that I can't remember when I last wore it.

"Stacy," TJ growls in my ear. I can feel his heartbeat against my back. "Admit that you're bored."

"I'm not fucking bored," I say. It sounds like the lie that it is, stiff and self-determined, angry because it has nowhere else to go.

"Come on, baby," TJ says, wrapping his fingers in my hair and tugging my head back so that my face is off the sheets, so that I can't hide in that silky fabric. "I know you better than that."

I struggle beneath him, struggle inside the cuffs that bind me. "Get off," I say because I have nothing else to say. Because I am worried that if I'm bored, then he is bored too. Because if we have all of this, everything we could ever want, and we're not enjoying the fucking, then what does that say about us? That we're done? I've loved TJ for so long, wanted him for so long. I still want him. So how can I be bored?

"No," he says. His fingers trace the side of my neck, that place where my pulse beats hard when I'm excited or pissed off or scared. "It's okay to be bored. You just have to admit it."

There is silence between us for a long time. Not the

good post-coming kind of silence or even the content kind of silence. This is a silence full of sharp edges and pressure. I can't breathe under him and I'm pretty sure he knows it.

"Fine, I'm bored," I say, and I have to be angry about it. Damn him. Damn him for always knowing me so well, for being able to read me like no other, for not even having to see my face to know if I'm telling the truth.

"Me too," he whispers, and that shiver of fear slides up through me, fast and hard. So hard it makes me certain I can feel tears pooling in my eyes. We're done, then. Our forever and ever bond is broken. I can feel it, feel him pulling away from me.

But he doesn't leave me. He stays on top of me. He kisses the side of my cheek, and that's how I know I am crying, because I can feel him pushing the teary streams against my skin. "Don't, baby. It's not us," he says. "We need to bring the *dirty* back is all."

There is the sound of a buckle jangling, and TJ's hands around my neck. I feel the collar, the one I'd been thinking about, and I wonder again how he can know me so well, how he is always one step ahead of me. The collar doesn't feel the way I remembered—it's not soft at all, but scratchy and broken. It pinches my neck in the places where it doesn't curve right. Somehow, that's all perfect. The pain of it, the discomfort, brings my body to life with little sparks. TJ's fingers wrap inside the leather so that it grows tighter around my neck, and a small growl rises in his voice. "Roll over," he says. "Spread-eagle. Eyes open."

He slides off the bed, leaving me on sheets with my arms and legs spread out. TJ's still talking and I'm following some of it, bits and pieces here and there about being tired of being so clean, so posh, but mostly my mind feels like it's short-circuiting, somewhere between confusion and desire.

He has rope in his hands, our old clothesline—where in the hell did he find that?—and he's wrapping one end around my ankle. His erection bobs with every wrap of rope, and I don't know which is making me wetter—the feel of his hands working so steadily to loop and knot the rope around my ankle or watching his arousal. He tucks the rope under the end of the mattress and then ties my other ankle. Already I feel bound in a way that I haven't in a long time. Immobilized. I'm so wet that I can feel it soaking my spread thighs. My nipples pucker and push into the air, aching for his touch, for the brush of the edge of a belt. Every time I pant or swallow, I can feel the collar, its tight pinch and choke.

"Hands forward," he says.

I bring my hands down to my belly, clasp them together.

"Good girl." The old, broken belt makes its way around and around my wrists. The buckle is still broken, so TJ ties it off, cinching it tight.

"Wiggle," he says. But I hardly can. My cheeks burn, and I am delighted and amazed at their flush. How can

I be embarrassed? We'd done this a hundred times, a thousand, but I always am. And it's been a long time since I was this powerless before him, in front of him.

He brings out the clothespins, squeezing them open and closed, his grin wicked. My nipples are so pointed they're easy to clamp. The wood bites into my skin, and I make a noise somewhere between a groan of pleasure and a swear.

TJ stands back, hands on his hips, and he inspects me. "So much better," he says. "I've missed having you all trussed up, all dirty." He walks around me, touching and looking.

He tweaks one of the clothespins, sending a jolt through me. When I cry out, he laughs, delighted. Two fingers brush the cleft between my legs before he brings them up, wet, to press them into my mouth. I taste of dirty thoughts and desire, of a hot want that seems ancient and timeless. He presses my tied-together hands between my thighs.

"Fuck yourself," he says. "While I watch."

My face burns hotter—I want to turn my head away, close my eyes—but I do as he says. I wet my fingers in my own desire, then rub small circles around my clit. He watches my eyes, his own green ones turning darker. With one hand, he takes hold of my collar, pulling my head up. With the other, he aims his cock toward my mouth.

His tip is glistening, the hole at the end wide and open, and I want him buried in my throat when I fuck myself. I want to feel him come deep inside my throat, to taste his sweet salt while he groans and shudders above me.

"Please, please," I say, just as his tip parts my lips. He doesn't sink any deeper, though, teasing me instead, wiping his arousal over my lips and tongue, holding me away from him by the collar.

"Oh, I've missed this," he says. His thrusts deepen, just a little, until I can take the whole head of him, suck him into the heat of my mouth. I focus on his length and taste, wrapping my tongue around him, urging him deeper.

He slips out, and I groan from the loss of him. "I didn't say you could stop," he says, and I realize I've let my hands go still.

"But I'm going to come if I keep—"

"That, I think, is the point," he says. He moves my hands back into position, rubs them hard over my clit, until I'm doing it myself, my hips bucking up as much as they can with my ankles tied.

"Now you can have my cock in your mouth," he says, and the groan I let out is part for the slide of my fingers on my clit, but mostly for wanting him, for the way he starts to stroke into my mouth, quick and whole.

TJ talks the whole time, his words sending small shudders of pleasure between my ears and my mouth and my clit. It's a tiny circuit that runs through my body; if it keeps speeding up, it's going to send me over. TJ knows this, of course, which is why he keeps talking, keeps thrusting, keeps reaching down to tweak the clothespins on my nipples.

"I've missed you being my cheap, dirty whore. Tied up in clothesline and broken belts. I'm going to throw out all the sheepskin and fleece and silk. I'm going to rub your nipples raw on rough cotton sheets. I'm going to bind you to the floor with the dog's leash, hands and knees, and fuck you until you've got rug burn. I'm going to hold that loud plastic vibrator to your clit until you beg me to stop and then I'm going to hold it there some more and listen to you holler as you come."

Fuck him, I think, for knowing everything I want before I even want it. Fuck him for giving me every-thing.... And then the short circuit goes into overload, runs mouth, nipple, clit, bam bam bam in time to TJ's thrusts. There is only the pleasure of having my mouth full of TJ's cock, of the pain in my nipples, of the flutter of my own fingers on my clit.

TJ's words stop too, fall away into a groan of plea-sure as he floods my mouth and throat. He tastes just like me, filthy thoughts and sweet heat, and I swallow him down as I come.

"Still bored, baby?" he asks a few minutes later as he unloops the belt from my wrists, watching my face with those green, green eyes.

"No," I breathe. I'm not sure where my brain and body are, but I'm having a hard time pulling them all together enough to answer him, much less think. "Not bored."

"See?" he says as he takes the clamps slowly off my nipples. "I told you it wasn't us. We got all clean and rich, but we forgot how to be dirty and rich."

"Filthy rich?" I say. TJ starts laughing, then he takes hold of the old collar around my neck and leans down to kiss me, soft, the laughter rolling from him to me, just another invisible bond between us.

"Exactly," he says. "Dirty, filthy rich."

LIFE DRAWING

Vida Bailey

The women were so beautiful. That wasn't something Rosie had anticipated taking from the sessions, when she signed up. Casual life drawing meetings her friend had organized, they didn't have the cash for a model, much less a teacher. Instead each woman took turns sitting, or standing, or in the case of the ones who did yoga, holding poses. She marveled at them, the set of their hips, the auras of curls or straight strands of hair, and somehow, most of all, at their wrist bones. There was such elegance, such strength and delicacy, in the braced poise of a woman's wrist, in her splayed fingers. She encountered enormous frustration in being unable to render what she saw with such clarity, what she looked on with awe.

When it was Rosie's turn, she sat as still as she could,

enjoying the peace of the concentration. It was refreshing to do nothing but be for a while. Hold a warm teacup and a pose. Remember to breathe. There was a strange acceptance to be found in doing it—holding someone's interest because of exactly what you were, being concentrated on without judgment. She saw herself become a curving tangle of lines, of light and dark. Each smile, each laugh became a picture. It was a welcome sort of attention.

People came and left the small space, weeks on and off. In week four, someone brought Arlo.

Amidst the bustle of cheery greetings and shivers at the start of the evening, Arlo entered, and there was a momentary hush. Rosie's friend Clara came in, and then the atmosphere in the room shifted. Behind her was a lean, dark-haired man, the first male to join the group. They'd all said that would be nice, and it was, of course, but the dynamic became charged the second he walked in the door.

Arlo smiled hello as the women greeted him and quickly sat down and started setting out his pad and pens. He waved at Rosie. They'd been in college together and had had mutual friends. She'd spent an evening talking to him at a boring party, but that seemed so long ago. He didn't look that different, though. He was still lean and well dressed, straight-backed in a way that made his modest frame seem taller. She marveled at the way he could walk into a room full of women without seeming ruffled or making anyone else uncomfortable. He looked like a man anyone would want to know better.

Arlo quickly became engaged in drawing Jane, a tall, slim woman with long, flowing, dark hair. Rosie watched his eyes flick from model to paper and back, watched him look through the woman leaning against the chair back. She took in the lean line of his cheek and his full lips, and her fingers itched to trap them on paper.

She watched him from behind the cover of her board. His dark hair fell into his eyes as he looked down and he would blow it away each time he looked up again. His hand moved deliberately. Clean lines, Rosie thought. After ten minutes, Jane called time. She stood and stretched, perhaps a little ostentatiously, and took her seat again. There was the usual who's-next? dithering. Rosie waited. She'd taken a turn fairly recently. She sat resolutely still, yet thought about how she'd feel, out there under his measuring gaze. She smiled to herself, tingling in her seat thinking about his eyes on her. Looking over again, she met his stare. He was watching her, too. Holding her eye, he stood. There was a smattering of appreciative noise as Arlo moved into the center of the room.

"I'm game, ladies, if you think I'll do?" A chorus of agreement broke out. "Where do you want me?"

"How about against the wall?" Jane called out, to a round of guffaws. Arlo just smiled. He took off his jacket, then bent to unlace his boots. He peeled off his shirt and socks and leaned against the wall in jeans and undershirt. Rosie looked around to see more than a couple open mouths. This was…a treat.

"Two minutes?" The women nodded. It was different, drawing a man. Rosie willed her fingers to work. How to draw him? She scribbled vague outlines, trying to learn the lines of him. It was frustrating, to see each line of tension, each smooth surface misrendered in pencil. She gave up and drew him in little segments; his hair, the line of his profile, his bare arm and shoulder. Engaged with his bicep, she forgot about the rest of him and was shocked to glance up and find him looking at her. Their eyes connected and she faltered for a second. Then she smiled and kept working, cursing the blush she could feel working itself into her cheeks.

They went to the pub after class that night. Arlo wove through the crowd, balancing pints in two hands. He sat down beside her.

"Are you busy Sunday?" he asked. She looked up at him, licking Guinness off her upper lip, eyes wide. She shook her head. "It would be nice to catch up. Would you like to grab some brunch, maybe? Stop by my studio first?"

"Come up and see your etchings?" She tried to make it come across light, and then worried she sounded like a dirty old woman. But he laughed.

"Maybe. I haven't gotten to draw you, yet."

Tit for tat, she wanted to say, but repressed the flip remark. "I'd like that."

His smile was warm and she felt her nerves burn

off as they chatted. She'd forgotten the feeling of his easy company; she liked the quiet attention. In college Arlo had been all energy, the kind of person who never stopped moving. Now he was unexpectedly still, and it suited him. She felt quite grounded in his presence. To the extent that she'd said yes to being drawn! Unless that had just been banter. It was hard to say.

That Sunday, at his studio, the stairs were broad and winding. Painted white. She felt her floral skirt swishing around her thighs as she walked up them, held tight to the banister so as to stay the boss of her heels. Above the concentrated grip of her hand, there was a framed photograph. A startlingly beautiful Japanese woman stared at her, lips stained with dark rose, eyes moist. She wore a silk kimono that looked traditional and expensive. Her arms were pinned behind her back, and her torso was bound with rope, above and below her breasts, binding her belly. She looked at the wisps of hair falling into the model's face, the only real evidence of disarray.

Rosie turned to look at Arlo, remembering he was standing behind her. Her mouth was open a little too wonderingly, maybe, and he smiled at her.

"Araki, that one. Not me. I've got lots of others," he offered, without a trace of a leer. Laying a gentle hand at her back, he moved just past her and guided her to another picture. This one was more explicit, black and white and artfully shot, a woman tied and stretched and her face a picture of repose above the white, bright-lit length of her taut neck. And beyond that, spread legs and smooth belly, black and white again, the Y of her crisscrossed with a girdle of black rope that framed her abdomen, her shaved pussy lips and protruding labia. A belly ring gleamed in the dark light of the photo.

Rosie forgot the sunlit day outside as she looked, so compelling were the shadows in the photographs, the lights and darks from which the women emerged. She looked at Arlo again, and swallowed.

"They're beautiful," she said, and was rewarded with such a smile she realized that it was he who'd been the nervous one. He hadn't intimidated her at all; rather, she was the one who was in a position to judge by being frightened away. Or worse still, disgusted. She wondered how many women had failed the test in the past.

In the studio, there were more pictures, some sketched, some painted, and lots of photographs. Not all were of women, there were couples too, even families. Arlo clearly drew people with their clothes on as well. The room itself was a beautifully lit attic, with a padded canvas floor. It smelled of wood and paint, and something sweet she couldn't identify.

"Did you mean it, Rosie? Can I draw you?"

Up until that moment, Rosie hadn't decided. She hadn't been sure if he'd meant it for real. And now she felt extraordinarily flattered by his request. She inclined her head shyly.

"If you'd like to?"

"Great. I thought we'd eat afterward? I don't want

anyone feeling self-conscious about a swollen belly." He rubbed his own, and winked.

"Am I taking my clothes off?"

The question hung, bald and final, in the honeyed air of the studio.

"If that seems like a nice thing to do on a Sunday morning, sure," Arlo answered, nonchalant. "Your heels, at least," he amended, reaching for them. They were burgundy suede pumps, soft, little worn. She slipped them off one at a time and placed them in his outstretched hand.

"Sit. Show me your toes." He arranged her chiffon skirt around her bent knees, his fingers lingering on its soft material, touching the tiny flowers of its print. "Pretty."

She looked up, into his face, which seemed startlingly close to hers. The dress was feminine, not a little girlish, she knew. It was provocative for that reason.

Arlo drew back, pulled up a chair and grabbed a big drawing pad. "Now it's my turn."

Rosie closed her eyes and settled into her pose. She spread her fingers on the floor and thought of how she'd felt when she'd drawn him, how he'd looked to her. She listened to the sound of his pencil on the paper, felt the warmth of the sun on the back of her neck. What could he see? She stretched her shoulders and looked past him, realizing that a coil of rope hung from the wall behind his head. He followed her eyes, turning to look at it.

"Would you like to touch it?"

She nodded. It wasn't rough hemp like the one in the first photo. It was black, and it looked...silky. He took it from its peg and brought it to her, placing it in front of her like an offering. She stretched out a finger and stroked its surface. The rope lay coiled between them, a neat thing. Rosie imagined it unfurled, its length a straight line across the floor, between them. She saw it looping around her wrists, her back, its soft strength binding her. She cleared her throat.

"I'd like to know what it feels like."

"Wound around you?"

"Yes. Would you draw me like the women in the photographs?"

"I'd love to."

He picked up the rope and unwound it. There seemed to Rosie to be a lot of motion, the swish of rope running through fingers, looping, tugging, repetition. At first there was just knotting going on, Arlo's fingers jerking at her back, running under her breasts, but she soon noticed that she was beginning to feel constricted—her chest was crisscrossed with ropes that formed a harness. He'd drawn her arms back behind her and folded them, and now they were immobilized. Her breasts stood out, tight cord above and below them. Rosie felt dizzy. A vertigo overtook her, as if she might fall from a great height. A sense of accompanying panic threatened her. She was sitting on the floor, but she felt an expanse open up beneath her.

"Breathe."

Arlo's voice came soft in her ear. He pressed a gentle hand to her breastbone. "It's fine. You're fine. Just don't forget to breathe."

She let out a breath she hadn't realized she was holding. He raised her chin and looked at her expectantly.

"I'm fine." She laughed, breathlessly, and breathed some more. "Yes, really, you're right, thank you."

"Good," he said, and went back to his pad, pacing round the room, viewing her from different angles. His pen scratched some more, reimagining her in black and white.

"Rosie, there's just something...I just want to see what happens when..."

She felt a gentle pressure on her shoulder, and before she could grasp what he meant, she found herself tipped over onto the soft floor. With her arms behind her back, she panicked going down, and her legs flailed a little bit. She lay there, hair in her face, her legs akimbo and her dress risen to crotch level.

"Arlo!"

"Shh. That's perfect. Stay there, please. Are you okay?"

"I'm upside down."

"Mmm-hmm. Not *really*." His tone suggested he'd seen far more upside-down women in the past.

Rosie pressed her face into the soft padding and tried not to wiggle. A hot blush rose in her cheeks when she thought about how she looked. Her arms were pressed tight to her back and her shoulders felt stretched. If she tried to get up she knew she'd flop about like a fish. So she lay there. She closed her eyes and thought about the woman in the photo, her mouth full and relaxed, her eyes closed as if in sleep. She had been laid on her side too, wrists and ankles tied, breasts bound. It was a much crueler position that Rosie was in, yet she seemed to revel in it. Rosie tested her bonds and found them strong. She was held by them. She tried to be aware of every point where the rope touched her, to sense the pattern of it as it looped and bound her body.

A shadow fell across her. She looked up.

"Hey." Arlo was looking down at her. There was another length of rope in his hand. "Would you like some more?" Rosie considered. "You're doing so well."

"Where?"

"Hmm?"

She blushed again. "Where would you tie me?"

He knelt beside her. Stretching out a hand to her, he ran his fingers around the inside of her naked thighs, up over her hips and around her waist, and then down, across the top of her mons and down toward the creases of her thighs.

"All around here?" he offered, stroking her buttock with butterfly fingertips. She tipped her pelvis toward him, greedy from the sensations he'd awoken. Her knickers were wet, she knew, and she knew he could see. Even smell, maybe. But it made her understand something. She had arrived in a place from which there was no going back. So she nodded. And she asked a question.

"Arlo. Would it be better if... Would you take off my underwear?"

His hand slid up to cup her cunt, pressed lightly there.

"That would be perfect, Rosie."

His polite response to her faltering request seemed ridiculous, but the pressure of his hand stopped her giggling, stopped her feeling embarrassed. She breathed deeply and waited while he rolled the elastic down off her hips, lifted her up off the floor as he pulled them down her thighs and dropped them behind him. Then his fingers followed the path they'd traced and soon her underwear was replaced with a girdle of rope that ran around her belly, biting into the soft skin there. It looped under her ass and framed her cunt and tied thickly around each thigh. She strained to close her legs, hide herself from his gaze, but he laid a firm hand on each knee and tsked softly, shook his head.

"Stay open for me." His eyes met hers, completely serious. "That's right. Good girl."

The rope felt hard against her soft places, the cushion of her inner thighs, her ass. His fingers tripped over it, not touching her bare sex. She longed for the feel of his warm palm against her again. But he withdrew, picked up his pad. This time, she felt scrutinized. It was the first time she'd posed naked in any way, and now she was not only naked but completely exposed. The dress that was rucked above her waist made her feel even more bare below, turned her sex into something a little more obscene in its contrasting nudity. Arlo's eyes on her felt like hands now, she was so completely aware of herself. She fought to keep her legs open. She wanted to please him, to be like the still, serene models in the photos on his walls. Not this heart-pounding, wet-snatched mess of a woman lying sprawled on the floor.

So she breathed. And tried to contain the urge to move her hips. She lay in the bonds he'd put her in and relaxed, as much as she could with the ache in her legs pulling at her. She risked a glance at him and was shocked at the intensity with which he was looking at her. His eyes were dark as they moved from the paper to her body with a keen, concentrated interest. His gaze met hers and locked, it seemed to penetrate all of her—her open legs, the way her flesh pushed between the ropes, her nudity and constraints peeled away by its force. His stare cut through the layers of self-consciousness and nerves and insecurity to whoever lay beneath. He'd tied her up and set her free. Rosie wanted to ask him who he saw. She bit her lip and closed her eyes and heard the reassuring scratching of pen nib on paper again. Her cheeks burned, but her modesty was overruled by the erotic impact of the thought that his pen was tracing the lines of her cunt. She could feel it, stroking there, feel him outlining her, drawing her anew.

It occurred to her that she was giving herself to him completely. She could withdraw and let him do what he wanted with her, make her into whoever he chose. It was a relief, almost, to have someone else in charge of her image. Rosie lay there while Arlo rendered her in ink. She found herself feeling quite safe after a while, settling into a drifting kind of peace. He drew and drew, staying close to her. She could hear his breath, smell his cologne as he moved closer.

"I think it's time to get up now."

She was going to protest, such was the languor that had come over her, but she stretched her fingers and found her arms buzzing. Arlo lifted her upright with ease and began working to untie the ropes, releasing her arms first. Red lines appeared as the rope fell away. She was marked all around, and the blood flowing back into the places where the ties had bitten tingled and sang. He rubbed at her wrists and shoulders, squeezing out the ache there.

Arlo stood and went to a shelf on the wall. When he turned back to her, she saw he had a camera in his hands. He pointed it at her as she stretched, easing out the tension and cramp, the pins and needles. The sleepiness stayed with her—her usual horror of being photographed remained a gentle tension in the background and she just looked up at him, intrigued by the concentration on his face, his measuring gaze. He knelt by her again, showed her the photograph he'd taken. In the tiny screen sat a woman she hardly recognized, softened and hazy.

"This is probably what I'll use in the end. This one,

when the ropes are unwound but their mark is still on you. When you don't think you're on show anymore, and you've relaxed. This is the one that looks like you."

Oh. A means to an end? It was hard to see it as a process, the rope, when it had felt like such an end in itself when she lay there.

"Rosie?"

She looked at him.

"Are you wet?" He knew she was. When she moved her thighs together she could feel the liquid smooth between them. "Will you touch yourself for me?"

I couldn't do that, she thought, and her fingers found their way under her dress, toyed with the softness of the rope that ran down between her legs, pushing her swollen sex lips together and pressing into the crack of her ass. *Oh, oh, I couldn't, in front of someone I don't know that well*, her voice sang in her head, as she slipped her fingers up and down her labia, into her wet cleft and back, back to her clit that thrummed as she touched it, rubbed behind it, first gently, then with increasing speed. Her bound hips lifted off the mat as she explored herself. She was framed for him, her legs bracketing the roped space between, sectioned. She heard the camera again. And she let out a little moan, an exhalation of all the arousal that had been building since she got ready that morning, never realizing where she'd actually find herself, tied on a floor and masturbating for an artist she hadn't seen in years with her fingers crammed inside her...oh...

Rosie came with a burst of warmth, flooded by light that shone into the warm little studio space. She strained her thighs against the ropes that held them, braced herself and shoved her pelvis down against the contractions that thronged inside her. Her head rolled to the side and the light found her face. She breathed through her mouth and felt herself floating somewhere. The tingling moved through her teeth, sang in her scalp, tickled the ends of her hair. She was limp and weightless, she was floating free. She wasn't even sure how she found herself standing, or how much time might have passed later, when Arlo suggested the café across the road for lunch. But she agreed, suddenly ravenously hungry.

She pulled her dress up to reveal the rope circling her thigh, looked at Arlo expectantly. She hadn't a clue where to start untying herself.

"Oh." He smiled at her. "Well, how about you leave it on while we eat, and afterward, we can come back here and I can take it off...or leave it there to hold on to it while I fuck you?"

She blushed again, knowing it would be ridiculous to pretend shock after she'd just come on his floor, in his bonds, and was looking forward to doing it again. And so she ate lunch, tied in his rope and the red marks that ran around her chest and arms, squirming in her seat and waiting for the new thing that had already begun to take flight and carry her with it.

CUTE BOY GETS SQUEEZED

D. L. King

Hey, Cute Boy, you should come over here. I got something fun for you," she said.

No "Hi, how are you"; no "This is…"; no preamble, nothing. It didn't matter; I'd know that peculiar cross between a Brooklyn and a Southern accent anywhere. And besides, Evangeline was the only person who called me Cute Boy.

Somehow, Eve had spotted my kink right from the get-go. She knew, even before I did. She could tell I wanted to be bound, controlled, placed in predicaments I couldn't get out of, my free will supplanted by the will of another, yada yada yada. You get the idea.

"So, Cute Boy, you comin' over or what?"

"Hi, Eve."

"Hi, Cute Boy." She said it with a sort of dreamy

quality. Eve was bizarre, but man, was she hot. I knew whatever she had in mind would be more than "fun"; it would probably be unbelievable.

"Tick tock, Cute Boy."

"Uh, yeah," I said, "Okay. But I don't know where you are."

"Sure you do. You've been here. Red Hook. Remember?"

Of course I remembered. How could I forget? It was the first time I'd been tied up since I was six. Eve lived in this huge industrial loft space that had been converted into part photography studio and part living space. Her roommate, whom I'd never met, was a photographer—a pretty successful fetish photographer, from what I gathered. Eve wrote dirty books. Maybe she did something else, too; I didn't know.

"But how do you get there?" I asked.

"It's easy, Cute Boy, just take a cab."

She gave me the address and I said okay. Okay— of course okay. I jumped in the shower, and while I shaved off the pubic stubble that had grown since the last time we'd played, I remembered the way the ropes felt against my bare skin. I thought about the way the prickly hemp felt between my legs and the way my balls bulged and stretched, tightly wrapped in rawhide. Just thinking about it practically made me come right there in the shower.

The sun was just beginning to set as I rang the bell and heard the lock click as the buzzer sounded. I stepped into the big, industrial cage and pulled the front gate down in order to start the climb to the top of the building. That's when the butterflies kicked in. This was only the second time I'd been here, and Evangeline was—different… I mean, I didn't think she was, like, dangerous or anything, but, well, it's strange what kinds of thoughts can run through your mind on your way to being made naked and helpless.

I rang the bell and a guy opened the door. Before I could say anything, Eve bounded up and draped her arm across my shoulder, pulling me inside.

"Cute Boy, this is my roommate Nigel. Nigel, Cute Boy."

"Pete," I said, holding out my hand to Nigel. "I didn't know your roommate was going to be here."

"Chill, Cute Boy, that's why I called you. Nigel's got this gig and we wanted to try something out before the shoot. I immediately thought of you. You're not claustrophobic, are you?"

"I don't think so. Why? You're not gonna lock me up in a closet, are you?"

"No! That wouldn't be any fun at all. So you're not, then, right?"

"I don't think so."

"You like rubber?"

"Huh? I don't know. Maybe. Yeah, I guess. What's this all about?"

"Take your clothes off."

I eyed Nigel, who was standing by the kitchen counter

drinking a cup of tea and futzing with a camera. "Wait a minute. Is he gonna take pictures? I don't know about that, and you have to tell me what the deal is." I was taking a stand.

"Don't worry, no one will ever know it's you, I promise." She put her hands on my shoulders and kissed me while she slid her hands up, under my T-shirt, grazing my nipples as she pushed the shirt farther up until I gave in and took it off. She petted my chest and stroked from my nipples down to my navel with the backs of her hands, her glossy blue fingernails skating over my skin, raising goose bumps. When she made it to the waistband of my jeans, she unbuttoned them and I let them fall into a heap at my feet.

"See, didn't I tell you? He's got the cutest little body and such a nice cock."

My "nice cock" had been getting all happy until she pointed it out to Nigel, and then it started to wilt.

"Oh, poor baby. Just forget Nigel's here. Go away, Nigel. Come into the living room, I want to show you something."

Nigel disappeared into another room and I followed Eve to a giant square of gray rubber stretched over what looked like a frame made of PVC pipe. I touched the rubber and it felt nice: cool and slick but not slippery—kinda smooth. "Hey, I've seen one of these online. This is a vac something, right?"

"A vac bed."

"Yeah, a vac bed." My cock started to wake up again.

"Wanna try it?"

Oh, yeah, I wanted to try it. I think there was a little drool at the corner of my mouth as I nodded, kneeling on the floor, stroking the rubber.

"I have some toys to go with it that I think will make it even more fun," she said.

I was so enthralled with the rubber and the whole idea of being squeezed between the sheets, I wasn't paying much attention until she said she was going to blindfold me. I wasn't sure I wanted to be blindfolded, but she said it would be better for my eyes and besides, I'd have to have 'em closed inside the vac bed anyway.

I suppose she had a point there.

After blindfolding me, she helped me kneel down on the floor next to the vac bed and told me to get on my hands and knees.

"Ever had anything up your butt?" she asked.

I thought of Nigel and said no, thinking I might not want anything up my butt. Before I could get the words out, I felt slick fingers teasing my asshole. "Um, Eve…"

"This'll be fun. You'll like it. Just relax. It's just a little butt plug."

I felt something huge slowly coaxing me open, but she kept stroking my cock and balls the whole time, which seemed to help. And after a while, it felt pretty good. I pushed back against it and my body just sucked it inside.

While I was shifting my weight from one knee to the other, getting the feel for the plug, I felt something wet and cold press against me, somewhere between my balls and my asshole. It almost made me jump out of my skin. Eve laughed.

"Cute Boy, you're so cute."

"What was that?"

"Nothing. Don't worry about it," she said.

"No, really, what was it?" I asked again.

"It's a surprise," she said. "I think you'll like it. It'll be fun. And if you don't like it, you can do a safe call thing. So look," she said, "I'll help position you between the rubber sheets and get the breathing tube situated. There's, like, a mouthpiece inside the sheets that you put in your mouth, and that way you can breathe 'cause, you know, you're gonna wanna breathe, and this way you can do it without breaking the seal. But then you won't be able to talk. So we'll have a signal. If I ask you a question, make one noise for yes and two for no. And if you don't like it and want to stop, just make two noises and we'll stop. Okay?"

As soon as I crawled between the rubber and felt it on my skin, my cock got happy. With each movement, the plug in my ass knocked against different parts of me and set off little nerve fireworks, but once I was situated and had the mouthpiece in, nervous anticipation took over. The cold of the rubber against my bare skin made me shiver, but by the time Eve locked the frame together, things began to heat up.

I lay on the floor, spread-eagle, with my cock sticking straight up as I heard the vacuum start up and the air being sucked out. I felt Eve's hands through the rubber as she played with and stroked my cock, which only strained harder against her touch. I could feel the rubber sheeting start to shift and close in against me and I fidgeted.

"Are you all right?" she asked.

I tried to say something but it was unintelligible.

"Grunt once for yes and twice for no."

So I grunted once and felt her guiding my erect cock toward my belly as the rubber began to wrap around it and squeeze me in tightly. I grunted, with feeling.

"Like that, do you?"

I tried to nod but couldn't move my head. The rubber had encased my cheeks and my forehead and I felt like I was in a velvet vise. The vacuum was still going and I could feel the rubber's hot embrace getting tighter and tighter until I could no longer so much as twitch. That's when I felt something trace up and down my hard-on. I must have babbled incoherent things because the torturous touching continued, but Eve told me to grunt once for good and twice for stop. I would normally have slouched into the feeling but I couldn't move enough to slouch. All I could do was produce one protracted grunt and take it like a man.

The noise of the vacuum stopped and I felt more than one set of hands. I felt fingers circling my nipples, causing them to get even stiffer under the tight bondage and fingers teasing my sac and the head of my cock, and as I acclimated to the dichotomy of sexual edge and the relaxation of strict bondage, everything but my body ceased to exist. I floated in the sensation of the tight cocoon—until, out of nowhere, my ass lit up like a Christmas tree. My ass was getting fucked from the inside, but the plug wasn't moving. At the same time, I felt an insistent throbbing just behind my asshole and I moaned.

"Is that a happy noise?" she asked.

One long grunt followed.

"I thought it would be fun to hook you up to electric toys. I guess you think it's pretty fun too, judging by the noises you're making." Once she got it set the way she wanted it, she went back to stroking my body through the rubber. I have no idea how long she played with me that way; I lost all track of time. When she ramped up the sensations in my ass and balls, I came back to myself to feel her concentrating her touch on the head of my cock. She swirled her finger around the sensitive part, under the tip.

I felt an electrical jolt go up my butt and, at the same time, I felt her fingernails bite into my cock, through the rubber.

You have no idea what an odd sensation it is to come while your body is under extreme pressure. My back wanted to arch, and the bondage of the vac bed wouldn't allow it. It was like straining against a wall of steel. Shortly after that, the pressure was released. I began to shiver almost as soon as she opened the frame. My body was covered in sweat and it pooled under my butt and my back, between my legs and under my arms. I took the blindfold off as Eve threw me a towel.

"How was it?" she asked.

"Fucking amazing," I said.

"Wait till you see the pictures!"

ON THE ROCKS

Heidi Champa

It was so damn hot. The air-conditioning really picked a hell of a night to conk out. The usually chilly airflow stopped completely right before the pub was supposed to open. Noah called the repair guy, but he couldn't come out to take a look until the day after tomorrow. We were stuck with the heat, and soon our customers would be stuck to the vinyl bar stools and chairs. We threw open all of the windows, but there was hardly any breeze blowing that night. The air was so damned thick, I could almost feel the moisture as it settled on my skin. The only thing we had to keep us remotely cool was an old fan we found in the storeroom. It moved slowly from side to side and managed to circulate the stale air just a bit. Noah and I stood in front of the squeaky old thing, gently swaying to stay in the fan's path. However, soon it became clear that moving around was negating the limited effects of the fan.

Margarita Wednesdays were always a popular night, but since the heat wave hit the city, the pub was slammed. It seemed the entire town was sweating, and the only cure for their condition was a frozen drink. The blender was constantly whirring and the two of us never stopped moving behind the bar. The ice machine was on overdrive, but it couldn't keep up and melting liquid drained in a steady stream, making the floor wet. Everywhere I looked, people were holding their drinks up to their foreheads, trying to cool off any way they could.

Between making the tropical drinks and the sweat soaking through my tank top, I was feeling sticky and salty. Every now and then, when no one was looking, I dropped an ice cube down my shirt, letting the freezing cube melt between my breasts and run down into my denim shorts. I noticed Noah staring a few times, taking in my cooldown technique, momentarily oblivious to the throng around us. Each time the cube heated up and disappeared into water, I let out a satisfied sigh, but all too soon, the relief was replaced by a fresh sheen of sweat on my skin. Noah made the best of a bad situation as well, scoring extra tips every time he raised his shirt and exposed his chest to get some fresh air. The show wasn't lost on me either, my stomach tightening every time I saw his bare skin. Each time we brushed against each other behind the bar, he'd lay a hand on my waist or my shoulder and make me quiver inside. He knew what he was doing to me and the bastard enjoyed every second of it. Talk about a heat wave.

"All right, everyone. Last call."

The words I had longed to hear all night rang out of Noah's mouth, the predictable groan that followed music to my ears. I started to pick up the glasses strewn all over the pub, pools of sticky liquid dotting the length of the bar. The last remaining stragglers were forced out into the wretched heat of the night, and just the two of us were left behind. We started our nightly routine, each one of us working in slow motion trying to stay as cool as possible, until the bar was as relatively clean as it was when the night began. Noah piled the glasses in the kitchen for the day crew to deal with; the thought of all that hot dishwater made my stomach turn. I grabbed the mop and bucket to clean up the spills that had made their way to the floor.

On my way by, I pulled open the lid of the ice machine, the arctic blast hitting me right in the face. It felt like heaven. Noah moved beside me, letting the cool fog work its magic on him, too. He reached into the vat and extracted a pair of perfectly formed cubes. He held one out to me, the heat making it drip as soon as it hit the air. I thought for a moment of doing the proper thing and grabbing it, but instead, I let my mouth fall open, waiting for him to place the cube of lovely coolness on my tongue. He obliged me, only hesitating for a moment, which allowed a few stray drops to cascade down my chest. Even surrounded by so much heat, it made me shiver as I sucked on the ice, tasting the saltiness of his fingers until he pulled them away. The flavor of his skin sent a rush of blood to my cunt, the heat between my legs ten times hotter than the rest of me.

I let my eyes close for a moment so I could enjoy the rush of cool that headed down my throat, but Noah surprised me back to reality with another flash of freezing on my skin. My eyes shot open, and there was Noah, running a rapidly diminishing cube over the skin exposed by my tank top's neckline. I found my voice a moment too late, only after a satisfied gasp first passed my lips.

"Noah, what are you doing?"

"Helping you cool off. Doesn't it feel good?"

"Yes. It does, actually. But—"

"But nothing."

He smiled and I clenched my fists to keep myself from touching him. He leaned in and spoke right into my ear.

"I have to say, it looks good, too, Tara."

As the last few pieces of his ice cube dripped down my skin, I actually felt goose bumps rising, despite the heat all around us. His wet fingers lingered over my chest, his skin burning against mine. I pulled back, trying to regain some sense. I wanted him. Plain and simple. But I knew I shouldn't. We shouldn't.

"I have to get back to work, Noah."

He stood in front of me, blocking my path, his eyes burning into mine. I feared the whole building would go up in flames from all the heat. Both outside and inside.

"You don't have to just yet, Tara."

I could barely breathe, but I swallowed hard, trying to tamp down the desire bubbling over.

"Yes, I do."

He still didn't move, at least not at first. He finally relented and let me past. I pushed the bucket around the bar and tried to focus on the task at hand. I was sweating again in no time, even the simple act of swirling the mop around in front of me making me perspire as if I was running a marathon. Noah moved slowly toward me, but I tried to ignore the look in his eye and the suggestive roll of his hips. He walked over the freshly cleaned floor, took the mop right out of my hand and pushed it aside. It hit the floor with a thud and the silence stretched out between us. He kept moving closer until I was backed up against the pillar that punctuated the center of the room. Beads of sweat ran down my spine, and when he smoothed a finger over my cheek, my pussy clenched.

"Noah, please don't."

"You don't really mean that, do you, Tara? You really don't want me?"

I sighed as he leaned against me, his lips on mine before I could even answer him. My arms wrapped around him, his shirt clammy with sweat. As his tongue probed my mouth, I felt my knees go a bit weak. I wanted to keep kissing him, but the heat between us was starting to overwhelm me. It took all my strength to push him away, but he didn't go far.

"Noah, I can't breathe."

I was nearly panting; the humid air leaving my lungs wanting more. Noah pressed his pelvis into my belly and I moaned out loud.

"You need to cool down, Tara. And I think I can help."

I pressed my hands to his shoulders, trying to get a little more space and a little more air. He was still too close, but he wouldn't budge another inch.

"You're just making it worse, Noah."

I watched with hazy eyes as he undid the small black apron where he kept his tips, the long black strings hanging limply in his hands.

"Trust me, I can help. I know what I'm doing."

I went limp against the pole as he was back in my personal space. I let him pull my arms around to the other side, his strong hands digging divots into my flesh. The full weight of his body was against me as I felt the damp fabric slide snugly around my wrists, growing tighter with each wrap of the strings. My chest was thrust forward, the thin fabric of my tank top stuck to my moist skin. I fought against the bonds, but the cutting pain of the straps made me stop. Noah placed a hot palm over my heart, his thumb lazily tracing my nipple until it peaked. His tongue ran up my neck to my ear, his teeth capturing my lobe. The voice that dripped into my ear was hotter than anything I'd felt so far that night.

"Now, how about we cool you down, Tara?"

His hands went to the hem of my tank top and yanked

it up and over my tits, leaving me exposed, the cotton still clinging to my sweaty skin. My body tensed as his eyes swept over me, the heat between my legs growing unbearable. Noah walked away and headed behind the bar. I could hear the sound of plastic crushing against ice and I licked my lips involuntarily, my dry throat desperate for another cool cube. He approached me with a pitcher of ice in each hand. I could see the water dripping onto the floor from his muscled forearms and I would have given anything in that moment to lick them clean. He set one of the pitchers onto a nearby table and approached me slowly. Our eyes met as he pressed the wet plastic against my stomach. I gasped, the cold both amazing and awful.

"Noah, Jesus, that's cold."

"That's the whole point, Tara."

He tipped the pitcher and let the ice-cold liquid run out over my skin. I cried out as the moisture seeped into my jean shorts and panties, dripping down to my most sensitive skin. I squirmed, but there was nowhere for me to go. He moved the vessel higher and let a steady stream pass over each of my breasts until my nipples peaked with cold and desire. My mouth opened to protest, but Noah kissed me instead, the heat of his mouth a momentary respite from the cold. For the first time all night, I wasn't under the spell of the heat, but it was a new kind of torture.

"There, now, isn't that better, Tara?"

I nodded as I watched him extract an ice cube from

the pitcher and wield it between his thick fingers. He started at my parted lips, pressing the smooth surface over my parched mouth. I licked at the ice, but he continued on, tracing down my neck. Shuddering as he neared my nipple, I could feel the slippery cold almost before it arrived, my voice echoing off the walls as the ice melted against my hot skin as he circled my nipple, making it impossibly hard. He grabbed another cube, then another, each one disappearing quickly as he teased and tortured my body with the exquisite cold.

His fingers were still cool as they slid down my stomach, flicking open my button fly with staggering ease.

"Noah, please."

"Please what, Tara?"

I once again struggled with my bonds, but it only elicited a laugh from him. His hand dipped into my panties, the chill of his skin sending shivers through me.

"Oh, would you look at that, Tara. I think I found a place on you that's still way too hot. What are we going to do about that?"

I bit my lip as his fingers dipped back into the pitcher of ice and retrieved a cube. I was shaking my head, but my voice was no longer working. He kissed me hard and as I writhed against him, the ice slid between the lips of my pussy. My mouth was freed just in time to cry out in a jumbled mix of agony and joy.

"Oh, fuck! Oh, god, Noah."

The ice danced over my clit, melting quickly in the

heat and creating a slick path for Noah's fingers to follow. He pushed a little bit further until he was moving it inside me, the cold heel of his palm strafing against my clit. I gasped as he took a drink from the pitcher, letting some ice flow into his mouth. He kissed a cube into my mouth before dropping his head to my nipple. As the cube shrank down to nothing, his rapidly warming mouth was a welcome respite from the frigid ice.

He dropped to his knees in front of me, setting the pitcher gently on the floor. My shorts and panties were soon next to it, my legs pushed apart by his insistent hands. I couldn't stop watching him, especially when he again filled his mouth with ice before moving his lips ever closer to my cunt lips. The shock of bitter cold made my eyes finally close when his tongue turned from frosty to furious as he devoured me. He sucked my clit and slid a finger inside me. I was eager to touch him, but all I could do was lace my fingers together in their prison. I tried to move my hips, to urge him on, but he lapped at me slowly, intensely, until once again I was sweating from the heat.

When he stood, I was ready to beg, which was no doubt his aim all along. He pressed his warm, damp forehead against mine and I breathed out the only words I could think of in that moment.

"Fuck me, Noah. Please."

He smiled, planting a kiss on my lips before shucking off his shorts and sliding on the condom. Grabbing my leg, he held it at his waist, opening me up. He entered me in one smooth stroke, my still-hard nipples strafing against his chest.

"Jesus, Tara. You are so fucking hot."

I was hot. Every part of my body, even the parts touched by such freezing ice, were scorching hot as I took him, his cock buried deep inside me. There was no teasingly slow buildup, just a good, hard fuck. Which was exactly what I needed. My eyes fell shut; the only sounds in the pub were our soft grunts and the constant hum of the ice machine replenishing its stock. I heard him digging in the pitcher on the table, extracting a few more perfect cubes as he fucked me slow and deep. He seemed to enjoy it so much, swiping the ice over my burning skin and watching me react. After each flash of biting cold, his hot mouth followed, warming my skin back up again. The cubes melted quickly, but each was quickly replaced by another, the warring temperatures overloading my already overheated mind.

When he reached down with cool fingers and toyed with my clit, my body could take no more. I was over the edge, his mouth swallowing my guttural cries as I came under his relentless fingers and his thrusting cock. I was nearly spent when he came, his fingers digging into my leg, the heat from his straining body making me heat up all over again. But this time, I didn't mind the warmth as we both stood panting, trying to catch our breath in the sweatbox the pub had become. He untied me quickly and my arms went around him, touching him for the first time. He ran ice over the red marks the apron made on my wrist, soothing my distressed skin. I looked into his eyes, so tender in that moment. We kissed until neither of us could breathe and had to pull apart out of necessity. And even more reluctantly dressed in our sticky, sweaty clothes.

With trembling hands, I reached for two more ice cubes, popping one in my mouth and offering one to him. He took it from me, sucking on my wet fingers for good measure. We chomped the ice in silence, letting the cool liquid slide down our throats.

After all the lights were off and the windows closed, we headed out into the burning-hot night, the heat wave still unbroken. Noah pulled me into his arms, kissing me hard before looking into my eyes.

"The weatherman said it's supposed to be just as hot tomorrow. I guess we'll just have to suffer through for at least one more night."

"I wouldn't call it suffering, would you, Noah?"

"No. I guess not. I just hope the ice machine holds up."

"Me, too, Noah. Me, too."

"GOLF" SPELLED BACKWARDS

Andrea Dale

I glanced up when the door to the pro shop opened, and sized up the man who entered.

Average height, decent build—he probably ran or swam—with thick brown hair in a style that tiptoed the line between corporate and rebellious. Someone moving up the ladder but not quite fitting in yet. I sensed intelligence as his gaze took in the shop, and me.

"Can I help you?"

"Hi, yes, I'm here for a one o'clock golf lesson."

I didn't have to look at the clock. "You're a little early."

He smiled, and it seemed genuine. "Better that than late."

"You'll have to wait until Jenna gets back; I'm covering for her while she's at lunch."

To his credit, he read between the lines. "You're the golf pro?"

I stepped out from behind the counter, hand extended. "Anastasia Schiff."

"Dan Emerson."

Firm grip. That would do well for him.

I watched him size me up, giving him another few points for not commenting on the fact that the Sandy Bluff Golf Course pro was a woman. I considered docking him a point or two for the way his gaze lingered on my bare legs and the swell of my breasts. Golf shirts and shoes don't exactly make for sexy outfits, and I'd be a fool not to appreciate that he found me attractive.

Plus, I don't believe leather and stilettos are necessary. It's all about attitude.

"My friend Craig Zable recommended you—well, the pro here," Dan added. "He didn't mention you were a woman."

I raise an eyebrow. "Is that a problem?"

"Not at all," Dan said. "I trust any recommendation from Craig."

I remembered Craig. My clit tingled pleasantly at the memory. Tall guy, sandy hair almost in a buzz cut, a little cocky—at least, until I'd given him a few lessons.

Then he'd been cocky in a different way.

Hmm... If Craig had recommended me, he thought Dan would be a candidate for the same treatment.

I licked my lips, and Dan's gaze followed the track of my tongue. I certainly hoped so.

* * *

As we rode the cart out to the driving range, I asked the right questions to learn more about Dan. He told me where he worked, that he was a junior executive, that he had pretty much guessed golf was one of the ways into the old boys' network. He wasn't wrong about that; I got a lot of my clients that way.

When I asked about a Mrs. Emerson and he said he wasn't married, my body reacted again, excitement thrumming in my veins. I didn't give my lessons to married men. If he mentioned a fiancée or even a serious girlfriend, that part of the training was right out. I have my standards.

He'd been golfing a few times, understood the basics, but—and he said this with a charming laugh—he had a lot of experience on the mini-putt course.

When we stopped and got out, I laid down the rules.

"I take this very seriously," I said. "I can't abide anyone wasting my time. If you're not on board one hundred percent, that's the end of your lessons."

"I understand," he said.

He didn't, not yet. But he would—I hoped.

"You will follow my orders without hesitation," I went on. "You may certainly ask for clarification, to make sure you understand, but you will not question my requests nor my judgment. Is that understood?"

He nodded. "Yes."

"Good." I smiled. "Then let's get to it."

I suggested the club he use, grabbed my own. He carried the bucket of balls from the cart without my having to ask. Good sign. My body hummed in agreement.

I hit a few balls, explaining what I was doing, discussing stance, technique, follow-through. I sensed Dan wasn't giving my lesson his full attention. Out of the corner of my eye I watched his gaze on my form.

My body, that is. Not my golf form.

Time to put him to the test.

I stood back, analyzing his swing. Yes, he'd had some experience, had the basics down. But he definitely had a way to go.

I stepped up behind him, reached around him to put my hands over his where they gripped the club. Of course, this meant that I was pressed against him, my breasts to his back, my groin to his ass.

"You need to adjust your grip," I said. "Up on the club just a bit. Your left hand should be about a quarter inch beneath the butt. Align both your thumbs down the shaft. That's it. Good job."

I stayed against him, guiding him through the swing in slow motion. My body moved against his. My breath was deliberately hot in his ear as I murmured instructions. My nipples were hard—not deliberately, although the cotton weave of my shirt was deliciously rough, and I wondered if he could feel the hard nubs.

I stepped back, slowly. His next swing went wild.

"Daniel!" I said sharply, and was gratified to see him flinch. "Pay attention."

I stalked around to face him. His next swing was better, but the tenting in his pants was clear. I bit back my smile.

"That," I said sternly, looking pointedly at his groin, "is getting in the way of your swing."

Oh, sweet boy, he blushed. Before he could say anything, I continued. "You see that copse of trees over there? Go and take care of that problem. Otherwise we can't continue."

We were alone on the driving range. It was always off-limits during my training sessions.

"Ex-excuse me?"

"Is that a request for clarification or a protest?"

I folded my arms across my chest, plumping my breasts up in the process and watching his eyes slide down, then dart back to my face when he realized what he'd done. I also watched the play of emotions cross his face, from confusion to understanding to panic to realization.

And then to acceptance, of a sort.

As he walked rather stiffly toward the trees, it was all I could do not to plunge my hand down my pants and get myself off.

He was hooked.

We didn't speak about the situation after he returned; I simply offered him a wet wipe, and his hand shook a little as he thanked me for it, and we went back to the lesson.

He was early again for his next lesson.

"Did you practice since our last instruction?" I asked.

"Yes." The flush suffused his cheeks again. I'd left the question deliberately vague, hoping he'd jump to a certain conclusion. Good.

"And did you think about what I taught you?" I watched him carefully, my belly tight with anticipation.

A hint of a smile, no doubt at the memories. "Yes."

"Good. Today we'll work on putting."

Today didn't start out as well as last time, though. He might have remembered jerking off in the trees at my command, but he'd forgotten how to hold the damn club. Maybe he was distracted, wondering what I'd do next, or by the fact that I was wearing a short golf skirt, but I didn't care.

I rearranged his hands on the club, told him not to move, and stalked off to the cart. When I turned back, I was thrilled to see he hadn't budged an inch, frozen in the leaned putting stance that would strain your lower back if you stood that way too long.

"If you're not going to remember a simple thing like how to adjust your hands, we'll have to keep them there with other means." I held up a roll of double-sided grip tape.

"But, Stacy—"

"Excuse me?" I snapped. He jerked, eyes wide. "You may address me as Ma'am, or Ms. Schiff, or Anastasia— I'm not a stickler there—but you will *not* use the casual diminutive of my name. Understood?"

He swallowed. "Yes Ma'am."

"Now, were you protesting my teaching methods?"

"No Ma'am." He set his jaw. I nodded. Good. He was willing to push it further.

"Good."

I wrapped the tape over his hands, most of it sticking to the golf gloves he wore. Ripping tape off his flesh wasn't the type of pain I was planning on…at least, not yet. Obedience first. Limits next.

His putting was adequate. I gave him some leeway for being distracted by his hands bound by tape and by the burgeoning lump in his pants—especially because I was pleased the former was helping to cause the latter.

We kept at it for as long as I could stand, ball after ball just missing the cup, a few making it in. Finally, I said we'd had enough, and I wanted to see him make a few drive swings, to reinforce what we'd gone over last time.

And to push things to the next level.

A few swings, and then in slow motion, and then as he was rotated back, prepared to swing, I said, "Freeze, right there."

He did.

I stood in front of him, locked his gaze with mine.

"We have to work on form and concentration. It's crucial: on the links, in the boardroom, in the bedroom."

His gaze flicked sideway, met mine again.

"Are you willing to do whatever it takes?" I asked.

"Yes Ma'am."

No hesitation. I liked that. I didn't stop staring into his eyes as I worked his belt free, popped his shorts open, slid his underwear down. Because of his position, the garments caught on his knees. His cock sprang free, red and swollen, a generous size.

I ran my nails along the underside of his shaft, from balls to tip. His breath hissed between his teeth. I had a tube of lube in my pocket; I greased my palm, reached down again.

"Daniel. I want you to hold that stance. If you lose the position, I'll stop touching you. Is that clear?"

"Yes, Anastasia."

His muscles trembled as I pulled on his prick. The closer he got, the harder it was for him to stay still, especially in that uncomfortable pose, arms up, body twisted. His breathing was harsh as I coolly jerked him off.

My clit pounded so hard, I considered stopping and making him get me off first.

But no. That wasn't how today's lesson was slated to go.

"How long, Daniel? How long do you think I could stroke you while you stand like that?"

He knew, without my having to tell him, that he needed my permission.

"Please." His forehead dotted with perspiration. "Please, Ma'am," he amended.

He hadn't answered my question, but we were early in his training, and I took some pity on him.

"Now!" I said, stepping to one side just in time to avoid the gush of semen that spattered and decorated the manicured grass. He did break the pose somewhat, but as his spasms subsided, he regained position. It was harder now, I could tell, with his muscles wrung out from his orgasm.

"Follow through," I ordered.

He swung.

Hole in one.

I finally did let him touch me, let him lick me and bring me off. It was on an overcast day, which somehow made the grass look richer, like it had when I'd played a tournament in Scotland, the birthplace of golf. The course was closed for "maintenance," and he caddied for me.

Naked, of course.

Over the course of the next few weeks, I put him through his paces, both in golf and in our personal encounters. I pricked his nipples, his inner thighs and cock and balls with golf tees. I spanked him barehanded and while wearing golf gloves.

Everything carried a lesson.

We talked about how the best way to get someone to do what you wanted them to do was to convince them it was what they wanted to do—ideally, to convince them that it was their idea in the first place.

Daniel hadn't specifically thought about jerking off in the bushes during our first lesson, but he'd certainly thought about jerking off. I'd just allowed it to happen.

And that was the real trick, I explained: to make the other person believe you were opening the door for them, when in truth you were encouraging them to do exactly what you wanted.

"You target their deepest desires," I said. "The ones they don't even know they have. You coax those desires out, all the while dovetailing those desires to your own."

His golf improved dramatically and, I could tell, his confidence. He stood taller, carried himself with more authority. He got his hair trimmed, just a little.

We never spoke of continuing our relationship; never spoke personally unless it involved his work (and even then, I didn't want to know what company he worked for, who his colleagues were).

As always, I felt the occasional pang of regret. Daniel had been a fast learner in all ways, and his skill at cunnilingus was as admirable as his golf game. He would make some woman very happy.

I hadn't yet let him enter me—that was a privilege to be earned—but I'd held that generous, hard cock in my hands enough times to be looking forward to feeling it inside me nearly as much as he was. I spent numerous nights fucking myself with a dildo of his approximate size, fantasizing. (Not that I told him, of course. On the other hand, he was required to tell me in detail about any time he jerked off...if I'd given him permission to do so ahead of time, that was.)

The leaves were shading to gold and red when we

played a round of nine holes. There was little I could instruct him on anymore. He had a natural talent that had surfaced fairly early on; I'd spent the time fine-tuning him, teaching him style and focus and little tricks.

"Are you ready for your final lesson?" I asked him.

"Yes Ma'am." Perhaps a little too eager, but I didn't have the heart to correct him. Our desires had dove-tailed quite nicely.

I used grip tape to bind his hands, arms spread, to the upright metal bars on either side of the golf cart. He sat in the seat, breathing elevated, watching my every move. Stripping off his pants and underwear was a challenge given the enormity of his erection. I tossed them in the back with his shoes.

From my pocket I produced a condom. He swallowed hard as I unrolled it down his weeping shaft. I suspected the knowledge of what might happen next had pushed him close to the edge already.

I slipped off my thong, pulled my skirt up, and straddled him, placing my hands on the seat back by his shoulders. "You know the rules," I said. "Patience, control. You'll know when you're allowed to come."

"Yes, Anastasia."

It was the first time he'd used my name since the beginning.

I sank down onto him, glorying in the sensation of being filled, just as good as I'd imagined. I was wet, as aroused as he was. I posted up and down for as long as I could, until my thighs, strong as they were, trembled not only from exertion but from the buildup of desire. Then I simply sat and ground down on him, grinding my clit into his groin as the pressure mounted.

A drop of sweat slid down the side of his face. His jaw was clenched with the effort of holding back. But he kept his eyes open, locked on my face, and that was what triggered my orgasm. My hips pumped even as I hissed, "Not yet."

Many of my clients never quite succeeded at this one. But Daniel held firm, somehow, although I could see how he quivered, could see how purple his cock was when I slid the condom off.

I set my foot on the edge of the seat and slowly but firmly pressed my golf cleats into his balls.

He came helplessly, spurting all over my shoes, the expression on his face a mix of astonishment and relief.

I unbound him from the cart, but in truth, I had already freed him.

I said that I never have a personal relationship with my clients, that once our lessons are complete, that's it. Oh, former clients often bring colleagues to the club to play, and if we run into one another, I'm introduced as the golf pro and they praise my tutelage. I might even join them if they're one short for a foursome.

After Daniel was through, I had some free time to catch up on other things, including some back issues of various golf magazines. I was flipping through, skimming rather than reading, and I nearly missed it.

A photo in a news column. Four men on a course, having won a local tournament. A congressman from another state, commenting on how he was sorry to lose one of his golfing buddies, who was moving to Sandy Bluff, transferring to the company office there.

I sat up straight, stared. Then I shook my head, laughing.

Daniel had played me. He hadn't come to me for golf lessons at all.

And it occurred to me that maybe, just maybe, I was going to have to invite him for a rematch.

EYE CONTACT

Derek McDaniel

When you give yourself to me, the first thing you'll do is suck my cock, and you'll do it exactly the way I taught you. You'll deep-throat, you'll swallow, and you'll make eye contact as you do it.

Don't worry about remembering, though; I'll remind you.

There will be no going out to dinner first; there won't even be an introduction. The only introduction you need to me is to drop to your knees and plant your face in my crotch.

You'll be trim and toned, your musculature defined beneath the skimpy clothes. Each missed appointment with your personal trainer over the last six months has been punished with a dozen strokes to your pussy, while you kneel, spread before the webcam, and count out each hard stroke for me. You learned to keep your appointments and put in your appointed hours on the stair-stepper and elliptical trainer. You'll be stacked, too, or something very like it. Your tits will be elevated by a push-up bra a size too small, so they spill out everywhere. You'll be dressed to the nines, wearing slutty black stockings, seams down the back and red ribbons centered front and back where the garters attach. Several inches' worth of garter is visible on each thigh, where the lace tops of your stockings don't quite come high enough to find the tortured hem of your skintight candy-red dress, already riding up so high on your thighs that I can glimpse your skimpy panties. You'll be perched on six-inch heels, having practiced for months to be able to wear them without falling down. (Not that you'll need to walk around very much; you'll spend most of the next three days in one of three positions: on your knees, on your back with your legs spread, or over my lap with your squirmy little ass in the air.

Your freshly blond hair will be teased to its limit, your face made up, your body tanned despite your protests.

You'll look slutty, yes, but even so, it'll all be premium crap, purchased at high-end emporiums. Even with your tits spilling out and your dress riding up and your nipples peeking through the dress, you'll almost look like a model—one who pushes the limits of good taste. Almost.

But you won't be a classy girl; you won't be a model; you'll be something far filthier, and two things will announce that you're not classy at all, you're a piece of kneeling trash, the plaything of a man you've never met before.

First, around your creamy throat, there will be a collar—black leather, its padlock engraved: *SLUT*.

That won't be very classy.

And over the stockings, you'll be wearing knee pads.

That's even *less* classy.

But you'll sure be glad you have them; those are eighty-dollar stockings. And pillows are so last century.

In seconds, you're on me.

You kneel before my armchair with your legs apart. Your slutty blond hair scatters all over my lap.

You kiss my cock through my slacks and reach for my belt buckle with your dagger-tipped fingers. We've been in the same room for one minute, and your face is in my crotch. *Good girl.*

You try to open my belt while you kiss my cock all over, through my slacks. I'm wearing a suit because I do that sort of thing. And this is our first date, right? You'll get lipstick on my pricey slacks while your slender hands try to work my belt buckle—and fail. You're not used to having the long, red nails. I made you grow them over the course of months, made you punish yourself every time you broke one until you were sufficiently "motivated" to let men get doors for you, among other things.

The sharp red nails make it hard for you to open my belt, even though I made you practice. The nail polish matches your lipstick: slut-red, bright as blood. Your lips are slathered with it—the color that only a truly shameless slut would wear to meet a man for the first time...even if she's already been having webcam sex with him for nearly seven months.

While your slut lips redden my slacks, I take pleasure in your struggles not to break a nail against the leather as you strive to unfasten my narrow belt. I don't move to help you. I let you struggle, smiling, pleased with your eagerness, pleased even more by your skill.

I sip my Scotch and puff my cigar as you gingerly work the end of the supple leather belt out of the buckle.

I think *Good girl*, but I don't say it.

It simply wouldn't do to reward you with praise—not yet. Not until my cock's in your mouth, at the very least.

You finally get my belt undone, looking up at me red-faced. You unbutton my pants; that part is easier. So is sliding my zipper down; you can pinch the zipper between two long nails and draw it down easily. Your slender, sharp fingers reach into my pants to get my cock.

You ease it out of my boxer shorts, out of my slacks, and against your other hand, caressing my cock, the head slick and glistening with precum. Your hands look pretty on my dick, just like your face looks pretty up against it. When I first saw your hands—on webcam, about one minute before I made you spread your legs and spank your pussy with them—they were so pale. Now they're a light golden tan, like the rest of you. I made you tan, despite your protests; you didn't want to be some dumb bimbo slut.

I told you, "Yes, you do," and I guess I was right.

Your pretty pale skin is now the color of a Jersey girl now; Guidos everywhere envy me.

You caress my cock. You're nervous, panting, your forced-up tits heaving so hard they seem almost ready to pop out of your dress. You look up at me shyly as you stare at my naked cock, inhaling its scent, preparing to suck it. You hesitate. Your face turns pink. Your new tan can't hide your blushing embarrassment—not entirely. I like to see you blush.

"Come on," I tell you, drawling around the cigar. "Don't pretend this is the first dick you've had in your mouth. Open wide. Do your duty."

You give a little shiver and a flutter of your black-caked eyelids.

No, it's not the first cock you've ever sucked. You've sucked exactly three, not counting silicone ones. You were a virgin till twenty-three, and had two boyfriends since then, plus a single one-night stand between the two. And now my cock is in your pretty face with its whore makeup, slut hair, a pair of red lips that quiver as you lower your face to suck me.

Your eyes look big and innocent; I've had you wear a garish shade of blue eye shadow and cake your lashes with black mascara. Your lips, red, slut-painted and pouty, circle the head of my cock. You slide your mouth down onto it.

Your lips feel plump, wet with drool, sticky with lipstick. Your tongue feels soft and eager and juicy. You start to suck my cock, bobbing up and down eagerly, whimpering softly at the back of your throat as you give yourself to me. You get me erect and take me deep into your mouth, swirling your tongue around hungrily. I'm very pleased by the feel of your mouth; I'm pleased still more by the feel of your firm, erect nipples brushing against my knees as you dance up and down on me.

But you've forgotten a critical step.

That pleases me even more.

I put the cigar in my mouth. I reach down and brush your massive cascade of bleach-blond hair back, gathering it in one hand. I expose your pretty face and watch as you take my cock in your mouth, the big wide shaft disappearing between your pursed red lips.

With one hand I pull your hair. I pull it till you whimper around my cock.

With the other, I slap your face.

Your black-rimmed shiny blue orbs go wide in surprise as you feel the sharp blow. It's surprise that could have translated to an unexpected bite, but I was ready to take that risk for the pleasure of seeing and feeling your shock in the very same instant.

I pull your hair again, harder, forcing your head back.

My cock slips from your plump red mouth with a pop.

You let out another cry, louder, your mouth open wide in surprise.

I slap you again—thrice more, harder each time. I don't hit hard enough to really hurt you—just to surprise you. It's hard enough to make you cry out in earnest.

I give you three more slaps against each cheek, your big eyes shamed and seeking.

Your face is so pretty, framed as it is by the pulled-up blond hair and the long hoop earrings.

Even through your paid-for tan and the makeup, I can see the red in your face.

You blush so prettily.

Your eyes roam wildly as I seize your chin with one thumb and forefinger, force your head back with the other hand tight in your slutty blond hair.

Your wide black-rimmed blue eyes start to brim with tears.

When they fall, they're jet black, coursing thickly down cheeks tanned and blushing—rivers of shame.

That's what I like.

I like to see you crying black tears rich with cheap mascara—the tears of a slut.

I watch the pretty tears go rolling down and make cooing noises.

"Are you crying, slut? Are you crying because your Master slapped you?"

I slap you again. More tears roll down your rosy-tan cheeks; you're not crying, and I know it. All that makeup just makes your eyes water, as does my cock all the way in your mouth. But it's really the bright lights overhead that are making your eyes go all watery; I put them there for a reason.

You look up at me, frightened and excited. Your nipples are hard against my knees, practically popping through the dress.

"I'm sorry, Sir, what did I—"

"What have I told you?" I growl around the cigar. "Always make eye contact the first time you take a man's cock in your mouth. That way he sees the submission in your eyes. Don't you remember?"

"There's just so much to remember," you whine, and I cut you short with another firm slap.

You squeak sharply, press your lips together for a second while another pair of tears rolls down your cheeks. I can feel you squirming and rocking against me; you can barely keep your hips from pumping. That pussy must be *molten* beneath your tiny little dress and your tinier little panties.

I slap you.

"What do you say, slut?"

Your moist blue eyes look up at me, widening.

"Yes, Sir. I'm sorry, Sir."

"Tell me what you do."

"I make eye contact the first time I put a man's dick in my mouth."

"Good girl," I say, caressing your face. "Forget again,

and you'll find yourself getting a very hard spanking."

I watch your face with pleasure as the threat sinks in. A shiver goes through you; I watch it ripple from your humiliated eyes to the glorious slope of your butt, propped up tight against your six-inch heels.

I seize my cock and slap your pretty face again.

It coaxes a tiny sob from your pretty mouth, and two tears from your face. You can't keep eye contact as you gasp and whine. I slap you again. You look up and let me see your shimmering eyes, topping the black rivulets on your cheek.

I ease up my grip on your hair, and you take my cock in your mouth. Your eyes stay aimed at mine. You never stop looking as you slide your mouth over my dick, halfway down the shaft, your tongue swirling. You bob up and down. It's an awkward position, but it's worth it; your face looks so very pretty with my dick in your mouth.

I pull your hair again, forcing your head back, taking my cock out of your mouth. You cry out. This time, there's a glistening string of spittle from your plump red lips to my lipstick-stained dickhead.

I seize my cock and slap you with it. This time you never take your eyes off mine. Again. Again. I hear you whimper and whine, your whole body trembling. Again. You're still looking at me.

Lesson learned.

I shove your head back in my crotch.

You try to keep your eyes upturned and toward me,

but it's not easy for you. This time I force your face in my crotch so firmly, pulling your hair, that you know I won't take no for an answer. You only struggle briefly; then you give up and let me do as I wish, trying to keep your eyes up toward me. But as you worship my cock, your eyes are often obscured. But you keep them toward me nonetheless... *Good girl.*

I can feel the soft, wet smoothness at the back of your throat; each time you go down, you press my cock-head against it more firmly.

I nudge you down with my hand in your hair, guiding you to take it in your throat.

As I push you down, I feel a shiver going through you again. You've really been looking forward to this part.

No, it's not the first cock you've ever sucked; there have been three, and not one of them has been down your throat. Not unless you count silicone ones—then three of the five that I sent you have been there. The other two were too big—far too big. The three were of increasing size, each of them flanged, starting long and soft and thin and progressing roughly up to the size of my cock. Each of them filled up that very pretty throat behind the dog collar you always wear when you suck cock on webcam for me. The one that says *SLUT* on its padlock.

Now it's time for the real thing, and you can't wait; your increasingly sweaty body is practically bursting with energy.

You lean forward, putting the weight of your upper

body in my lap. You try to look up at me the whole time as you get ready to take me down your throat. Your pretty ass wiggles in its candy-red dress as you lean more fully forward to straighten your neck and get some leverage.

I feel your throat open up, the muscles accepting the entry of my cock. You gag a little as you swallow me; you come up for air and make love to my cock, your head bobbing up and down, your lips around my shaft. They leave faint streaks of bright red lipstick. You go down again. You hold it deep, this time; ten seconds, twenty; you come up gasping, panting, drooling everywhere.

You catch your breath and go quickly back down on my drool-wet cock...until your red lips are circled around the base, and you can't look up at me till you tip your body back a little.

But you do. You look up at me again, excited, shamed, your eyes pouring black tears.

With my cock down your throat, you make eye contact.

You keep eye contact with me for five seconds, ten... Very good. You're letting me see your blue eyes filled with shame, with arousal, with hunger. Not just hunger for cock—that part is easy. Hunger for submission; hunger to be kneeling before me, just like this, wearing knee pads and tarted like a slut.

You come up for air; my dick comes free with a pop. Drool runs everywhere.

You go right back down, but quickly this time; then you're making love to my cock, rubbing it all over your face, bobbing up and down intermittently and lavishing affection on me with your mouth, your tongue, your face. You smear tears and mascara everywhere, even into your hair; sticky precum and spit form strings between your chin and my cockhead while you lap at my balls, easing them out of the deep worsted V formed by my fly. My balls are tight and high with arousal, so you can't quite take them into your mouth, but you work them just far enough from my body that you can caress them all over with your tongue. You part your lips and slide them up and down my shaft, your tongue working drooly and crazy, all over me. You tease the cockhead, and something in the way my breathing changes tells you not to push your luck just yet. I think I see a smile play across your cock-spread lips; I'll have to spank you for that later. You obediently lick your way back down to my balls, caressing my shaft but not stroking too hard; we both know you've learned your lessons well. I could cum on your face any moment.

But I hold back, and you help me hold me back. You worship my balls just long enough to let me cool down.

Then you look up at me and make eye contact again, sitting back slightly on your heels as your slut-blond hair scatters everywhere.

You ease your body heavily against me again. At some point your tits have popped out of your dress and your push-up bra—that, or you popped them out. You push your tits together and slide my cock between them, smearing messy mascara and lipstick all over your firm, tanned mounds. You pinch your own nipples as you hold your tits tight, forming a channel for my cock. Your upper body undulates sensuously as you fuck yourself onto me. You make eye contact again and again, pleasuring me with your tits.

But by now I'm mounting toward a hard, wet cum all over your tits. So I stop you. I put my hand in your hair and pull you back and force you down and slap your face with my cock again.

That almost makes me blow my load. I freeze and pull your hair, feeling my cock throb as tiny hot squirts of jizz stream out on your face. Your mouth forms into a wide *O* of tender surprise as you feel the semen hit you. You nostrils flare as you smell it. You shudder all over. At the scent of cum, you're like an animal in heat. You let out a desperate little gasp, your tongue lolling out as you lap hungrily after the warm touch of cum. You get a good lick in—but I haven't quite blown just yet. It's not exactly a false alarm; I'm just teetering on the edge.

And that's a good thing; now you've got cum on your face, two little streams of it across your mascara-smeared cheek, the scent of it making you crazy. It drips down onto your lips and you lick it as I pull your hair and slap you again—with my cock, my hand, my cock, my hand.

Your eyes turn back to me, looking up with the mingled shame and pride of deep submission. Tears roll out as I slap you; when I guide your mouth down to my cock again, I let go of your hair and let you work.

I take a pleasant suck at my big cigar; I take a sip of my Scotch as my breathing quickens and my grunt comes hard and insistent from my lips.

You know what I want.

You look up at me, pleading. You take your hands off your tits and put them on my cock. You open wide and stick your tongue out and stroke my cock, moaning softly as you guide me back to the brink.

You cup your tongue and look at me, your blue eyes watery with effort.

Thick streams shoot into your mouth.

You catch it, at first, but then you show me, proudly, displaying the creamy load of cum on your cupped tongue as you make eye contact. Doing that, you have to tip your head back, and you dribble as you show off.

Then you swallow most of it, but a steady drizzle runs down your chin and down your neck, and when I grab your hair and sit you upright, I watch it run down to your tits.

Your eyes stay on me, making eye contact, showing me your deep submission—and I know it wasn't an accident. That eager gulp you made was just too perfect, the spillage down your chin too awkward. You did it on purpose, or half on purpose.

Your big eyes show me just how smart you are— how badly you want to go over my lap for spilling my precious seed.

But I can't bear to do it; I can't bear to spank you. Not on your ass, at least.

Don't get me wrong; I want that ass. I want to bend you over and give it to you hard, blow after blow on your perfect pert buns. I want to see your ass pink and punished.

But right now, I don't want to tip you face-down, ass-up.

If I did, we couldn't have eye contact.

"Take off your panties," I tell you. "You need to be punished."

Your body trembles as your slender hands work the skimpy red panties down. You've worn them on the outsides of your garters—like a true slut.

But when you obediently try to get over my knee, face-down, I grab you.

I pull you roughly into my lap—facing up. I manhandle you into position, until I'm cradling you in my arms and forcing your thighs open wide.

I put my hand in your hair and force your head back, so my face is close to yours.

I look deep in your eyes as you whimper.

My hand traces a path up your slender thigh, and I see the fear in your eyes as you realize what I have in mind.

"Time for your spanking," I tell you.

I draw my hand back and bring it down sharp—right between your legs.

You close your eyes and gasp in pain as I cradle you

and spank your pussy. But you never look away, even when it hurts. Your big blue eyes stay locked on mine, pouring dark mascara tears as you gasp and moan and squirm in my lap, taking every blow to your pussy like a brave little slut.

Looks like you've learned your lessons about eye contact after all.

But you still get that spanking.

DOUBLE DUTCH

Giselle Renarde

D amn, girl!" Nakesha tore Jansey's rope away. Hurling it to the ground, she stomped on it with the ball of her foot like she was crushing a cigarette. "How many times we been over this? It's Crouger first, then into the Awesome Annie."

"I know, okay? I made a mistake." Jansey bent to pick up her jump rope, but Nakesha's foot wasn't moving. In her peripheral vision, she noticed Ruby and Beatriz skulking at her sides. She felt claustrophobic between the pair.

"Yeah, and what's with all the doubles?" Ruby sucked her teeth. Jansey hated that noise. "There's just the two doubles to start things off, then into the triples and quads."

"I was only marking it this time." Jansey's voice

sounded small and weak, even to her. "I'll do it right in competition, obviously."

Beatriz muttered "lazy ass" under her breath, but loud enough for Jansey to hear. Why was everybody always picking on her? They made mistakes too.

"And when you gonna cut your hair?" Nakesha folded her arms in front of her chest, and Jansey watched her spandex suit shimmer under the fluorescents. "All that little Dutch girl frizz gonna get caught up in your rope one day."

Jansey ran her fingers through her ponytail. It wasn't all that frizzy, was it? "Well, what about Ruby and Beatriz?" she shot back. "They have long hair too."

"Ah, yes," Ruby mocked, petting her hair like it was a fur coat. "But my fine Oji-Cree tresses don't tangle."

"Neither do my lovely Spanish locks," Beatriz said in that same teasing tone.

Ruby shot Beatriz a glare that seemed to say *don't steal my thunder*. "Yeah, well, Indian hair is sacred, bitch."

Nakesha put her foot down. "Women! We've been a team too long to start getting catty now. You two shut your yaps and, Jansey, cut your hair."

She didn't want to. She liked her hair. "You guys are bullies, you know that?"

"Yeah?" Nakesha swooped down to grab Jansey's red plastic rope and stretched it out end to end. Those arms of hers were toned, all sleek black muscle. She was the fittest of them all. "Well, learn the routine and we won't bully you so much."

"I know the routine!" Jansey sounded whiny now, and she knew that wouldn't go over well, but why did the girls have to be so mean?

Jansey held out her hand, silently asking for her rope back, but Nakesha didn't give it. Beatriz said, "White girls can't jump rope," and they all laughed. All except Jansey, of course.

"If I couldn't jump, I wouldn't be on the team," she spat, hoping that was actually true. "Anyway, how would you feel if I said Indian or Black or Spanish girls couldn't jump? Huh?"

Ruby and Beatriz exchanged cunning grins before creeping up at her sides like Nakesha's henchmen. Grabbing Jansey's arms, the girls pulled them behind her back so hard it hurt.

"Oh, but we *can* jump," Nakesha said. "That's the difference." And she tied Jansey's wrists together with that translucent devil-red jump rope. "You wanna see a solid routine? We'll give you a show."

Jansey was too shocked to react. They'd tied her arms behind her back? Why would her skipping team do that to her? And, god, was it ever hard to stand when she was bound like this, her wrist bones rubbing one against the other, the jump rope tight even around her forearms. A dull ache began in her shoulders and bled down her back. As the other three girls took up their ropes, Jansey eased herself down on her knees. That was better—or, at least, the best she could hope for in such a strange circumstance.

"You pay attention, little girl." A strange smile crept across Nakesha's lips. "Let your big sisters show you how it's done."

When Nakesha turned on the boom box, the beat soared through the gymnasium floor, rocking Jansey's calves. The music ran up through her thighs. It got right inside her spandex one-piece, vibrating inside her pelvis, making her instantly wet. Music could do that for her. That's why she'd always been an easy lay at dances. The beat made her hot. Even underneath her skintight spandex, she could feel her nipples hardening to tight little buds.

Restrained and kneeling on the floor of this public school gymnasium they rehearsed in after hours—after midnight, after the tippling security guard had dozed off—Jansey watched her team perform their skipping routine without her. They always started off with Speed Steps and Criss-Crosses, usually punctuated with a Side-Swing or two. Judges weren't too fond of the latter, so they kept 'em to a minimum.

Nakesha, Ruby, Beatriz—they executed the triples and the quads without breaking a sweat. Their matching ropes were like extensions of those bodies clad in black spandex one-pieces as they went Crouger into Awesome Annie, the trick she'd messed up earlier. Then it was time for some of Nakesha's incredible freestyle while Ruby and Beatriz went with can-can variation jumps. They finished up with impressive Donkey Kicks, their hand-stands in perfect form, their lean limbs always where they should be, their ropes along for the ride and never getting in the way.

They were right: Jansey wasn't anywhere near as good as they were. White girls couldn't jump rope.

Nakesha stopped the music. "Well, little girl? What do you have to say for yourself?" Her almost flat chest expanded and contracted in swift repetition as she breathed hard. The other two took sips of water.

"I suck." What else could Jansey say? "You guys are amazing and I suck." She looked at Ruby and Beatriz leaning against one another like twins, almost, in their matching outfits. They were roughly the same height, Ruby a little shorter, a little more athletic in build. Even their breasts were about the same size and round like navel oranges, though Beatriz had sharper features to Ruby's moon face.

Nakesha was taller than any of them, strong and thin and dark as night, her kinky hair cut close to the scalp but on a queer angle, like a tidal wave. She dropped her head, shaking it. "That's exactly the opposite of the point I was trying to make, little girl." She bent down low, perching her arm on one knee while the other met the gymnasium floor. "If you sucked, we'd have cut you a long time ago. You just gotta get your pretty little head in the game. You're dropping the ball out there."

The hardness in Nakesha's gaze melted into caring, and that downy expression ignited Jansey's loving desire. She squirmed against the damp crotch of her spandex one-piece. It was truth time. "I just can't stop thinking of what we did...that night. You know...that one time...after Manitoba Jumps?"

She'd known for a long while that Ruby and Beatriz had fallen in love, but one time, after a big win in competition, that love had expanded to include Nakesha and Jansey, too. It was the greatest night of Jansey's life, and the most intense pleasure she'd ever experienced. Every time she rehearsed a skipping routine with these girls she'd known so intimately, she revisited that event in her mind. She had to go back there.

A wicked smile broke across Nakesha's lips and the other girls broke out laughing. "That's what this is about?" Nakesha asked. "You're just horny?"

Jansey squirmed against the rope binding her wrists behind her back, and against the ever-more-confining crotch of her one-piece. Her pussy lips were thick and throbbing, and she'd give anything in the world to touch herself right now. "Well, you make it sound like I'm horny in a general way. I'm not. I'm only hot for"—she lowered her eyes and her voice—"only for you guys..."

Ruby and Beatriz chuckled once again, deeply this time. They were holding each other now, and Ruby cooed, "You gotta beg for it, little sister."

A glimmer of hope shot through Jansey's embarrassment. "Oh, I beg you...please!"

Beatriz approached, inching slowly across the gymnasium. "Gotta do better than that, kid."

Why did they always call her kid, little sister, little

girl? All four of them were the same age, all in their third year at university, and she wasn't that much shorter than Ruby or Beatriz. Maybe it was her manner. Granted, she was a little more childish than the rest of them—gullible and naïve at times too.

"Please," Jansey said, this time with all the desperation she felt in her body. "I need you to touch me and kiss me and lick me in all the right places, like you did that night."

"I don't know," Ruby teased. The three of them closed in, looming tall above her. "How can we be sure it'll improve your performance?"

"It will!" Jansey cried. She felt anxious now, her skin itchy, clit pounding, like if they didn't do it she would just die. Her heart hammered so loud it was all she could hear. "Please...I promise...please..." Her mind was so muddled by lust she didn't know what else to say.

Beatriz grabbed her under one arm, and Nakesha did the same on the other side. At first, Jansey felt self-conscious because she knew how much she'd been sweating, but that all fell away when Nakesha said, "Well, since you asked so nicely..."

They pulled her to her feet, then yanked her toward the wall where there was a mural of a man riding a serpent, the great thunderbird in the background—a legend of Ruby's people. Jansey felt limp in their arms, like she couldn't possibly stand without them.

"What are you doing?" Jansey asked, panting. She was so turned on her legs scarcely supported her.

Nakesha quickly untied her arms. "Oh, you'll see, little girl." Beatriz raised them up above her head as Nakesha wove the red rope through an iron hoop plunged deep into the concrete wall. The school surely used it for stringing up a volleyball net or something, but these girls had other ideas. Nakesha and Beatriz secured her to that hoop in the wall, tying her wrists so tight she was sure her hands would turn purple.

Meanwhile, Ruby collected two more skipping ropes and brought them over. All three whispered, pointing to the iron hoops near the floor, one on either side of each foot, but at a distance. That must be where the gym teacher tied up the kiddie goal nets for indoor soccer and floor hockey.

"Open those legs, little girl." Nakesha's command, but it was Beatriz who stepped up and slapped the insides of Jansey's thighs. The smack of those flat hands rang out against her spandex, and it stung a little, but not as bad as flesh on flesh. How she wished they would strip her bare and spank her all over: slap her naked thighs and her tits, smack her cunt over and over again.

"Open wider," Ruby instructed, kneeling to tie one of Jansey's ankles with a red rope. Even through her sock, it felt tight.

Beatriz did the same on the other side, and that was even tighter. The confinement made Jansey feel like Godzilla, and when the girls secured her ankles to those metal rungs, her ass clenched and her pussy rang out. If it wasn't for the spandex, Jansey knew her juice would be dripping all the way to her knees by now.

Her legs were spread, her arms above her head, and she watched that pack of wolves lick their lips in unison. They wanted her—she could see the lust in all six of those dark, gleaming eyes. And what they wanted, they could have, they could take, devour.

"Please…" Jansey didn't know quite what to ask for. Her head was buzzing with desire. "Just take me. Do anything."

For a long moment, nobody moved. Nakesha was the first, and she only ran to her gym bag, returning with a Swiss Army knife. Jansey's throat went dry as she watched the blade flip up, its sharp edge gleaming against the fluorescent lights in cages on the ceiling.

"What's that for?" Jansey stammered.

"For this." Pulling on the top of Jansey's one-piece, Nakesha sliced the spandex down the middle, all the way to her belly button. "And also…for this." When Nakesha's hand touched down on the crotch of Jansey's one-piece, she nearly fainted. She was so needy, so chock full of arousal, that even the quick brush of fingers weakened her knees.

As the other girls looked on, Nakesha pulled the spandex away from Jansey's body and cut a jagged hole. She never wore underwear with her one-piece, since it had a sort of built-in crotch, and now not only did her tits swing free, but her pussy lips were kissed by the humid gymnasium air. She'd shaved her pussy that morning, and she was so tender and bare Nakesha's firm touch made her shudder with so much pleasure it was almost painful.

"Oh god…" Jansey backed into the cool painted wall when Nakesha's long fingers slipped between her pussy lips. Through rivers of juice, Nakesha stroked Jansey's clit, already so throbbing and distended it protruded rudely beyond her naked outer lips. She felt like she had her very own cock down there, and it was getting hard as she imagined what might come next.

"Turn on the music," she heard herself pleading. She wasn't sure where that request had come from, but the idea made her quiver.

"Why?" Nakesha asked, rubbing her clit in tight circles. "You want to visualize the routine while I'm eating your cunt, little girl?"

Jansey's knees buckled. If it wasn't for the skipping rope binding her to the iron ring in the wall, she would have fallen right to the ground. "Yeah," she said, fuzzy-headed, desperate. Her arms strained and she forced her spread legs to hold her upright. "Music…"

Ruby turned it on, and the bass line rode up her thighs, rocking her pelvis. She'd felt it stronger when her core was closer to the ground, of course, but now Nakesha's deft fingers seemed to guide the beat straight into her pussy.

"Yes," Jansey moaned, holding that *s* until she ran out of breath.

It was a club beat, a remix, and it got her so hot she wanted to dance. She swayed a little as Nakesha watched her, amused, stroking her sopping wet pussy slowly now.

"Come on," Nakesha shouted over the music. "Suck our little girl's tits while I lick her sweet pussy."

Jansey's heart thumped like crazy, like she'd been shot up with epinephrine or something. She watched Nakesha sink to the floor until that tall beauty disappeared behind a cascade of black hair.

Ruby and Beatriz closed in fast, tearing sliced spandex away from her chest and locking on to her tits. The pleasure was so immediate and so vast, Jansey didn't know what to concentrate on: Sweating hands cupping her breast? Plump lips encircling her nipples? Tongues licking those hard buds, mouths sucking them? Or maybe just the expressions of pleasure in the girls' eyes as they gazed up at her? Jansey watched the stress lines disappear from their foreheads, and she felt as though she'd given them something good.

And then Nakesha's tongue touched her clit, and the world went black.

Jansey felt herself slipping down on Nakesha's face, and she tried to pull herself back up but her arms and legs were weak with arousal. Nakesha gripped her thighs hard, pushing her ass flush to the wall, licking Jansey's clit as the sliced-open spandex at her crotch retreated, curling around her naked pussy lips, pushing them together. She could feel the pressure on her clit and she found herself rocking, though she wasn't sure how she was doing it. Maybe the music had her in its grips. No, that was Nakesha, grasping her ass now and swaying her body with the beat.

Just like Ruby and Beatriz, Nakesha locked her mouth down on Jansey's body. When Jansey closed her eyes, she could see that mouth clamped around her shaved pussy through that jagged hole in her leotard. She still couldn't believe Nakesha had ruined her uniform, but this pleasure was definitely worth buying a new one.

Nakesha was sucking now, just like Ruby and Beatriz, like everybody was giving her body one big blow job—tits, clit, pussy lips, everything was getting sucked inside somebody's warm, wet mouth.

She was going to come so fast like this, all strung up from above, legs parted, feet tied to the wall. If her hands had been free, she would have cupped Ruby and Beatriz's heads, pressing them harder against her chest, forcing them to choke on her tits. As it was, she found herself bucking against Nakesha's face. She didn't mean to. Her hips moved to the music, thrusting into Nakesha's mouth like she was fucking the woman's throat, faster and faster.

Any minute now, she would explode with cum—at least, that's how it felt. Their routine hadn't even crossed her mind, but this was no time for work. Sex was the sport of queens, and she writhed with her teammates, the girls who'd taken regionals, who would one day hold the cup. Her body moved like a wave against their mouths.

That familiar sensation rested deep in her belly, wanting, waiting to come out. It liked Ruby and Beatriz.

It liked Nakesha even better—Nakesha whose fingertip slid easily up inside her pussy. God, she was wet. She was so damn wet Nakesha's slim, long fingers slipped right up there.

All the girls kept licking her, sucking her skin, savoring her body. Nakesha finger-fucked her, petted her insides, fucked her again. Swift alternation. She couldn't keep up with everything that was happening to her body. It was like a whirlwind, a tornado of lust tearing her apart. The sensations blew Jansey's mind. Her whimpers turned to yelps and hollers as Beatriz nipped at her tits.

"Fuck me, fuck me, fuck me, fuck me," she kept repeating to herself, and to Nakesha, whose fingers gave her such intense pleasure—not that anyone could hear her low growls over the loud music.

It was getting to be too much now. Jansey fucked Nakesha's face while Nakesha fucked her pussy. Ruby sucked hard on one tit while Beatriz bit the other. Hopefully that security guard really had passed out from the booze, because if not, her screams would surely summon him. She didn't exactly want to be caught strung up like this, but she couldn't stop. She didn't want to. Her whole body bucked against the girls, writhed against the wall, back and forth, rapid fire.

And then she popped.

The buzz in her belly overwhelmed her and she screamed until her throat felt as raw and red as her poor little pussy. Jansey pushed forward and pulled down until her arms strained, muscles blazing. She pushed against her heavy orgasm, bore down on the fingers and tongues, and all at once it was too much, too much, too much. It was more than she could handle. She would have kicked them all away, but her feet were still tethered to the wall. Instead she hollered, "Stop!"

And they did.

"You okay?" Ruby asked. Her lips were all red and swollen from the sucking. So was that small stretch of skin between the top of her lip and the bottom of her nose. Beatriz looked much the same, but Nakesha… Wow! When she stood, her face was gleaming with juices, and when she wiped them with the back of her hand, Jansey's knees went weak for about the fortieth time tonight.

It wasn't just Nakesha's chin that gleamed, though— her eyes did too. When Ruby had inched away to turn down the music, Jansey said, "That was amazing."

Nakesha replied with a simple "Yeah."

"You think you can concentrate on the routine now?" Beatriz untied her hands first, while Ruby worked at her ankles. Their presence hardly registered at the moment. Jansey was too wrapped up in Nakesha's loving gaze. It took a few moments before she even realized she was loose again. There were new ties binding her now, and they weren't made of jump ropes.

"We might have to do that again," Jansey said, gazing into Nakesha's depths.

How could everything change so fast? But it could. It could.

"Any time, little girl." Nakesha peeled off her one-piece and shoved it down to her ankles, pressing her small, dark tits against Jansey's bare chest.

They'd seen each other without clothes before, but Jansey knew this was the first time she was seeing Nakesha *naked*. And when this woman, her teammate and leader and lover and friend, kissed her with all the sizzling sensuality a pair of lips could pack, Ruby and Beatriz cheered from the sidelines.

SENSELESS

Stella Harris

Lana sees the two striking men across the room and decides to take a chance. If she doesn't do it now, she'll never work up the guts. She's been fantasizing about them for months, since the first day she saw them on set. Sean Mitchell and Jason Crane, daytime heart-throbs. On their own Sean and Jason are intimidating enough; together they are almost unapproachable. Lana screws up her courage and marches forward.

"I know what you guys are up to," Lana says, cocky grin in place, eager to display a confidence she doesn't actually feel. *Hot men, like dogs, can smell fear*, she tells herself. Lana's met with matching looks of inno-cence, Sean's joined by a raised eyebrow. "Oh, come on. Everyone *knows*," she insists, not willing to be deterred so easily. She's gone over this conversation in her head countless times, determined to be ready for every contingency.

"What're you fishing for, Lana?" Jason asks, like he couldn't care less about what she's hinting at, but there's an undercurrent of wariness. She knows they have to be carful, that Jason and Sean are worried about their professional reputations. A sad truth of the business is that gay, or even bisexual, men don't get cast in leading roles.

"I was just wondering what a girl had to do to get in on it," she answers, not quite meeting either of the men's eyes. But even her indirect gaze can't miss the way Jason almost chokes on his sip of beer and the way Sean goes stiff and a little pale.

They look at each other, a silent exchange as though they can read each other's minds. And hell, maybe they can. That would explain why they work so well together, why their presence is larger than life when they're on the screen, as if the energy between them jumps right out to grab the viewer. After a pause, Jason speaks. "If we're gonna do this, we're doing it our way." Though he says *our*, he clearly means *my*. It hasn't escaped her notice that Jason is the type of guy that likes to take charge. Not that Sean isn't strong in his own way, but he seems to like letting Jason take the lead, especially in social settings.

True to form, Sean doesn't speak, but the look he gives her is a challenge. She hadn't expected it to go this far, she thought she'd have to pass the whole thing off as a little harmless teasing. But if they're serious, she certainly isn't going to back down.

Lana arrives at the hotel room not knowing what to expect. She'd received an email from Jason telling her where to be and when, and reminding her to be prepared to do as she was told. She's afraid she'll find out this is all a big joke, but her curiosity won't let her walk away. She has to knock on that door.

Jason answers, predatory smile firmly in place. If she didn't already know him and trust him, she'd be worried. A man of his size with that look on his face? Trouble. He's dressed to his best advantage, the way he always is. Or maybe it's just that anything would look good on him. He's tall and muscular, with big strong hands that Lana can't tear her eyes from as he waves her in.

Sean is across the room, leaning against the sturdy hotel desk with a drink in his hand. He doesn't speak, but the look he gives her is appraising. His silence and scrutiny make her nervous. Sean is as attractive as Jason, though in his own way. Sean isn't as tall as Jason but he's still a tall man; both of them tower over Lana. Sean's features are softer than Jason's—she imagines he would have looked almost feminine when he was younger. Maybe he still would if he didn't cultivate a five o'clock shadow at all times.

Jason moves into the room to stand next to Sean and picks up a drink of his own. Neither of them offer her anything. She's not sure if she'd want it, anyway. Her nerves are on edge, but she wants to be sharp for this, doesn't want to miss anything. Lana knows this is a one-time thing.

"Strip," Jason commands from his place by the wall. She knows he wants to be in charge of this encounter, but hadn't fully realized what that would mean.

"Excuse me?" Lana's surprised, not used to being addressed in that tone. She kind of likes it. Jason exudes confidence and authority. Something deep inside her longs to obey. But this is so far from the fun-loving Jason she knows that she's taken aback.

"I told you this would be on our terms, so if you want to stay, then strip," Jason explains in an even, firm tone, like it's the most reasonable thing in the world. She eyes them again, thinking that maybe this was a bad idea—a terrible idea—maybe she should just turn around and leave now. But when her glance reaches Sean's eyes, she stops. The look he's giving her, it's...hungry, and that's enough to get her in the game.

Lana drops her purse and starts to strip as instructed. She's too aware of being watched to make it sexy, so she settles for trying not to fall over herself. She's always been clumsy, it's one of many things she's self-conscious about. She toes off her shoes, then pulls off her shirt. In just jeans and a bra she glances at the men and sees that they haven't moved. They offer no word or gesture to encourage her, but Sean licks his lips, and intentional or not, it gets her moving again. She unclasps her bra and lets it drop unceremoniously to the growing pile of clothes on the floor.

Lana pops the button on her jeans and unzips her fly. She looks up to meet first Jason's gaze and then Sean's. They're still watching her as she slides her jeans and underwear down. Once she's done undressing they break eye contact and let their eyes roam over her body.

She stands totally nude in the middle of the room while the boys are still fully dressed. It seems unfair, but she does her best to stand proudly, chin raised, and not look uncomfortable. She makes a living on her looks and yet has never achieved the confidence most people assume goes along with that. Lana finds herself not only waiting for the next instruction but even eager for it. The wait is terrible. She wants to fidget, to ask questions, to take action.

Perhaps deciding she's suffered enough, Jason finally speaks. "Get on the bed, on your back." His tone is a little softer this time, but it's still an order, and her heartbeat quickens at the sound of it.

This is the last step. If she does this, does as he says, this becomes real. She lets herself take one last moment to think, to compose herself. But, she reasons, she's come this far, she may as well take it all the way. Lana moves over to the bed and climbs on. It's one of those high hotel beds, the edge nearly reaching her waist. These beds always make her feel young, make her want to swing her legs over the edge.

Lana positions herself in the middle of the bed and

lies flat on her back. Her heart is pounding with anticipation and it's difficult to resist asking questions. But even without being told she knows they'd be unwelcome, so she lies there and waits.

She doesn't have to wait for long. Jason sets his drink aside. The sound of the glass hitting the wood of the table fills the silence, and Lana tries not to flinch. Jason reaches into a bag on the floor that Lana hadn't noticed before and his hand comes out holding a strip of black cloth. It takes her a moment to realize that this is a blindfold. She opens her mouth to protest, but a look from Jason is enough to silence her before she's begun. Lana closes her eyes in submission and tingles from the tip of her head all the way down to her toes in anticipation of giving up her sense of sight.

Jason fastens the blindfold across her eyes and ties it to the side of her head, so she's not resting on the knot. His hands move with an assurance that makes it clear he's done this kind of thing before. Lana is suddenly plunged into darkness. It's a strange feeling when she knows that all the lights are on in the room and that she is still perfectly on display.

Lana hears a sound, her hearing now more acute to make up for her loss of sight, and then something is being snapped around her right wrist, her arm pulled above her head. It isn't until her left wrist and arm undergo the same treatment that it really sinks in that she's being tied to the bed. A small voice in her head panics, thinks she should object to this. But she trusts

Jason and Sean. If she didn't she wouldn't be here. She resolves once more to hold on tight and enjoy the ride, wherever it might lead.

Her ankles undergo the same treatment as her wrists, being bound into a cuff and then stretched apart and secured to the bed. The hands doing the work move with the same efficiency as they did when securing her blindfold and she knows it's still Jason binding her.

Now fully secured, Lana feels every passing second more acutely than ever before. She is hyperaware of every part of her body; not knowing what is going to happen, or where she will be touched, puts every inch of her flesh on high alert. It's not an unpleasant sensation, it's almost like a meditation exercise, and she lets her awareness flow to one part of her body and then another. She only has to think of her breasts on display, and possibly under scrutiny, to feel her nipples harden.

For what feels like hours but is probably only a few minutes, no one touches her and nothing happens. But when she listens carefully she hears the rustling of fabric. The men are undressing, maybe undressing each other. The idea that they are stripping right in front of her when she can't see a thing is so much hotter than it should be. She's already imagined them naked. She came here because she wanted to see the real thing. And yet she isn't disappointed. She gets to have this experience and still maintain her fantasy. Somehow, it's the best of both worlds.

Lana hears what must be the sliding of skin, of

bodies moving together, and then she hears a wet sound. She realizes with a jolt that the men are kissing. They're right there and they're kissing. Fuck. She wants to see this. Wants to know what they look like together. Just knowing that they are so close to her and are touching each other is enough to make her wet.

A moment later she feels the mattress dip and knows they're climbing onto the bed with her. There's the seemingly unintentional brush of skin against her skin. She doesn't know who is touching her or what parts of their bodies she's feeling. And then there's a hand. She doesn't know whose. It's trailing down her chest slowly, onto her stomach, and then stopping, moving up again, lazily stroking at her body. She can feel the slightly rough texture of calluses on the fingers, the occasional scrape of a carefully manicured fingernail. Lana imagines the hand belongs to Sean. That he's still looking at her with blatant desire. Or maybe it's Jason, with Sean hungrily watching him touch her. She's not sure which idea she likes better.

The bed moves again and she realizes they're on either side of her—she can feel two sets of knees. And then they're kissing again. There's nothing else that could be making those sounds. The wet slip of lips and tongue. The soft breaths and barely there moans. Her imagination is so vivid she can almost feel those lips, can almost taste them. A hand falls to her body, cups her breast as fingers tweak her nipple. It's her turn to moan. She can't help it; she's so amped up that every touch sends sparks through her body. She tries her bonds but they hold. She hears a chuckle, sure it's Jason. He clearly loves this. Loves that she has no control. And she's beginning to find that she loves it too. They've barely done anything and yet she's already wet. Doesn't think she's ever been this wet in her life. Her inner thighs are soaked with it. She's almost embarrassed.

Someone is getting on top of her, she can feel the mattress shift again, feel hands and legs on either side of her. There's breath against her cheek, it's warm and moist and it smells like whiskey. Someone is right there and she can't do anything about it. There's a wet noise again, but this time she knows it isn't kissing. There's only one person in front of her, of that she's sure.

Her mind starts to spin, imagining all the things that could explain what she's hearing, and then there's a gasp right by her ear. The startled sound morphs into a full-throated moan and a plea for more. That's Sean's voice, she's sure of it. Sean is on his hands and knees over her body and Jason is doing something that is gently rocking the bed and making Sean beg. She can hear every little hitch of breath perfectly and she imagines the look of ecstasy on Sean's face that must go with the sounds that he's making. Lana wonders if his eyes are screwed tightly shut or if he's looking at her, at her blindfolded face, her parted lips, her goose-pimpled body.

"Gonna use your juices to work him open," Jason's sex-deepened voice warns just seconds before she feels his massive fingers sliding against her, into her. She cries out, she can't help it. Jason's fingers are working into her, his thumb absently brushing against her clit—as if it wasn't already clear that her pleasure wasn't the focus this evening. And then his hand is gone as quickly as it came, leaving her throbbing and wanting, all of her awareness focused sharply between her legs.

The bed moves again. It's Sean being pushed forward and thrusting back. It must be. Lana's sure she knows what they're doing now. What Jason is doing to Sean. Jason's fingers are inside him now, they must be. The same fingers that were just inside her.

The pace of the breathing by her ear is ramping up now, coming in ragged little gasps. "*Oh, fuck. Fuck, yes. Jason, please.*" The word *please* is so elongated it's barely a word. Sean's hissing right into her ear, and the sound of his broken begging gives her chills.

Lana feels something wet hit her belly, and her mind reels for a moment trying to imagine what it could be until she realizes with a start that Sean is so aroused that he's actually dripping on her, leaking. That's somehow both the hottest and most disgusting thing she can think of. It would be one thing if she was involved. If she was coaxing the fluid out of him with her hand or her mouth. But this is different. They're paying no more mind to her than to the bed. Dirtying her up as carelessly as the sheets that will be housekeeping's job to clean up.

But she's not going to ask them to stop. If this is as close as she's going to get to having them, she's going to take it. Even if it's frustrating, even if it's unsatisfying, it's still maybe the single hottest experience she's ever had, and the fantasies from this are going to last her a lifetime. She wants to memorize the sound of Sean's desperate pleading, play it back in her mind on nights when she's alone and touching herself.

There's a shifting of weight on the bed again. There's moaning again too, and this time it's both of them. Sean's voice by her ear is ragged and Jason's, from further away, is deeper—almost a growl. The movement on the bed increases. Jason must really be fucking him now. She can hear the slap of skin on skin over the grunts and gasps, all the private, intimate sounds they're making.

Her whole body is tingling with arousal. She should be annoyed, hell, she should be pissed. She's being treated like furniture, like a prop, or at best like a sex toy. And yet she's not bothered at all. There's something so perfect about experiencing them together this way. She thinks, now, that it would have been a shame to take all the mystery away.

The bed is rocking so furiously that she's almost getting motion sick. Sean falls forward a bit, his arms brushing against hers and his forehead on her shoulder. He's damp with sweat—she is too, she realizes then. Lana arches up toward his body, strains forward as much as her bonds will allow, seeking any contact she can get.

Teeth bite into her shoulder and there's a hot splash against her belly. She gasps, knowing exactly what it is, what it means. She wonders if Jason's hand was on him, or if he came untouched. *"Fuck, Sean,"* comes out as a growl above her and she knows that Jason is coming too. After just a moment, the motion of the bed stills, and she can feel them climbing off the bed. "Don't be impolite to our guest, Sean, clean her up." These words are followed by warm wetness against her stomach. Sean is *licking her*, eating his own spend off her flesh. Her stomach roils and she shudders. All of her awareness focuses on the hot drag of Sean's tongue against her skin; long stokes and little kitten licks. She longs to feel his mouth move lower, to feel his tongue between her legs.

All too soon Sean's mouth leaves her body and after a moment of unidentified noises hands begin to work at her ankle, undoing its bindings. The hands work systematically until she's untied, and then the blindfold is removed, too. She blinks up at the brightness of the room, slowly bringing her arms down and bending her knees, feeling the blood move back into her limbs with an unpleasant tingle. She rubs at her wrists, feeling where they're marked from her struggles. Lana wonders how badly she'll be bruised, hoping for a physical reminder of this night, even if only for a few days.

Her eyes focus and fall upon Jason. His jeans have been pulled on, but not buttoned, and he hasn't bothered with a shirt. He's tossing a towel into the bathroom before coming back into the room to stand at the foot of the bed and smile at her. She smiles back, lazily; she's still in a daze even though she didn't do more than lie there. No words come to her, so instead of speaking she looks for Sean, finding him sprawled in the arm chair, wearing boxer-briefs and a T-shirt, a drink back in his hand. He returns her lazy smile.

Lana pauses, not sure if she should be waiting for instruction, but after a moment it's clear that their game is over. "So, um..." she manages to say as she crawls off the bed and fumbles for her clothes. Jason turns away from her to retrieve his drink as she quickly gets dressed. She doesn't know what to say. What the hell does someone say in a situation like this? *Thank you* doesn't seem right. *See you around*, maybe.

She finishes dressing before turning to look at the men again. Jason has perched on the arm of Sean's chair. There's a careless intimacy between them that wasn't there when she walked into the room. As if to emphasize this, Sean's free hand comes to rest on Jason's thigh.

"So, I'll let myself out, then," she says, feeling awkward. "And, uh, this'll stay between us. Of course. I mean, I won't tell anyone." She's babbling now, but she can't stop herself as she moves toward the door— ready to exit the room and leave this strange experience behind.

Jason gives her a wink and says, "What's to tell? You didn't see anything."

JUST DESERTS

Kiki DeLovely

She's got me hog-tied, face-down on the floor. Although quite the aficionada for being restrained, put in challenging positions and the like, this is one of the very few times I've been bound so restrictively. Certainly I've never been trussed up and simultaneously closed in with a floor against my face. Being somewhat claustrophobic, I'm delightfully surprised that I don't feel panicky. In fact, this predicament is having quite the opposite effect on me. It quiets my mind for the first time in days and I can finally experience my body completely, without interruption; the voices around me seem far off, I feel the rope digging into my flesh. And for a tactually motivated person like myself, being tethered like this is heaven.

She runs her palms over the ropes and then up my

thighs. "This isn't supposed to be a scene—I'm only allowed to give brief demos tonight—but, damn... You sure are tempting..." Pushing it a little further, she inches up my skirt just a bit more and inadvertently locates the single most erogenous place on my body. That spot where ass meets inner thigh just shy of pussy. I inhale sharply, not loud enough for her to hear me in such a large crowd, but my body must be whispering secrets to her fingertips because she lingers there, lets her knuckles dig in. I close my eyes, exhale, and feel every last nerve ending on the surface of my skin. The connection emanating from touch. The rope just tight enough to be delectably uncomfortable. The mastery of her obvious skill. The general humility of her nature is refreshing—she's not overly cocky like so many. All this gets me hot.

Tonight's ties are only a taste of what's to come for me tomorrow. Still, the simplicity of this hold gets me out of my head, calms my spirit while exciting my body at the same time. I want to experience a rope suspension and she eagerly agreed to rig me up, but it would have to wait for the next day. Quite the endeavor that isn't without its risks, the full weight of my Amazonian body suspended midair using only rope. But I trust her. Handed over in a flash, she was telling me about her craft, going over safety information, and I caught a look in her eye. My shyness evaded me long enough to finally take in the green flecks in her eyes, bound in a gaze that I was somehow able to sustain, despite my nerves. It was then I knew. And now my body feels it too. There's something about the energy she puts off—I find her enticingly compelling—so quietly sexy, she almost flew under my radar. Almost.

This is my first camp. It took me thirty-some-odd years to finally experience what I had so envied in my childhood friends. Summer after summer, I stayed home while they had gotten to experience the adventures of camp; though this was definitely a more unconventional and very...adult...version thereof. Camp is so very unique from any other gathering I've ever heard of—connecting with nature, acres of wooded land in the middle of nowhere, while experiencing your darkest desires. More than that, you witness, take part in and perhaps even manifest fantasies you never knew were possible, let alone hiding inside you. There's no judgment, just an open air of loving (and lustful) support that lends itself to the unearthing of clandestine salaciousness. Camp really is all about the community experience.

As the resident pastry chef, I spend a good portion of my day in the kitchen whipping up tasty treats for the campers, all of whom are assigned volunteer hours. And that is how I met her—in my kitchen. She was on prep duty and we were in the weeds. I was beyond stressed. She had a calm, charming way about her, despite me freaking out over the twenty pounds of butter gone missing and an overflowing chocolate catastrophe in the oven. At one point, I had swung by her station to give further instructions, and as I walked away she called out, "Yes, chef. Thank you, chef." A smile crept across my face, a spark hit my panties and I threw her a look over my shoulder. A perpetual bottom everywhere else, I often forget just how toppy I get in the kitchen.

We meet in the dining hall the next day to share breakfast and some thoughts before our hot morning date. But really the heat begins instantaneously. She asks me what I like about rope and I struggle to find the words. How does one put language to that which exists almost entirely in the unspoken? Being bound is meditative, gives me a sweet respite from the maddening constancy of wheels spinning uncontrollably and slams me firmly into my body in the most delicious way. When I'm in that space, there are no words. It's all such an inexplicable, ethereal experience. To be forced to feel.

Stumbling over my thoughts, I decide to turn the tables, "Why are you drawn to rope? What does rigging someone up feel like for you?" I realize immediately I wasn't quite prepared for her answer. She's smart. Even smarter than me. Possessing quite the impressive vocabulary, and though she's far from abstruse, her command of the English language is daunting. Obviously having put a lot of thought into a question she's answered before, she throws out a few esoteric words, one of which I've never even heard before. This, of course, gets me wet. Well-matched intelligence is always a huge turn-on, but when I'm clearly out of my league? That's a rare day. Where some would be intimidated, I'm sucked in, dying to know more, to learn from her. My intellectual boner raging. She likens each rope suspension to a snow-flake—each one utterly unique, perfect and evanescent.

When I ask what else she's passionate about, a string of complex language flows from her lips directly into my cunt. It's as if my questions give her permission to share with me her incredibly provocative thought process. This is the most seductive kind of foreplay for a girl like me. Turn me on with your mind and your hands can do as they please. Impress me with your critical thinking and I'll do just about anything for you.

Her eyes light up when she gets into academic mode, a glint of obvious avidity. Not dissimilar to the look of playful delight and attentive dedication as she contemplates her rope in regard to the body before her. Lost in thought as to where she's going with this, I take advantage of the opportunity and study her face, suddenly privy to how she takes in all of me, carefully considering every curve of my body—I see her plotting out loops and ties, discovering how this snowflake will be strung up. My first rope suspension, rising in her eyes.

She leads me out the back door of the dining hall, through the field, up toward her cabin. Squeal. (My favorite cabin.) I have such a fondness for its members, its energy and sex appeal. I sneak them treats from the kitchen late at night. It started out as a gift to a top who aptly suggested that a gooey chocolate delivery from a girl who wants to get cut would make a good impression. Quite quickly, it became habit. The cabin-mates praise my skills, appreciating how the treats fuel them after scenes, give them a boost for what's to come. During one late-night delivery, I sneak a peek at "the board," getting a rush from seeing my name with more than a few check marks after it. Members of Squeal pride themselves on being very dirty players and like to keep tabs on all the conquests of the cabin, à la notches in the bedpost. Except that it's them keeping score for everyone outside of the cabin—quite the hot little nonconsensual game—and they give out awards at the end of camp. (I've been assured that I'm a shoo-in.) Secretly I wonder who claimed their stake first and got to add my name. It's open for wide interpretation what one might consider check mark–worthy, which is why I don't know for certain, but my money is on my rigger.

We stop a short distance shy of Squeal. The playground. I look up and consider the metal crossbeam just above us. Swinging beside the swings. An achingly sexy choice for a scene. The exposed, public nature of it. The fact that it's right outside her cabin (almost as if she's showing me, and our scene, off to her cabin-mates). The idea that our scene won't be in the dungeon and instead bringing it back to the community-based (and exhibitionist-prone) sensibility of camp. All of these factors play a role in the heat mounting inside me, between us. The understated nature of our chemistry lends itself to a slow boil. Such involved rope work inevitably takes time and patience. I delight in every sweet second of buildup.

"Turn around, hands on your head." Her terse

orders make my clit jump and I spring into position. The hemp fibers drag purposefully across my flesh, surprisingly soft, as though one would have to really try to make them burn. Constriction, on the other hand, they facilitate with ease. As she ropes me in, the lengths draped over her shoulders take on a momentary illusion of a harness across her chest and I can imagine how hot she looks bottoming. But this thought is a flash in the pan, as she assertively pushes and pulls me however she pleases, wrapping around my body again and again. Clearly, she's the one in control. I close my eyes briefly to take in the feel of it all. Before my mind has a chance to figure out what this binding is doing to my body, I'm being grabbed and reined in by an intricately knotted harness. She latches onto it right between my breasts and yanks me around, facing away so I can't see her. My nipples, already stiff from her rubbing against them with every pass of the rope, begin to harden all the more with candied agony.

Just as she's pressing her body up against mine from behind, pulling me into her hard, we hear a passerby call out, "Looks like someone's getting her just deserts!" The semantics geek in me can't help but relish this twist. He obviously means that I'm being properly rewarded for my efforts in the kitchen and his usage is clever, tying it to me being a pastry chef. But I'll never be privy to whether or not he actually knows that the saying has absolutely nothing to do with desserts—even though it is pronounced the same, the idiom stems from the

word "deserve," is spelled with just one "s," and literally means "to receive that which one justly deserves."
Then it hits me that here I am, in the middle of a scene
where I'm about to be suspended midair for the first
time ever, by this lusciously skilled rigger, no less, and
I'm pondering word play. I am such a nerd. Luckily, she
is too. I can only imagine that her mind got stuck there
for a second too.

Having loosened her grip momentarily, she snaps
me back into my flesh by whipping me around and
continuing to work the rope around my legs, dangerously near to my cunt. I never know when to expect the
touch of her hands next, where the cords will trail, twist,
tighten. Every time she creates a new knot, the remaining
lengths of rope must be pulled through, and feeling the
falls raining down on my skin is exquisitely delicious.

As she pulls through each loop that is then tightened
into a knot, I feel the erotic energy behind her patience and
deliberate contemplation put into each action. Sadistic
love breathed into every knot. The concentration in her
face alone is pristine in its lasciviousness. There's a beautifully even-tempered art to rope bondage; she steps back
occasionally to get a more distanced view of her canvas.
Once again grabbing hold of the anchor conveniently
located between my tits, she pulls me forward until my
feet run out of earth. I have a moment of panic, thrown
off balance, fear that I'm falling, and then suddenly I feel
gravity give way. Her smile says it all. Mine does too,
once the terror is pushed aside and absolute bliss takes

over, it stretches wildly across my face. Every last inch of my body is on display—a showing of her kinky artwork. Floating in the breeze leaves me feeling sweetly objectified, hanging helplessly for the whole world to see. Or at least all of camp.

I exhale into the ropes, settle into the pain. With other challenging play, I usually try to breathe through the white heat, attempt to go beyond it; but as I'm suspended here, I find myself wanting instead to breathe into it. So I inhale and submit to the purest form of pleasure.

My rigger grins, snaps on a black latex glove, and smooths a layer of lube across it. Entering me in one swift, fluid motion, she works her fist in my cunt, gradually gaining momentum. A particular flavor of ecstasy permeates me as I give my lungs permission to open up and emit the most primal, guttural screams—a freedom that doesn't exist in the real world. Here at camp, I know that all within earshot are delighting in the shared experience of my pleasure. My eyes want to roll back in my head and so I fight it—I need to take in every second of this once-in-a-lifetime view—the look of glee and satisfaction in her face, the pine trees reaching up into an expansively open sky, the feathery clouds that drift by. She twists her wrist and I begin to squirt. Feeling my cum shooting through the air as I glide back and forth with rhythmic swinging, my vision blurry and unfocused, I can take in the vastness that surrounds us. I feel as though my arc will stream endlessly through the sky, forever defying gravity.

I realize that I've misplaced some time when the next thing I feel is the sweet, sensual friction of the ropes sliding across my chest as she works at releasing me. Her instant recognition of how hot this gets me, the sensation of it flickering throughout my body and the tension sparking hot and fast between us. That awareness and arousal in her eyes draws me in further. At last the weight of all the rope falls to the ground and I still feel like I'm floating, light-headed and dizzy. She sees it in my eyes and pulls me into her, tightens her arms in place of the rope, supporting me. She holds me there until I'm steadied, then kisses me slowly, her tongue wrapping around mine, before freeing me one last time.

Smiling as she coils up her ropes, she tells me I'm a natural, that I was up there for a long time, especially given this was my first suspension. She has another date and has to leave before me so I stick around and clean up, realizing too late that she left her jacket on the slide ladder. It sparks an idea in me and so I gather up the rest of my belongings, scurry off to my room and locate my cherry pin. Every camper gets a pin. But the cherry pin is not theirs to keep. The assignment that comes along with it is to give it to someone who pops your cherry in regard to an activity you've never before tried. And since my rigger popped my suspension cherry in a major way, I thought it only appropriate to attach it to her collar. I grab my journal and her newly pinned jacket, make my way back over to Squeal, and ask one of her cabin-mates which bed is hers. Folding it up neatly, I decide against leaving a note. Leave *her* in suspense for a change.

I meander back out and decide to write while lounging in the open field, the sun kissing me lightly. Playing with her took me out of my head in a delicious way and it takes a few minutes to get back into it, but suddenly the words come rushing over me and my pen struggles to keep up. After scribbling continuously for a while, language slows and I look up. The playground equipment we made such good use of is now occupied by another group. The handsome top who had marked my back with a brief, intense flogging the night prior (and who will, in a matter of a few hours, run a scalpel across my flesh) is now swinging playfully just inches from where I had been strung up. Several others are crowded around, creating a completely different formation of hot scenes. I imagine the energy my rigger and I left lingering there serves to electrify their play all the more. I stroll back to my bed for a quick nap, all the smacks and bellows echoing through the field and her sweet, sexy energy vibrating on the surface of my skin. The impression and effects of her ropes are embedded in my flesh for days, but the experience will always live inside me. It's undeniable: After just one hit, I'm addicted to suspension. Yes, this pastry chef did indeed get her just deserts.

BALANCING
THE BOOKS

Lucy Felthouse

A bead of sweat ran down the side of Philip's head and trickled into his hairline. He'd been lying flat on his back on the cold parquet floor for what felt like hours. Realistically, it probably hadn't even been one hour, but because he'd been trying so hard not to move a muscle for fear of toppling the stack of hardback books resting on his abdomen, every single minute was torture.

And yet, at the same time, it was complete and utter bliss. Giovanna was sitting on a wooden chair, the legs of which were either side of his hips—as were hers—and she was using the pile of books as a table. She idly flipped the pages of the weighty tome she was pretending to read, and studiously ignored Philip, as though he really were nothing but a table.

Philip's cock had never been so hard. He was torn.

Part of him wanted the books to fall so Giovanna's beautiful eyes would flash with anger and she would punish him the very best way she knew how. The other part wanted to please her, in the hope that she might let him bury his face between her thighs and lick her delicious pussy to orgasm, and maybe, just maybe, be allowed to come himself.

Another droplet of sweat followed the first one into his rapidly dampening hair. Philip's erection strained beneath his clothes, and he decided to try and distract himself by thinking of something else. *Trees. Taxes. Tridents.*

It didn't work. Instead, his mind wandered to how he'd gotten into this predicament in the first place.

Giovanna was Philip's boss—in the usual employment sense as well as the mistress and slave sense. Just a few short weeks back, he'd been wandering the high street of the town he lived in, and had come across an amazing-looking bookshop. He'd peered through the window, fascinated. The slightly gloomy interior was all dark wood and spiral staircases, and was a book lover's wet dream. And Philip was a book lover. Turning, he made for the door. As he reached it, he noticed a sign stuck to the pane of glass in its center.

EXPERIENCED BOOKKEEPER WANTED.

COMPETITIVE RATES.

APPLY WITHIN.

Philip didn't need a job. He was, in fact, a highly qualified accountant, and some of the past investments he'd made had come good and meant that he could live very comfortably off the profits. In fact, it wasn't worth his time to work, as the tax man would pinch even more of his pennies.

Philip didn't need any books, either. His custom-built home library was fully stocked with an abundance of fiction and nonfiction, and he really needed to read and get rid of some of them before he started purchasing more.

He peered through the door, catching sight of a voluptuous bespectacled woman standing behind the till, writing in a notebook. She sure was easy on the eye, with her long dark hair pulled up into a high ponytail and the hint of ample cleavage peeking out of the top of her blouse. She must have caught sight of him out of the corner of her eye because her head snapped up from what she was doing and she looked straight at him. Peering over the top of her glasses, she continued to gaze at him unsmilingly. Many people would have found her demeanor cold, unapproachable.

Philip pushed open the door and walked in. Before he knew what he was doing he'd walked straight up to the counter and the aloof woman behind it and said, "I'm interested in the job."

She put down her pen and raised an eyebrow. "And what are your qualifications?"

He was, in fact, vastly overqualified for the job she

was offering. He could do the paperwork for the book-shop standing on his head. With one hand tied behind his back. However, the cool, unimpressed stare the woman gave him made him *want* to impress her—and so he gave her the full whammy of his qualifications and experience.

The woman's face had remained impassive.

"It sounds as though you're used to much bigger accounts than you'd be dealing with here. Why on earth are you interested in *this* job?"

Because I want to fuck you.

"Because I live off the profits of some wise invest-ments and don't need to work, but I *do* need something to fill my time, before I go stir-crazy. There's only so much golf a man can play. I figure you can pay me in"—he'd been going to say books, but as he tore his gaze away from her steely one and onto the tantalizing curves of her body, his brain substituted the word for a much more inappropriate one—"kind."

The bookseller's eyebrows shot almost into her hair-line.

Philip gulped. *Stupid idiot, what did you say that for? She'll have you done for sexual harassment!*

Narrowing her eyes, the woman paused for a few seconds, then asked coolly, "What's your name?"

Unable to cope with the intense glare he was being subjected to, Philip lowered his eyes to the counter between them and mumbled his name. He also pulled in his shoulders protectively, fully expecting her to flip her lid and give him a tongue-lashing before throwing him unceremoniously out of her shop.

"Well, Philip, I *do* need someone to balance my books. And"—she looked him up and down—"it certainly seems as though you're more than up to the job."

She thrust out a hand. "I'm Giovanna. And you're hired."

Philip took her hand and shook it. It was cool and dry, much like her demeanor.

And that had been the start of their relationship. Giovanna had taken charge immediately, leading Philip into the tiny room behind the counter and showing him where everything he needed could be found. He'd followed that rotund, swaying arse willingly and decided there and then that he'd follow her anywhere.

She'd watched him as he'd leafed through paperwork and tried to make sense of it—she'd obviously not been doing any bookkeeping at all until he'd showed up. There were bits of paper, scribbled notes, receipts and invoices shoved randomly into box files, and although Philip was exasperated at the amount of work he would have to do to even get the stuff in order, let alone balance the books, he was also secretly pleased. It meant more time spent in the company of the divine Giovanna. He was already so besotted that he'd happily watch paint dry, if it meant being with her.

Hopefully she'd be so grateful that he'd sorted out her paperwork nightmare that she'd deliver on the promise her eyes had given as they'd looked him up and down.

Under Giovanna's watchful gaze, Philip continued his job with renewed vigor.

Later that day, Giovanna had indeed paid Philip in kind. When he'd padded out of the office to where she was dusting the banister of the gorgeous spiral staircase, she'd peered at him over her glasses, her cold blue gaze pinning him to the spot.

"Done?" she said curtly.

Philip nodded meekly. "Yes. I've got everything pretty much sorted out, but I'll come back tomorrow with a proper ledger to get everything recorded so it's easy for you to refer back to, if you ever need to."

"Yes what?" Giovanna asked.

"P-pardon?"

"You said yes, when I asked if you were done. And I'm now asking you, yes what?"

It took Philip a good few seconds to understand what she was getting at, but as those piercing blue eyes continued to burn into him, he suddenly understood. Or at least he hoped he did.

"Yes, Mistress."

Giovanna gave a satisfied nod. "That's better. Now finish cleaning this, and then you can go."

She tossed the duster at him, and Philip immediately set to his task. Giovanna climbed the staircase, giving him a tantalizing view of her rump as she did. Then, just as she reached the top and he was about to silently lament the loss of the spectacular view, she turned and sat on the top step.

Philip's already semi-hard cock sprung to full attention. Giovanna had positioned herself so that anyone looking up at her from below would be able to see right up her skirt. This would have been enough to drive Philip to distraction, but Giovanna had taken it one step further. She wore no underwear, and her bare pussy was completely on display. Philip had no idea if he was supposed to look at her or not, but he couldn't tear his gaze away. Licking his lips, he eventually clawed back the presence of mind to turn his eyes to Giovanna's face, which wore a smug grin.

"Like what you see?"

Philip's throat was suddenly so dry that he opened his mouth to respond, but couldn't make the words come out. Instead, he nodded vigorously, desperate to palm his cock and enjoy some temporary relief, but instinctively knowing that would be the wrong thing to do.

Not without permission.

Where had that come from? Since when did Philip, the big-shot, wealthy accountant, wait for permission?

Giovanna's grin widened, and she pulled the hem of her skirt up, parting her generous thighs at the same time. Philip's attention immediately snapped back to the beautiful pussy that was being displayed before him; the splayed and swollen labia, the sheen of juices and the nubbin of sensitive flesh that resided at its apex. He wanted to eat her; pleasure her delicious cunt until she came all over his face.

"Want a closer look?"

Now her smile was as wide as the Cheshire Cat's. An arched eyebrow seemed to punctuate her ridiculous question. Ridiculous, because the answer was so obvious that the question might as well have been rhetorical.

Eager for Giovanna to allow the very thing she was asking, Philip swallowed and forced the response from his mouth.

"Yes, please, Mistress."

Her slick pussy was so tempting that it took all of his willpower not to dash up the stairs, grab those luscious thighs in his hands and eat it for all he was worth. Instead, he waited patiently for her response. His cock, however, wasn't so well-behaved. It strained against his clothes, making every movement both painful and incredibly stimulating at the same time.

Giovanna said nothing, and the two of them stared silently at one another for a good few minutes, until eventually, she said,

"Come."

Philip would have liked nothing more than to come, but he knew that wasn't what she meant. He dropped the cloth in his hand and scrambled eagerly up the stairs until he was two steps down from Giovanna, which, when kneeling, brought his face almost level with her cunt. Still, he waited, resisting the urge to rub his swollen crotch against the edge of the step in front of him. She'd know exactly what he was doing, and he was damn sure she wouldn't approve. He wasn't going to risk pissing her off because there was no way she'd let him lick her pussy then. And he really, *really* wanted to taste her.

His good behavior was rewarded when Giovanna finally uttered the words he'd been longing to hear.

"Make me come."

"Yes, Mistress."

Philip didn't need telling twice. As soon as the words left his mouth, he shuffled forward, slipped his hands beneath her creamy, fleshy thighs and lowered his head to the prize between them. As his tongue touched her heated, swollen cunt, his cock leapt. She was *delicious*, but then, somehow he'd known she would be. How could such a woman be anything else?

He ate her pussy the best way he knew how: enthusiastically licking and nibbling at her labia, dipping his tongue into her saturated channel and sucking her engorged clit. Giovanna spoke no words of encouragement, and not so much as a moan or a sigh issued from those perfect lips, but the occasional involuntary twitch or thrust of her hips told Philip all he needed to know. Plus, he felt sure that if he was doing something wrong, she'd soon let him know. Giovanna wasn't exactly backward in coming forward, which is how he'd ended up eating her out on a spiral staircase in her shop, having met her only a few hours previously.

In all of his previous sexual encounters, Philip had found that when going down on a woman, the noises she made were important to help him gauge how he was doing. The absence of any sounds from Giovanna, however, just made him try harder. If he could wrench even the tiniest moan from her, he'd be thrilled.

A tidbit of delight was thrown to him when, rather than making a noise, Giovanna moved her hands from where she'd been leaning back on them and tangled them into his hair and pulled him more tightly to her crotch. He took that as a sign that she was close to coming, and, remembering that her order had been "make me come" with no specifics as to how, he shifted his right hand from where it had been gripping her ample thigh and slipped two long fingers up inside her pussy. Maneuvering so he was stimulating her G-spot, Philip was hugely gratified when he heard a sharp intake of breath from Giovanna.

He decided there and then he was going to get a noise out of her, even if it killed him. Capturing her clit between his lips once more, he began to suck and nibble it as he stroked the soft pad of flesh deep inside her cunt. The walls of Giovanna's pussy clenched tightly, and he felt a fresh surge of blood to his dick as he imagined how it would feel to have his shaft buried deep inside her instead of his fingers. He wondered if he would ever find out. He really hoped so.

Soon, the rippling of Giovanna's pussy made him forget all about fucking her and concentrate solely on giving her the orgasm of her life. He worked his fingers roughly against her sweet spot and flicked at her clit with his tongue until his jaw ached. Suddenly, Giovanna's grip on his hair tightened, and he heard a series of tiny grunts before she let go and her orgasm washed over her.

Philip whipped his fingers from her cunt and replaced them with his mouth, so he could taste the delicious juices that trickled from her. Tart, and yet somehow sweet at the same time. Philip couldn't help the groan that came from his own lips as he sucked at her lower ones while she bucked against his face.

Giovanna's movements slowed as her climax waned, and Philip felt the feeling come back into his scalp as she released her hold on his hair. As Giovanna then leaned back on her hands for a few seconds while she got her breath back, Philip expected her to recline on the steps for a little while. But no, she was made of tougher stuff than that.

Suddenly, she stood and snatched her skirt back into place before looking down at where Philip still crouched on the step. He paused, wondering what she would do next. A curt nod, perhaps?

Giovanna managed to surprise him again. She leaned down and patted him on the head, not unlike the way you'd pat a dog, and said, "Very good."

Heat rushed to Philip's face. He'd pleased her, and that pleased him. He still had a raging hard-on, but somehow, he didn't care. Making Giovanna happy was more important, and he suspected that he'd get rewarded at some point.

Several weeks later, and he was still waiting. Giovanna was really making him work hard for his reward, which was why he was flat on his back being used as a human book rest. Sure, over time she'd given him little rewards, like more pats on the head and even allowing him to rest his head in her lap, but she hadn't yet allowed him to come. She'd even forbidden him from masturbating, claiming she would know if he did it when he wasn't with her. Philip was too frightened to take the risk.

He wasn't miserable, though. Far from it, in fact. From the moment he'd set eyes on her, Giovanna had awoken the submissive inside him that he never knew was there. Every time he was allowed to feast on her tits or her pussy, rub her feet and lick her shoes was a reward to him. He adored her. Worshipped her, even.

Back in the present, Giovanna had obviously realized that Philip's mind had wandered. She slammed the book she was reading closed, causing the pile of books beneath it to teeter dangerously. Philip scarcely dared to breathe, in case the movement turned the teeter into a topple. He didn't want to let her down. Not now. Not ever.

Quietly, she asked, "What were you thinking about?"

"You, Mistress. How we met, the things we've done..." He trailed off. He daren't confess how much he wanted to come because if she knew how much he desired it, she might just make him wait even longer. And at this rate, his balls would soon drag on the floor when he walked.

"Hmm."

Philip wasn't sure if she didn't believe him or whether

she wondered what he was going to say before he stopped himself.

"You have done very well in the time that we've been together. Especially for a novice."

"Thank you, Mistress. I just want to make you happy."

A curt nod acknowledged his words. Then she stared into the middle distance for a few minutes before snapping her attention back to the pile of books in front of her and the man beneath them. She stood carefully, then pulled the chair from its position across Philip's body.

Philip's heart thumped hard in his chest as he wondered what she was going to do next. He worried that the thump-thump-thump would dislodge the books, but as Giovanna straddled his lower legs, he knew that there was no way he could calm his thundering pulse.

When Giovanna reached for his belt, Philip knew the books were done for. It was just a matter of time. She undid his belt and fly, then eased his straining prick out of his boxers.

Philip gulped and stared at the pile of books as though he could pin them into place with his gaze. Adding to his torment was the fact that the books being there meant he couldn't see what Giovanna was doing. And she was a seriously unpredictable woman. The last few weeks had proven that.

A gasp escaped his lips as Giovanna's hand wrapped around his swollen shaft and began to stroke it. Slowly, at first, then faster until Philip felt his orgasm hurtling toward him at an alarming speed. The books swayed dangerously as his lungs pulled in the air he so desperately needed. He sent a silent prayer to any deity that might be listening to just keep those books upright until he'd come. Once he'd come he could deal with anything, including any punishment Giovanna might see fit to dish out after allowing those goddamn hardbacks to hit the floor.

As it happened, the acts were simultaneous. As Giovanna's expert fingers teased a climax out of him, the resulting jolt from his body sent the books tumbling. Luckily, the heavy tomes went off to one side, rather than hitting either of them. Even more luckily for Philip, Giovanna didn't stop touching him. In fact, she continued to work his cock until she'd milked every last drop of spunk out of him until he was spent and gasping like a man starved of oxygen.

As he struggled to get some semblance of normality back to his breathing and demeanor, Giovanna stood and stalked away. Philip frowned. He hadn't exactly been expecting a cuddle, but to walk away without a word? His unasked questions were answered as she returned with a tea towel from the kitchen and dropped it into his lap with a smile—the first he'd ever seen from her.

"Clean yourself up," she said, her eyes twinkling. "It's month end. You've got some more books to balance."

MELTDOWN

Jax Baynard

When you do what I do, you do your job better if you're not angry. I was so angry I was shaking with it, which is why I called to cancel my one o'clock appointment. Morgan listened, then said, "Come anyway," and hung up on me. I fumed for a minute, then mentally shrugged. It was his back.

But I walked uptown instead of taking a cab, hoping to walk off some of the fury. The cause of it was an incident with a friend, in the neighborhood of betrayal, which made for bad real estate. The relationship was probably over. The shock was made more nasty by the fact that it was a friendship of long standing—one deep into the territory where one assumed (stupidly, I was learning) that such dangers were long past. I walked and obsessed, turning it over and over in my mind, decided to call and scream at her, decided never to call again, called Morgan twice more to re-cancel and got no answer because he wasn't picking up. Because he wanted me to come over there and beat the shit out of him? I would, in the mood I was in.

He lived in a townhouse on the park, a nondescript building in a pseudo-Georgian style, built early in the previous century. It had been expensive then and it was still expensive now. Morgan—I didn't know if that was his real name, but it was the one we used—owned the whole top floor. I didn't know what he did for money and I didn't look anywhere to find out. He paid me in cash and it was none of my business. His floor had its own foyer and wood paneling on the walls and marble on the floors and carpets from Turkmenistan and Kazakhstan and a bunch of other stans I couldn't remember. Everything I knew about interior design I had learned from my clients. Some of them didn't want me in their homes so I also knew a thing or two about Motel 6 and the Plaza.

My clients ran the gamut. I took on anyone who followed the rules: don't fuck with me. Okay, so there was just the one rule. Morgan buzzed me in when I rang. This man actually had a majordomo, but of course he was never there on Thursday at one. He was sent off to do whatever majordomos do in their spare time. I hadn't gotten that far in my research. Morgan opened the door wearing what he always wore for our appointments: nothing. He was, as usual, tall and dark-haired with wide shoulders and sleek buttocks. It wasn't a requirement for the job, but I liked his back. I had kissed it in a variety of ways every week for almost two years.

Unusually, I would have sworn he was all ablaze with suppressed curiosity. "How are you?" he asked, lambent gaze upon my face. It wasn't concern I saw in his eyes. Nothing like compassion, but it wasn't only lust either. I could smell it on him when I came in. Not lust for me, but for what I was going to do to him. He lusted for that. I was only the delivery girl, tricked out in black boots and leather under my staid Burberry trench. I couldn't read what was in his eyes and it bothered me.

"Fuck you," I said. "I shouldn't be here at all."

He smiled at me, a quick flash of white, expensive teeth, unruffled by my hostility. "But you are," he said. "You are here."

What was that? I wondered. Some sort of challenge? Opting to reject the niceties, I let my bag slip off my arm and hit the shiny floor with a thunk. My trench followed it. Morgan turned and waited for me. I swayed toward him in my black boots. No matter what you're into, I am something to look at. My insides might be as cruddy as the next person's, but the outside was top-notch. There was no point in being modest about it. The Ferrari dealer on Tenth kept his cars all clean and shiny, too.

I followed Morgan into the game room and he stood at the appointed spot. I got the restraints and latched them around his wrists, one at a time, being rougher than I needed to be about it. He let me manhandle him, watching my face.

"How are you, Faith?" he asked softly, and now he did sound concerned. That wasn't my name, just the one I'd given him.

"Just ducky," I said sarcastically and winched him up until his heels were off the floor. "What's the safeword?" I asked him. Most of my clients only had one and we used it over and over. Morgan liked to change them up every week—not a good idea for obvious reasons, but it was mostly a formality, so I let him.

"Yes?" he suggested. Morgan's idea of a joke. An affirmative where a negative was more helpful. I waited. An unholy amusement lit his eyes. "Forgiveness?" he suggested.

Ignoring that, I stalked to the rack on the wall. "Which one?"

He pointed with his chin to the one at the end.

"This one?" I asked, touching it, wanting to be sure of his choice. I stroked the leather handle, remarkably soft and shaped more or less like a phallus.

"Yes," he said calmly.

It was a twelve-strand plaited Australian stock whip made of kangaroo hide, a working job. Serious. I could do a lot of damage with it if I wasn't careful. Rage boiled up inside me, a black wash, coloring everything. "You are really pushing your fucking luck," I said through my teeth. He flipped his wrists so that he was holding the restraints instead of them holding him. I wondered if his arms were already starting to ache. He smiled at me, feral, a look I had never seen before on his civilized face, and I snarled. "You asked for it," I said and moved around behind him.

I snapped the whip a couple of times, limbering up, trying to think calmly. What was he after? If I knew what it was I could either give it to him or not, my choice. But I didn't know, and the anger and the hurt running beneath it, the hurt I was trying frantically to stay on top of, made it impossible to think rationally. So I hit him. Despite my threats, I pulled a few punches. I pulled all of them, actually, practicing restraint as a cautionary measure. After a minute or two he said conversationally, "You probably deserved it."

"*What* did you just say?" I asked.

"You heard me," he said, which, of course, I had.

I snapped the whip, the fine tip at the end making a crack. If I hit him like that, he would bleed instantly. It was the same as being sliced open with a knife. They don't pay me so much for nothing. I was good enough to be blunt, hitting him hard without breaking the skin. He jerked with the force of it.

"You're probably a real cunt," he said pleasantly. "I've thought so for years."

That stung, as if he had turned the whip on me and hit me hard when I was least expecting it. Was I? Was that why my friend had betrayed me? The whip hung from my fingers. I waited, breathing hard, making him wait, too. I lifted my arm. "You shouldn't have said that." I saw him brace himself. Then I hit him, again and again, until his back was a mass of red welts, until my arm ached and instead of every strike being smooth, they fell rough and unaccomplished across his back and ass and thighs. He did not protest. He did not say anything. He barely moaned.

The part of me that didn't feel anything, the part of me that was watching, told me when to stop, that if I kept going the welts would break open and blood would run down his back and down his legs and drip onto the impervious stones. I lowered my arm, forcing my fingers to unclench. The whip landed on the floor and lay innocent at my feet. I stood, the breath sawing in and out of my lungs. This was new. I had allowed a client to goad me into hurting him—really hurting him. I had little idea of what to do next. Apologize? Refuse to take his money? I felt hollowed out, sick, near to tears, which was Not. At. All. Like. Me.

Morgan was still strung up, balanced on the balls of his feet. I walked around in front of him. His head hung down, but he lifted it for me. No one said anything. I saw details: the harsh look of his mouth, set against the pain. The line of ropy muscle going from deltoid to bicep. The flat plane of his belly and the erection jutting upward from it. I sighed, involuntarily, and without planning to, without quite meaning to, I went down on my knees and took him into my mouth. I could take away the pain, at least for a little while. I sucked him, learning the taste of him, cupping one hand around each buttock and holding him to me when he began to pant and twist. I was as gentle as I have ever been with another human being, using just enough pressure to send him over the edge, and I let him come when he needed to and not when I wanted him to.

I stood up, fighting my own weight, and let him down slowly. He folded neatly, an origami man, one knee under him and one up. His fingertips rested on the smooth tiles like a runner in the blocks, but Morgan wasn't running anywhere. I went back and knelt in front of him. "What's the safeword, you stupid bastard?" I tried to manufacture a semblance of my old self, but I didn't sound fierce. I sounded scared.

"Dinner," he said, not lifting his head.

Something like despair rolled through me, uncontrollable. "Wrong, Morgan," I said quietly.

"No," he said. "Have dinner with me tonight."

I reared back in surprise. "Like a *date*?" Even to myself, I sounded suspicious.

"I don't know," he said, and I could hear the drag of pain in his voice. "Call it what you want. We will meet at a place where food is served. We will eat it together. When we're done I will pay the tab. All clear?"

There was an edge to his voice now. Unaccountably, it made me smile. I sank my fingers into his hair, damp with sweat, and lifted his head so I could see his face. "Why did you push me so hard?"

The lids dropped down over his eyes, as if he didn't want me to see him. "Fucking Christ, Faith," he said.

"It was the first sign of human emotion I've seen in you for two years. Of course I pushed you."

The tendons in his neck were quivering. I released him and with a sigh he lowered his head. "At such cost to yourself, though?" I said, bewildered as well as frightened. "Was it worth it?"

A corner of his mouth lifted. "That depends," he said, "on whether or not you have dinner with me."

I stood up. It occurred to me that he wanted to lie down right there on the cold floor and that he wasn't going to do it in front of me. "Leave me a message," I said, "with a place and a time."

"And maybe you'll show and maybe you won't?" There was no inflection in his voice. He might have been asking the time.

I was already at the door, tying the belt of my coat into a neat knot. I stared at him; even crouched on the floor, even drawn in pain, the lines of him were beautiful. I went back to him and curled myself up smaller than he was and put my head next to his, so our faces were touching. The high heels on my boots made it awkward. I kissed him on the lips, something I had not done with anyone in a long time.

"No, Morgan," I said. "Leave me a message with a place and a time and I will be there." I caught the fleeting movement of his mouth with my fingertips: a grimace under any other circumstances, but in these, a smile.

YOU SAY THIS IS A TESTAMENT

Maria See

The next time you pee, I'm coming with you," I say.

You don't respond.

You knew this was coming, after all. You started preparing for it yesterday. The first time I heard you pissing, while I was half-awake in bed, I knew what you were doing. I knew you were trying to get used to having less privacy. To not having a closed door between us.

I didn't tell you I had noticed. I waited until you did it the next time you had to pee.

"Have you been leaving the bathroom door open?" I asked you when you were done.

"Yeah."

You didn't tell me why. I already knew. You were afraid you'd freeze when I was there, in front of you, demanding that you piss.

You've always been extremely pee shy. In fact, you swore you would *never* pee in front of me. Never. *Never.* You were adamant. It wasn't a limit; it was an edge. And it became a marker to me. A means to measuring your trust in me.

Never didn't last. You started to waver. Your responses to my desire started to change. At first you simply weren't so strong in your *no*. And then you stopped saying no and didn't respond at all when I initiated conversation to check in. Soon, "But you won't pee in front of me, will you?" was met with a new response from you: "I might."

And now—now you give in, don't you?

If you could get used to peeing with the door open, knowing I could walk by, or even come in, at any time, you would be less likely to freeze when it would matter, when it would mean disobeying me. You don't like disobeying me. You want me to know that you can please me, that you'll do what it takes.

I usually bring you a glass of water after you orgasm several times, after I've worn you out. But last night your water was waiting for you on the floor, in a large stainless steel dog bowl. I watched you drink your water, checking to see if your head fit okay, if you liked the bowl—*my* preparation for today, unbeknownst to you.

The size of the bowl was perfect for you, and you did like it. "I like that I can see you in the bottom of the bowl, looking down at me," you said.

I liked that, too.

It's time to play, and you are dressed for the occasion, wearing your collar and nothing else. I have two balls: a tiny one and a tennis-size one. I also have a plastic doggy chew toy.

We play fetch with the tiny ball, and when I throw the tennis-size ball you push it back to me with your nose; it is too big to fit into your mouth. Playing fetch is about you showing me that you're a good girl; that you're obedient; that you'll get the ball and bring it back because that's what I want you to do.

The chew toy is shaped like a barbell. Sometimes you chew on it, but we also play tug-of-war with it. You bite down hard and fight me for it when I try to pull it away. Sometimes I let you keep it, but other times I'm determined to rip it from your grip.

After we play, I set down two of the same bowls we used yesterday. One is full of water. The other is for small cheese puffs you chose at the store earlier today. The water bowl is full to the rim, whereas I have yet to give you any food.

You are on all fours in front of your bowls. "Drink your water," I say. I wait for you to finish at least half before I empty cheese puffs into the other bowl. When I do, you eat them up. "Drink more of your water," I say.

You finish all of your water, and you think you're done. But I take your bowl, and I bring it back full again. I give you more food. You are drinking your water slowly this time, and it is annoying me. I want your bladder full, and I think that you want to make this difficult.

I grab your hair and shove your face into the water. "Drink it!" I scold. You start to push your bowl, and I shove your face into it again. You whimper and start to drink.

When you are done with the second bowl of water, you come over to me and place your chin on my knee. I pet your head and ask you if you've had enough water. You nod.

"Good, let's go for a walk. We'll walk to the bathroom," I say, and I get your leash.

You take your time on the walk to the bathroom, stopping along the way to pick up one of my flip-flops with your teeth. "Bad! Put it down!" I yell. I pull it from your mouth and place it back on the floor. We move along.

We get into the bathroom. I look at you and motion to the toilet seat. "C'mon," I tell you. "Come up here." You sit on the toilet, legs open. I'm standing between them, in front of you. I'm playing with your hair.

"You're going to be a good girl, aren't you?" I ask you. "If you don't go, I'm going to keep forcing you to drink more and more water. I know you don't want that to happen. You've already had so much to drink. That's not what you want. Is it?" You shake your head no.

I bring your head toward my chest and hold you

there. You begin to pee. You pee for a few short seconds, and you stop. You are nervous.

"Are you done?" I ask. I don't wait for you to reply before I continue: "Let me know when you're done." My tone has changed; I am patient, caring now. I am pleased with you, and I start to wish I had strapped on a dick before we started. I feel hard, and I want your lips around my cock.

You tell me you're done, and I reach for the package of wipes. I am so slow and intentional pulling out a wipe that you can hear the wetness as I unfold it. I want this to be slow and painful. I know this makes you uncomfortable. I want this because it makes you dependent.

I wipe you gently, except for when I press down on your clit as I slide by it. You are silent.

RIVER OF BEAUTY

Sharon Wachsler

Mayra stands in the center of the room, taking it all in: the furniture against the walls, the people in evening dress seated in a line of chairs in front of her, and at her side, dominating the room, the wheel. Nearby, a small table holds her sponges, brushes and arty cakes. Underneath it is a sealed case of champagne. Cattiveria isn't normally open on Mondays, but the owner is a friend.

The new art is up and lit—an assortment of time-pieces in acrylics, with a twist. Her favorite piece hangs behind her. The pussy is lifelike, in mauves, purples and browns. The lips unfurled and swollen, the cunt fairly drips arousal. She's particularly pleased with her use of trompe l'oeil: the second hand appears to be moving—ticking back and forth over a pulsing clit—while the minute hand snakes into a glistening slit. A short, fat hour hand, shiny with cum, rests on the labial fold at *10.*

Mayra's gaze falls on the femme sitting by herself below the picture. Her straightened black hair hangs like a curtain, concealing her face. She is shrouded in a black dressing gown, the collar flipped up to hide her neck, the bottom trailing on the floor hiding her feet. How long it's been since Avril sashayed through the door to Cattiveria in red leather, pink fishnets or spike heels, her head thrown back in laughter or tilted forward in flirtation.

Mayra turns her attention toward the wheel. If not for the setting, it could be mistaken for a kitchen table—except for the Roman numerals around the perimeter and the sheepskin-lined restraints. That would make for interesting dining.

Mayra beckons Avril to her side. Clutching her robe about her, Avril moves in her uneven gait toward her Mistress. Avril's stuttering steps tonight are not solely due to her right leg. Her hands, never affected by the accident, tremble, and her olive skin is deeply flushed. Mayra's groin tingles. A blush of embarrassment can turn to a blush of arousal, the heat of shame to the heat of pride.

Mayra steps forward. "Thank you so much for coming," she says. "Especially those who helped me create—" She gestures to the five-foot-diameter horizontal wooden wheel next to her, covered in canvas painted doeskin, stippled and lined to suggest human flesh.

"As you can see, it's on its way to being the last in my series." Mayra nods at the hourglass painted at the bottom between the *V* and the *VIII*. It's an odd image. The small pile of sand in the upper bell doesn't rest in the neck, but defies gravity, clinging to the roof of the bell. A straight line of sand falls from it, through the neck to a much larger pile on the bottom. The hourglass is tilted back, conveying movement, with the base sliding forward.

In the heavy silence Mayra feels her pulse in her neck. All the quiet discussions and loud arguments that led here fill her head with buzzing. She remembers the night, lying in bed, when she finally asked, "As an artist, as your lover and Mistress, after all we've gone through—do you trust me?"

Avril whispered, "Yes," with eyes blazing, and kissed her ferociously. After making love, Mayra began to sketch the wheel.

Avril's touch on her arm brings Mayra back. "It's time," Mayra says.

Time for their Cattiveria friends to see Avril without the scarves, turtlenecks and long dresses she's been wearing for two years. Time for Avril to see them seeing her. Avril lifts her head. Everyone's accustomed to Avril's face by now, except... Tonight she's not wearing the heavy foundation the medical cosmetologist gave her to cover the purple-red scar running up her throat and across her right cheek.

Avril unties the sash with fumbling fingers. Then, holding her breath, she lets the gown fall to the floor, gasping like she's ripped off a bandage that took away hair and skin.

"Breathe," Mayra instructs. Avril nods and exhales in a whoosh. She clenches and unclenches her hands as if yearning to grab the gown pooled at her feet.

Mayra takes in Avril's generous curves at breast and hip, the pouch of her belly, her strong hands. The scars that keep growing, adding dark layers of irritated collagen, are part of Avril's uniqueness. Though the keloids are painful and itchy for Avril, Mayra can't find ugly what marks her partner as a survivor.

"Come," Mayra says, helping Avril slide carefully into the center of the wheel, ass-first. Lying on her back in the center, she splays her arms and legs, resting her hands at two o'clock and ten o'clock, her feet at eight o'clock and five o'clock. Mayra has no intention of forcing Avril's right leg to four o'clock. She's learned that symmetry is unrelated to beauty.

Mayra starts at ten o'clock with Avril's left wrist. The shackles come together, metal on metal, shutting with loud finality. Then she spins the wheel 360 degrees. Avril tenses and flattens at the unexpected movement. Mayra could have simply rotated to two o'clock to cuff the other wrist, but she wants to build Avril's sense of unreality and lost control. Along with the disrobing, loss of equilibrium should tip Avril nicely into bottom space.

Abruptly stopping the wheel, Mayra snaps her fingers above Avril's face. "Hey!" she barks.

The femme stares guiltily, even though she's behaved perfectly.

"Is your right hand at two o'clock, where I told you to put it?"

Avril's eyes widen. She gropes for the shackle. "I—I think it is," she stutters.

"Yes, it is. Good girl." Mayra runs her hand down Avril's arm to her breast, caresses it once, then squeezes her nipple hard before pulling her hand away. Before Avril can react, Mayra clangs her wrist inside its shackle. Leaving no time to catch her breath, she spins Avril again.

"Gosh," Mayra says to the crowd. "This is like *Wheel of Fortune.* I wonder what I'll land on?" She licks her lips. Their friends chuckle.

She stops the wheel at eight o'clock and strokes Avril's thigh. "I notice you shaved your pussy for tonight. Why did you do that?"

Avril blinks. They talked about the stripping, the wheel, the shackles, the paint. They didn't discuss roles.

"Your pussy," Mayra muses. "It's all smooth and pretty and"—she cups Avril in her palm—"warm, isn't it?"

"Mmm-hmm." Avril nods, her eyes glazing slightly.

"Because you wanted everyone to see the lovely parts you still like?" Mayra spreads Avril's lips, discovering wetness.

"Yes," Avril whispers.

"Let's do that properly." Mayra abruptly pulls Avril's foot to eight o'clock, spreading her legs. She spins the wheel, stopping it so Avril's feet are a yard from the guests.

"You just lie still and let everyone get a good look at your pretty cunt," she says.

Avril blushes furiously, sweat popping out on her skin. Mayra lets a minute pass as Avril's jagged breaths fill the room, then spins her back to put her ankle in the cuff. She fiddles with the shackle noisily before clanking it shut.

Again, Mayra spins the wheel and stops it when five o'clock is in front of her. Mayra sits on the edge, gently stroking the bent foot, crosshatched with keloids.

"We need to be careful with this foot, don't we?" She asks.

"Yes, Mistress," Avril murmurs.

It's been so long since Mayra's heard the honorific that she's stunned; heat balloons in her chest and shoots to her cunt. She looks at Avril's lolling head, her limp limbs and her dilated eyes. Avril has become her blank canvas. Mayra's arms tingle. She wants to start painting now.

Saying nothing, Mayra lifts Avril's foot into the cuff and locks it in. Then she kicks off her loafers, baring her feet, and rolls up her jeans cuffs. She strips off the checked shirt and turns her cap's brim backward.

Taking a moment, she checks Avril's position. She has planned perfectly: the hourglass is completely visible just below Avril's pussy, creating the illusion that it's slipping out between her thighs.

Her first task isn't true painting, but documentation: to outline Avril's body on the wheel. Mayra brushes in a thick black outline around Avril's head, arms, torso and legs.

Now Mayra pulls the table with her tools closer and clambers onto the wheel, sitting between Avril's feet. After sending a prayer to Saint Catherine of Bologna, Mayra wipes her sponge three times across a square cake of doeskin body paint, then swipes the color onto Avril's left leg in large strokes. From thigh to arch, stretching out and down, again and again. She lays down the rich, creamy color in arcs, ripples and curves, the basis for later detail work.

While her body recognizes the movements of art, there is also a strangeness. These paints and tools are more intimate; the silken consistency of the cake paint is unlike that of acrylic. Avril's skin is smoother and more elastic than canvas, and even though her girl lies as still as she can, she's breathing. Her pulse is beating. There's an aliveness connecting them. Mayra finds herself matching her strokes with Avril's rising and falling chest.

Mayra reloads her sponge and reaches to sweep paint onto Avril's outer thigh, hip and the side of her ass. Avril moans, rolling to meet her caress. Mayra slaps the opposite asscheek hard. Avril yelps.

"Hold still. You know what we're doing here,"

Mayra chastises, continuing to paint Avril's ass and thigh. Peripherally, she sees Avril hang her head.

"What are we doing here?" Mayra prompts, not looking up.

"Making art," Avril says.

Mayra smacks Avril's inner thigh with the handle of a filbert brush. Avril cries out, a dark welt rising.

"Not just any art, a beautiful work of art. Look at everyone and tell them what they're here to see." Mayra pauses to watch.

Avril lifts her head as much as she's able, saying tremulously, "You're here to see a beautiful work of art." There's a tear in the corner of her eye.

"That's right," Mayra purrs. "But you don't believe it, do you?"

Avril shakes her head, eyes cast down.

"But you believe in my artistry, that I create beauty?"

"Oh, yes!" Avril nods.

"You think I can't transform this." She runs her finger up the thick, brick-red jagged line that begins at Avril's right ankle, crosses her calf and thigh and ends below her hip.

Avril shakes her head. Tears are streaming down her face. "Not so much that one...." she whispers.

"Oh," Mayra breathes. She lightly touches the other long keloid scar. Tracing the purple rope from Avril's collarbone down between her heavy breasts, over her belly, past her navel.

Avril shakes her head.

"Maybe I have more faith in my artistry than you do?"

Avril starts to protest, but Mayra slides her thumb across Avril's clit, and Avril moans instead.

"That's for your honesty," Mayra says and returns to painting.

Where thigh meets hip, she sweeps toward Avril's cunt. Avril attempts to slide toward Mayra's hand, but the wrist shackles hold her. Mayra grins but keeps working. Repeatedly she sweeps the sponge up Avril's inner thigh, letting her knuckles bump Avril's pussy. Avril's cunt is swollen now, open and trickling juice. She mewls but has given up attempting to move.

Mayra hops off and spins the wheel to keep Avril disoriented. She rolls her shoulders to stay loose while grabbing new tools. Stopping the wheel at her girl's left shoulder, Mayra creates the clock's hour hand. She paints a straight, thick black line the length of Avril's arm. Then, instead of a typical arrow point at the end, she paints a small vulva, lips open like an inverted heart, its clit facing the X. She spins the wheel and switches to blood red for the minute hand—a thinner line with a little pulsing vulva pointing to *II*.

She loads a fresh cake with dusky mauve and climbs onto the wheel, now sweeping an arc of undulating waves from Avril's left shoulder to breast to belly to abdomen. Leaning over Avril, Mayra feels the femme's breath caress her breasts through her thin top. Mayra's used to "breathing life into" her materials, but having her materials breathing on her is…different. Pleasurable. Distracting. In response, Mayra reloads for maximum saturation and smears color repeatedly onto Avril's left breast, especially her nipple, until it's round as a pebble. She lifts her breast to paint underneath, and Avril arches up to maintain contact with Mayra's hand. But Mayra carefully works around the exquisitely sensitive area, continuing to shade Avril's skin.

She goes to her table, grabs the two-tone cake she special-ordered—one half a rich plum, the other slightly lighter, velvety mauve—and swipes a fresh sponge across it. To reach Avril's belly, and to block Avril's view, Mayra places a knee on either side of her girl's head, straddling her face. Avril's breath comes faster, making Mayra's cunt throb. She's sure Avril can smell her excitement. As tempting as the idea of grinding against Avril's mouth is, the colors in her hands—and the scars—call more insistently.

Beginning at the base of Avril's throat, Mayra angles the sponge so that the darker shade is on the inside, along the scar, the lighter tone working out. Riding outward over Avril's breast, then back in toward her navel, Mayra applies the two shades. Down the other side of the scar, plum inside, blending into mauve outside. She reloads, flips, swipes, reloads, swipes, flips. She can't move fast enough to create what's coming through her. She senses, distantly, that Avril has turned herself over to Mayra's urgency, embracing her role as her Mistress's canvas.

She's sure Avril feels when the sponge touches her scars—they are always sensitive and raw. However, Avril had enthused that the discomfort would be nothing compared to having them transformed. Mayra is transforming them, all right, but not by their erasure. With paint filling in either side of her biggest, darkest keloid, it is more visible than ever.

Mayra keeps sponging up new paint and extending the shadowed valley of the scar down Avril's torso and abdomen. The colors meet at the apex above Avril's moist cunt. Any closer and her paint will run. Mayra flips the sponge back and forth, sometimes using one side, sometimes the other, until from Avril's neck to her mons is a crevice of dark flesh tones, melding together. Then she finishes the right leg with doeskin, to match Avril's arms. Just as on her torso, the leg scars show purple-red under the paint.

Now the detail work. Mayra's blood pumps as she hops off and gathers an assortment of brushes and colors. Despite her excitement, Mayra's steady hand outlines a four-inch-diameter clitoris at the base of Avril's throat. Not knowing what's blossoming on her throat, Avril swallows self-consciously as Mayra fills in the clit. Shaded with eggplant, its hood recedes in arousal. Adding gray to her brush, Mayra creates the pearl's contours and twirls her scruffy brush to bring out the plumpness she has seen so often on a much smaller scale. She mixes in shiny white to create the pearly wetness that glistens on the swollen clit. Mayra leans back to check the angle. Yes, the clit rests right above the scar on Avril's throat.

Mayra switches to Avril's face. The fine-tipped filbert brush must tickle, for Avril laughs. Mayra hadn't told her she'd be twirling and swirling black curls onto her chin, cheeks, nose, even her lips. Soon, Avril's face is a mask of sumptuous curls, eyes and lips mysteriously peeking through.

"You're adorable," Mayra says, impulsively kissing Avril on the nose. She hears a chorus of *aws* behind her.

"Oh, shut up." She waves without looking up. Everyone laughs, including Avril.

Mayra rotates the wheel 180 degrees and climbs between Avril's legs, moving up to reach her torso. Alternating gray and chocolate, she creates the outline and shadow of two labia majora—forming above the clit on Avril's throat and joining all the way down above Avril's clit. Mayra is about to dip her brush into her water can when she gets an idea of another way to moisten the colors that have dried on Avril's skin. Cleaning one hand with a baby wipe, she slides a finger between Avril's lips. Avril gasps, but Mayra's hand is gone. She smears the cunt juice down Avril's breast and belly.

"This is my idea of mixed media!" she announces. She continues to dip into Avril's wetness, which is increasing, using it to blend texture and shape into the existing mauve and plum. Soon, soft folds cover Avril's breasts and outer torso.

Then, on either side of Avril's sternum, Mayra creates the inner labia. To make the inner ripples of the engorged smaller lips, she adds some pink to the mauve and chocolate. Again, where the paint has already dried, Avril acts as water jar, moaning each time Mayra's fingers slide in.

The center of the cunt is next. She fills in the area on either side of the keloid with brick red, making the heart of the cunt, the deep crevice, the darkest part. She continues to shade and shadow to bring out the plump succulence she knows so well.

Almost at her climax, Mayra's in a fever. She paints the birthing of the hourglass—pink and silver tumbling out of the cunt on Avril's torso and down her thighs. Mayra assesses the effect. Yes, the sandglass on the canvas now looks like it was born there.

Mayra whoops in anticipation of the final metamorphosis. Taking a very clean, soft brush, she loads it with translucent silver. This she stipples down the keloid scar on Avril's cheek, transforming the strands of tissue into shiny strings of cum. Down her neck, where the clitoris is already gleaming, down through the huge pussy she's created, she turns the rope of scar into a stream of desire. Where the scar has spread between and below Avril's breasts, there now appears a pool of juice. This overflows the labia painted on Avril's right hip. Mayra extends the stream down Avril's right leg, painting the keloid silver.

The last touch is a dusting of silver glitter to really

make the river of cum pop. She dips her brush into the glitter and plays it along the scars. Instead of hiding them, she is highlighting them. The redness is still visible underneath, but now it's the pulse of arousal and desire.

She collapses on a chair. She realizes her top is sticky with sweat, her throat dry, her arms shaky. She could use a drink. She's sure Avril could, too, but hopes there will be time for that—for celebrating—later. She gets to her feet and stands at Avril's head, facing the crowd.

"Please, join us." She gestures.

Everyone gets to their feet and encircles the wheel. Mayra pulls a bag out from under it. "I've got a dozen cameras," she says, handing them around. "And two photo printers over there. Since we can't hang Avril on the wall, your pictures will form a collage as the final piece of the installation. Please write your title for each photo on a stick-it note and put it on the back of each picture."

Everyone moves around and starts clicking. Some back up to include Mayra in the shot, some move in for close-ups of one section of the canvas. Some stand on chairs to take pictures from above. With no task in front of her, Mayra tries to pace but keeps getting in people's way. She realizes she should check on Avril.

"I'm nervous," Avril says above the clicking.

"Me, too," Mayra whispers.

"Yes, but you're not lying naked on a table with no idea what you look like!"

"I'm sorry!" Mayra smacks herself in the forehead and gets Avril's dressing gown and a chair, then releases her. Avril collapses onto the chair, dropping the gown in her lap.

The others are grouped around the whirring printers, talking and labeling their photos.

"Is it time for bubbly?" someone calls.

"Help yourself," Mayra yells back. "I'm not moving from this spot!"

She hears a chuckle. Soon happy chatter and the popping of corks echo around the room.

"Time to see what the critics say," Mayra says, wishing she was joking. She wipes her sweaty palms on her jeans and crosses to the printers. She carefully scoops up the photos and brings them back.

Mayra and Avril put their heads together.

They're surprisingly good quality. The first one is a shot of the entire table from above. Avril gasps. "Mother of god," she says. "You made me into a big cunt!"

"I wouldn't put it that way." Mayra tries not to let her hurt show. "Let's see how the others see you."

She turns over the picture. The stick-it note says *Beauty*.

Avril gasps and puts her hand to her mouth.

The next one is a close-up of the silver scar. On the back is written *River of Beauty*.

Tears well in Avril's eyes. She opens and closes her mouth, but no words come out.

The next is of the hourglass, but taken from the

opposite side of the wheel—the sand fuller on top. The note says, *All the time in the world.*

A close-up of Avril's face: *Beauty.*

A shot of Avril's right hand: *Two years ago, time stood still.*

A close-up of Avril's cunt: *Beauty.*

A shot of Avril's left hand: *Happy Tenth Anniversary.*

Tears are flowing down Avril's face. Mayra's worried they'll ruin the pictures. She grabs her abandoned checked shirt to give to Avril as a hanky and realizes that she has tears on her face, too.

"Here," she says, "we each get a sleeve."

Avril laughs and sobs at the same time. "There are so many of them," she says. "How will we get through them all without dissolving into two puddles?"

"Beautiful," Mayra answers, "we don't have to do it all tonight. Remember," she taps the photo of the inverted hourglass, "we have all the time in the world." Then she does what she's wanted to do since Avril first stood up and dropped her robe—pulls her in for a deep, long kiss.

After they separate, Avril sighs and rests her head against Mayra's shoulder. "We should join the party," Avril says.

"Okay," Mayra agrees and stands up.

Avril takes a moment to slip her arms through the sleeves of the dressing gown. Mayra feels a cold lump fall into her stomach. But, she reminds herself, is it fair to expect Avril to walk around naked when everyone else is clothed? Even without her scars, she'd probably feel funny.... Maybe.

"Help me tie this, will you?" Avril says. She's holding the back of the gown in the small of her back with one hand and handing the sash to Mayra with the other.

Mayra reaches to bring the gown around to Avril's front.

"No, no." Avril slaps her hand. "I want you to tie it all in the back! My shoulders are cold is all."

"Oh!" Mayra gathers the gown with trembling fingers and ties it behind Avril's back.

"That's perfect," Avril says. "It's like a cape! Now I can show off my *River of Beauty*." She limps to the crowd of people holding champagne flutes and calls, "I deserve ten of those!"

Someone replies with a comment Mayra doesn't hear. She's watching Avril's head thrown back in laughter.

WHEN MY BOYFRIEND HAS A PARTY

Devin Phillips

When Jason, my boyfriend, has a party, he ties me up before his friends get there.

I don't mean he ties me all the way; that'll wait until his friends are ready to take me. Before they get there, Jason just ties my hands behind my back, and usually a tight little harness over my shoulders so I'm forced to stand up straight.

He wants my back arched so his friends can see my breasts hanging out of my top. He wants his friends to be able to get to my tits and my ass as I greet them at the door and invite them to touch me.

"Hello and welcome," I'll tell them with a smile. "Would you like to feel me up, Sir?"

This is after Jason has locked the dog collar around my throat and helped me get all made up so I look hot for his friends. He's picked out my outfit—usually something very tight in front, with no bra underneath, so my tits are hanging out. A low-cut blouse, or a shirt that buttons down the front so he can leave two or three more buttons open than I would if I were going to work or somewhere else respectable. He has me wear stockings, of course, and high heels, and sometimes he has me wear hot pants or even cut-offs, and other times he has me wear a skirt. I never wear panties, except the time when I was *only* wearing panties.

The stockings are stay-ups because he doesn't want his friends to have to monkey with a garter belt. Guys don't understand those things. He's had me wear fishnets sometimes, or white stockings, black stockings; right before Christmas he once had me wear red. Red. They looked garish and slutty. I still get wet and embarrassed. I still get red myself looking at the videotapes.

The heels are always very high. When we started playing our game, I had some trouble walking in them.

I'd always been a bit of a tomboy, never dressing too girly or wearing high heels. I even had shortish hair—a little shorter than a bob or something. Jason made me grow it out. That was a year ago; now it's long and getting curly. And then a month ago, Jason had me go to the salon and bleach it blond.

I was nervous at first; I thought I'd look stupid with pale blond hair. I'm very light-skinned; I really thought it would look terrible. I'll admit I look pretty washed out without makeup. But I wear lots more makeup now than I used to. Jason likes it, and I like it. I always wear makeup to work; I even put on a fresh coat—lighter than usual, of course, just a hint—before I get into bed. And when Jason has a party, I wear *lots* of makeup. Now that I'm blond I look even hotter, even sluttier. Especially the way I hang out of my clothes.

And his friends get to do all sorts of things with me.

It's not *all* of Jason's friends who come over for these parties, of course. It's only the cool ones. Once it was clear what I wanted and what he wanted to give me, Jason asked around. He'd made some friends at kinky parties on websites over the years. Jason picks his friends very well; they're all big and strong but gentle—but rough when I need them to be. We've got a safeword and everything, but I've never had to use it.

He invites twelve friends to each party. Usually eight to ten make it. I've gotten to know them well, even though I don't socialize with them outside our parties...so I really only know certain things about them. Certain *sexual* things. They're sexual objects to me the same way I am to them. There's Eric, who's tall and has this great jawline, who really loves to feel my tits and likes to give me rim jobs. There's Stu, who has great eyes and yummy hair and these *incredible* fingers; he can sometimes make me cum just with his hand. Then there's Alejandro, beautiful and young-looking, even though I think he's in his thirties. He's only about an inch taller than me when I'm wearing my heels, but...well, he's not just long but thick...really thick. I've had his dick in my mouth a few dozen times, and it's really hard for me to get my lips past the halfway point. Everyone else, I can deep-throat, no problem. I can even deep-throat Dylan, who's got this amazingly long cock, because it's slightly narrower than Alejandro's. They like that I can deep-throat so easily; they like that I like it. I *love* it, in fact. Usually, I'm totally in control when I'm giving head. But sometimes, when I'm feeling really raunchy, I let them fuck my face. Probably the most inveterate face-fucker among them is Chris, who likes to lay me out on the couch with my head hanging off and give it to me rough and deep, right down my throat in easy, slow thrusts at first while his hands caress my hair or reach down to stroke my clit and pussy. Then he fucks me rougher and rougher, until I'm gagging, always knowing how much I can take, how much I *want* to take. Maybe it's because he usually has his fingers in my cunt by then; he can feel me tense up when it starts to be too much. Then he backs off and does me more gently…and he can keep it going for half an hour. I'll be drooling and gagging and my face will be covered in precum…but I'll be completely in heaven, and the look in my runny eyes shows it. Jason catches it all on videotape.

There's plenty of others. There's Jerry, Joel, Isaiah, Hunter…some other guys I'm forgetting the names of. A few have visited from out of town, friends of friends, but all cool. All of them have been tested; Jason arranges that. He uses the local office of a professional service that works with porn stars.

I guess I *am* a porn star, sort of—because Jason videos

everything. We watch it sometimes when we're alone; I get as hot as he does…maybe hotter. He gets a couple of hours of footage at least each time he has a party, but it's not for other people. Jason's never let the files out of his sight. What he does is play my hottest moments on the television in the living room. He has the DVD player locked down so even if one of his friends wanted to palm a copy, he couldn't. But anyway, they're not that kind of guys. They like what they get from me, and they like that I give it so willingly. *More* than willingly.

But Jason still likes to have me tied up.

We all go down to the playroom in the basement. It's got cheap couches with vinyl upholstery so they don't get too dirty. With twelve guests it's a little crowded—fourteen people is too many for our basement, but we don't mind getting cozy. Eight is just about right for me.

There's a sling and a soft padded table with metal tie-downs to tie me to. My hands tied behind my back, I walk on my high heels for them; the men all look at me and give me gentle, firm orders, like "Bend over," "Show us your ass," "Let's see you jiggle those titties." They're never rough with me, except when I want them to be. I'm always wet as a faucet before ten minutes have passed—before Jason gives the go-ahead for them to start undressing me.

Their hands snake out; their fingers pluck my buttons open and they start caressing my tits. Their hands go down into my shorts, or up my skirt. They touch my shaved, pierced pussy and feel how wet I am.

They unzip their pants and guide me to my knees.

While I'm kneeling like that, someone usually takes off my skirt or my shorts and unbuttons my top all the way. They tell me to spread my knees and someone gets a vibrator, sometimes a dildo, sometimes a butt plug, too. I kneel and give head as they pleasure me—my pussy, my clit, my ass. Sometimes they put tit clamps on me. Usually I finish one or more of them in my mouth—guys who can't wait to fuck me, or don't want to this time, for whatever reason. Sometimes they cum on my face. More often, I let them cum in my mouth, and I swallow or drool it down my chin and onto my tits. They like it when I drool, but I really like to swallow.

I give three or four blow jobs on my knees, hands tied, while they play with me, tease me—never letting me cum.

Not until Jason gives the go-ahead.

Then they take me two at a time—sometimes three. Usually one will penetrate me gently, going slow; they know I'm fairly tight, all things considered. Their cocks make me wince a little at first. It doesn't take long before I'm moaning in pleasure and begging the man inside me to fuck me harder, while I suck another one's cock and some more line up alongside me, playing with my tits or brushing my hair back.

By then, they've played with me so much that the first cock inside me is what makes me cum. The first time. And sometimes a second.

They tie me up then—all the way, not just my hands.

It's pretty silly of me to act like I'm struggling, but it's kind of hot. They like it, too; it's hopeless. Any of them could hold me down and tie me up. With eight or ten or a dozen? It's easy.

They tie me to the table—face up, face down, depending on their whim. At first, Jason took the lead, telling them how to tie me, how to fuck me. Now he lets them decide.

The table's nice and comfortable. Padded...secure. I can struggle if I want, and they keep taking me. Sometimes they blindfold me, so I don't even know who's inside me at any given time. I like that. They like that. It's really fucking hot.

Sometimes, all of them fuck me, taking turns. Just as often, it's two at a time—usually one in my mouth and one up inside me.

Sometimes, they're satisfied long before I am.

Then they break out some toys.

They leave me tied up as they get me off at their leisure, again and again. Jason zooms in close, getting video of my face as I cum and my pussy as they get me off with fingers and dildos and vibrators. I know he'll make me watch it later, and I'll blush and be embarrassed at what an insatiable whore I was. But secretly, I'll like it. Well...not so secretly.

They make me cum until I can't cum anymore. They get me off until I'm *totally* satisfied.

When my boyfriend has a party. I *always* get satisfied.

Afterward, when the guys have gone, Jason will wipe me with a damp towel and sometimes let me sleep a little on one of the mats in the basement. He'll carry me upstairs, where sometimes he's run a bath for me; other times he helps me into the shower and washes me all over with the shower wand, supporting me with his naked body.

Sometimes I feel these pangs of fear, and I ask him to fuck me. It's not that his friends haven't satisfied me; it's that I want to feel together with him. I want to be intimate, knowing he loves me, knowing he wants me— even though I'm a dirty little slut who lets men do this to me.

He always fucks me gently, never trying to make me cum; he just adds his pleasure to the endless line of pleasure I've brought men that night.

I like that.

I'm always too exhausted and limp with pleasure not to sleep soundly. I cuddle up alongside my boyfriend and feel his naked body, so like and yet so unlike the others.

As I sleep, I have dirty dreams. I wake up purring and proud. Proud of my man; proud of me; proud of his friends. I wake up happy.

When Jason has a party, I *always* wake up happy.

BUTTER
THE BIRD

Sommer Marsden

Motherfucking cocksucking son of a monkey!" I yelled. And then I went utterly mental and started flinging butcher's twine around the kitchen.

The bird stared at me. Well, as much as an abdominal cavity can "stare." The place where the eyes had been was long gone.

"I am becoming a vegetarian," I hissed at it. It was mocking me. I could feel it. Even stuffed full of carrots and lemons and rosemary for a lovely herbed taste.

The hair on the back of my neck stood and I cringed. He was there. I could feel him. There. Watching me. Witnessing my…lunacy.

I turned and winced to see my sixth sense had been correct. "Calvin," I sighed.

He nodded. "Faye."

"Go ahead," I snapped. At the end of my rope. Too fucking past caring if someone laughed at me. It was very empowering. Sort of like when you finally lose the last sane shred of your mind and then...you just don't care!

"Go ahead and...?" He played innocent.

But I saw him. Oh, I saw him, pressing his plump, kissable lips together in a tight line to keep from laughing at me. Schooling his face in an expression of confusion. But he was not confused. He'd seen me get bested by the bird. The infernal fowl.

The...possessed...poultry!

"And laugh," I seethed.

"Never." He took a step into the kitchen.

He was tall and lanky and his hair was the color of bleached wheat, his eyes pine-colored with small striations of rich brown. He was beautiful and maddening. The last part because he was good at everything. Everything! He could write a financial report with one hand and smoke the perfect salmon with the other. Paint, build, write sonnets, do laundry. The man was a jack-of-all-trades, master of all.

Annoying.

But I loved him, so my annoyance lasted only a few heartbeats. Once in the room his energy brushed up against mine, feeling very much like a phantom cat twining around my legs, sliding sensually against my skin. He never belittled me, always helped me and found me highly amusing.

I'm not sure how I fell ass backward into Calvin but here he was, once again, examining the situation that was currently making me foam at the mouth.

"Can I help?"

"Sure," I sighed. Feeling suddenly tired and defeated.

"Dinner?" he asked, nodding toward the bird.

"Yep. I thought nice roast chicken and some garlic mashers and some beets. Fresh ones. Roasted with sea salt and the greens, all drizzled in olive oil."

He touched my shoulder. Just my shoulder. He was even touching me through my thin blue sweater, but the effect was the same as if I'd licked a lightning bolt. My body tingled and my toes flexed and I felt a rush of color to my face.

"Sounds wonderful," he said. I could smell the cigar smoke on him and knew he'd been outside in the yard with a beer and something nice, maybe a Partagás. And here I'd brought him up by going full-throttle hissy fit on a poor dead bird.

"Yes...I hope. But it's fine. I'll figure it out. I didn't mean to... Go back to your cigar."

"I was done," he said, eyes on the roasting pan. "So what's the problem?"

"I'm supposed to tie the legs. So it stays all nice and tight and juicy."

I hadn't meant it to sound that way. So dirty. But as soon as I said it, my cheeks blazed with heat and his eyes seemed to grow darker.

He half smiled at me and shook his head. "Faye," he

sighed. His bigger hand took mine and he pressed my palm to the erection he was suddenly wielding. But he said nothing at all.

I curled my fingers against him, my breath stalling out. But then he pushed me away and said, "Where's the twine?"

I looked at the floor, ashamed. Then I sort of flung my hands about and said, "All over."

Calvin chuckled and found the piece of cardboard the twine had been wrapped around. He snipped off a small section after winding it all back onto the board nice and neat and tight. "It's not so hard. You tie it in a circle. You loop it around this way…"

He demonstrated. But I couldn't concentrate. All I could focus on was the flexing and bunching of the muscles in his big forearms.

"Um, yes," I sighed as if I was following him.

"Then you pull this section through and you tuck this under and…voilà!"

I eyed his bound bird and shook my head. "Okaaaaaaaay," I said. "Show me that about sixty more times and I might get it."

"Faye," he said again. He was washing his hands with hot, hot water and sandalwood-scented soap but he was watching me. And I could see it in his eyes. He was interested in way more than poultry at the moment.

"Yes?"

"Take off your clothes." He was twisting the twine around his hand and then unraveling it. Twist. Unravel.

It was like watching a metronome, only with the promise of sex.

My pussy went soft and wet instantly; the heat and the moisture made me feel plump and ready and damn near mindless. I pushed my yoga pants down and he made a noise to see me bare under there. My sweater hit the deck next. Calvin was the one to unhook my pretty pink bra in the front and take it off. His mouth covered my nipple and his finger slid into me to test me.

"You're all flushed and wet," he said.

I thought he meant my cheeks were flushed, but I wasn't sure. When he added a second finger in my pussy, I didn't care.

"Turn around," he said, biting my nipple hard enough to make me jump.

I turned. He kneed my thighs apart just so. My stance wider than when my knees were pressed together but much less than shoulder width apart. When he began to wind the twine around my thighs—just above my knees—I found myself panting. My head was buzzing, my stomach a tangle of knots and excitement.

"Tying the bird is to help keep it pretty. And to help keep it juicy."

I bit my lip when he said juicy.

"Now you are always pretty. And always juicy. And I truly do doubt that anything could keep"—he pushed his fingers back inside me, from behind this time—"these juices in. Not really."

I moaned, hanging my head. The kitchen was sunny,

and outside the sky was blue, the air cold. I heard the wind chimes on the side porch banging merrily in the wind.

"Try and move your legs, sweetheart," he said, lips pressed to my ear so my nape prickled.

I tried and couldn't.

"Good," he said. "Now you're supposed to butter the bird, did you know that?"

I nodded. I hadn't gotten that far yet. I had failed my Bird Binding 101 and had a fit.

"But I prefer a healthier alterative to butter. I prefer oil. Olive is good. It's nice and healthy and"—his lips pressed to the back of my neck and goose bumps raced along my shoulders—"slick."

I sighed, watching him reach past me and pluck the large bottle of olive oil from the counter. He drizzled his fingers with the light green oil over the sink so I could see his hands but not him. The bulk of him was crushed to the back of me, his breath hot on my skin.

"But just for the sake of audible pleasure, I will say I'm *buttering* the bird. You being the bird, of course."

He laughed softly and then reached around my hips, pushing his pelvis to the back of me even as his now-slippery fingers invaded me from the front. He pushed his fingertips between my already moist folds. Parted my nether lips and stroked all around my clit so that I moved restlessly against him. I heard myself talking but didn't know what I was saying.

Then I realized it was, "Please, please, please..."

"Hush, Faye."

So I hushed, biting my lips to seal off the chant.

My reward was his slippery finger pressing and twirling and teasing my clit, so I tilted my hips forward to get more. To make it easier for him.

His fingers delved into my cunt, testing me and then teasing me so that I was within an inch of coming. Then he pulled his hand away and began a slow and somehow sinister tour of my back, kissing and licking and nibbling the back of my neck and down along my shoulder so I danced with energy. His mouth played over my shoulder blades and then settled on the middle of my back, where he placed a slow, warm kiss on every knob along my spine. I heard his knees pop a little as he squatted down to lay more tender kisses along my flanks.

I shimmied and swayed and tried to keep quiet even as one moment it tickled and the next it had my pussy flexing with need. It was torture. And it was perfect.

He found my clit again by reaching through my legs and rubbing me with just the right pressure. All the while his kisses rained down on the swell of my ass and the crack between. I hovered on the edge—praying he'd make me come, praying he wouldn't. Caught in the luscious world where orgasm was within kissing distance but hadn't quite arrived.

Calvin surprised me by plucking my clit between his fingers and biting my bottom at the same instant. I came fast and loud, my shaking hands planted on the ugly green countertop. My bound legs shook like I might fall.

"Ah, now my bird is good and juicy." Calvin chuckled. His zipper sounded like the buzz of a chain saw. His belt buckle hit the tile floor like a bomb going off.

My entire body was on red alert. All my senses heightened. All of me bright and brilliant chaos.

He turned me slowly and pushed my shoulders gently. Helping me kneel, he walked forward and traced my mouth with the tip of his cock. My tongue darted out to gather the small sweet drop of precome and he made a low sound. Fingers threaded in my hair, he drove into my mouth, sliding with leisure along my tongue. It was only a few thrusts, and when he pulled away I chased him with my mouth to try and get a few more.

"No more of that," he said. He held my shoulders to steady me so I could stand. Then he kissed me almost chastely and said, "I have other things I'm interested in."

And I was being turned again to face the bird. The. Bird. The bird that had mocked me and was now all trussed up, looking like a food magazine spread.

"Tell the bird you're sorry," he said. I could almost hear him smile.

"I...what?" I chirped.

His big hand came down on my right cheek—it was a cracking hard blow that made me jolt. "Tell. The Bird. You're. Sorry."

"Why!" I yelped.

Another two blows that crisscrossed the first, and my skin burned and tingled with heat.

"For losing your patience," he said. And then he did chuckle.

"I... This is silly—" I started. Three fast blows this time to the left cheek stopped my words. My pussy thumped in time with my runaway heart. I imagined my skin arcing with electricity and pain. A small bit of fluid fled my body and I thought how the juice was not staying in this bird.

"Say it and you'll be a happy little bird."

He wrapped my hair around his fist and very slowly levered me forward a bit over the counter. It was as if I were addressing the bird.

I said nothing.

He ground his cock to the back of me. Letting me feel the heavy length of his erection and what I was missing. "Go on..." he singsonged.

Feeling like a total moron, I said, "I'm sorry, um, *bird*, for..."

For what? For what! It was hard to think with my pulse racing and my cunt flexing and my bottom beating with heated thumps.

"Impatience," he whispered against the back of my neck.

More of my juices slipped free of me and I licked my lips, trying to calm down. "I am sorry for my impatience."

Calvin stepped up against me, his cock a hard presence he took a moment to nestle between my buttcheeks. He gripped my hips in his strong hands and licked a straight line up the back of my neck. My scalp prickled; my nipples stood out in super-sensitive points. He reached up and plucked them.

"Vin," I sighed.

I was the only person allowed to shorten Calvin to Vin, and only in times of desperate arousal. Hearing that, he kissed down each shoulder and then placed a hand at the small of my back and pushed me forward a little more. My hair—which he'd released—hung over the stainless steel sink.

He tortured me for a moment, running the tip of his cock over my slit. My legs were bound so close together he only had enough room to maneuver, and the friction was maddening. He breached me, penetrating slowly, whispering things I couldn't make out and didn't care to, given how intent I was on him pushing into my body.

When he was in, he stilled, not moving a lick, and I let out a sound that was more sob than cry. "Please, please…"

I had no shame.

"Hush now." He reached around me, still filling me, and found my distended clitoris with his fingers. Fingers that knew my body almost as well as I did. He pinched-pinched-soothed and then started to move. Short staccato bursts of his flesh into mine. Thrusting hard enough to make me sway, toes barely keeping contact with the floor.

Swirls and whirls and revolutions of his fingers on my clitoris, and his cock driving into me hard enough that my arms shook as I held myself up.

"Sorry, sorry, sorry," I found myself saying to the bird.

I heard him laugh and his strong hands were on my shoulders, anchoring me as his rhythm became frenzied.

"Touch yourself," he growled, and I nodded. I did it, my trembling fingers taking up right where he'd left off.

It was only a moment, I was so swollen, so amped up, before I was chewing my lip and trying not to come. Not yet. Not without him.

But he saved me. He always does. He banged into me, hard enough to move me forward so my hipbones clipped the edge of the counter. He could feel my pussy flexing. He could hear my breath. He knew my signs. So he knew I could obey when he rasped "Come" in my ear.

And I did. I think I was still apologizing to the chicken. I'm not sure, because my bound legs were shaking and tingling with pins and needles and my pussy was spasming around him as he emptied into me, his teeth latched to my shoulder.

It was like a series of gunshots, our climaxes, and the fallout was deafening. Silence filled our sunny little kitchen but for the sounds of us catching our breath.

Then his hands were splayed around my waist and he held me. I turned my head and he kissed me, even as my bottom beat with risen blood from his blows.

"Do you know the best part of what we just did, Faye?"

"The orgasm?"

"Nope."

"What?"

"That's going to be the best chicken you've ever eaten." He laughed.

"I'll never forget that fucking chicken," I said. "Or the chicken-inspired fucking."

"You know it," Calvin said. And smacked my ass one more time. When I cried out, he grinned. "That one was just for garnish."

THE BONDAGE PIG

Kristina Lloyd

Ralph brought the pig home when I was out, whether by accident or design, I couldn't say. I got back from the community garden, dumped a bag of veggies on the kitchen table and immediately sensed a presence, a dark anticipation lurking in the house. Dread is too strong a word for what I felt. It was more akin to the unease experienced before a thunderstorm, that time of waiting when you long for release but the imminent violence bothers you.

"What?" I asked.

Ralph was rinsing a pan of pearl barley in the sink. "What's what?"

"Dunno. Something's up."

Ralph shrugged. "Nothing's up. You okay?"

"Sure."

Ralph put the pan on the hob, paid too much attention to the dial, then straightened. He smiled, thumbs in the pockets of his jeans, looking guilty. "I have to work tonight, sorry."

"No worries. What is it?"

"A repair," he said. "Looks a bit of a bastard. Not sure how I'm going to tackle it."

"Repair of what?"

Ralph shrugged. "Just a, um, Victorian curiosity. Anyway, sorry, Sim. I need to…"

"Honestly, it's fine. But try not to be too late coming to bed, eh? It's been ages."

"Yeah, sorry."

Ralph's always sorry.

I took a bath later that evening. I could hear Ralph clattering above me in his attic-workshop. I was aching and dirty from an afternoon's gardening followed by two hours of squashing sodden newspaper into a press to make bricks for the fire. The gardening I enjoy, the brick-making's a chore, but Ralph and I are committed to ethical, green living. The bathwater around me was gray, its surface filmy with soap, and the subaquatic shadow of my pubes was a lonely, ominous rock on a seabed of flesh, my nipples cresting in two coral peaks.

Bath time makes me dreamy. The room was smudged with mist, a great cloud lit from within by the diffuse glow of a shaving light. Outside, the sky was black and, on the windowsill, a large fern glittered with sequins of peeping moonlight, its green fronds veiled by the room's haze. My body became mysterious and charmed, a powerful primeval thing in a land of carboniferous forests, swamps, stars and lumbering, long-necked monsters.

I listened to Ralph pacing to and fro as he does when there's a problem to solve. I fancied it would be the repair troubling him rather than the real problem: us, grown dull and old too fast, doing the same thing week in, week out. I heard him sawing and hammering, pictured his lanky frame hunched over his workbench, straggly blond hair tucked behind his ears. I hung on to silences until my thoughts wandered off, a thump or a scrape returning me to the moment. I drained away water, topped up with hot. Steam curled lazily in the half light. I was hoping to emerge from the bath when Ralph had finished work, then lie down on the bed, pink and clean, and have him sully me with scents of sawdust, sweat and leather, his fingertips rough from labor. Unfortunately, he appeared to be in no rush to leave the attic.

I pinched my nose and sank my head underwater, wondering what the repair was. I wanted to stay submerged a long time, enveloped by fluid, not breathing. It was peaceful and warm. When I came up for air, I thought I heard a faint cry of pleasure from upstairs. I held still, listening. A few seconds later, I caught the noise again. Then again, louder this time and almost pained. Was he…? Yes, he was! Ralph was jerking off!

I was angry, embarrassed and humiliated: angry because he should be saving that for me; embarrassed because we had a lodger, Jack, who was probably home by now and could well be within earshot; and humiliated because if Jack heard, he would know Ralph no longer desired me and I'd rather those mortifying, domestic intimacies were kept private, thanks very much.

A series of long, guttural groans shivered through the house, each cry stretched thin with torment and incredulity. I remembered, with the anguish of loss, how it used to be when Ralph would grab me by the hair and bang me six ways till Sunday.

Despite my resentment, the noise from the attic, so strangely and horribly potent, snagged at my cunt. As Ralph's cries rose to a pitch of near-bestial abandonment, I hooked my fingers inside myself, thrashing my clit in a frenzy of tiny splashes. I kept my moans as soft as I could. When I came, someone paused the universe. I shattered into a million little pieces and was blasted across time, at one with the dinosaurs and space travel and everything in between. Angels danced in my thighs, their revelry light, perfect and joyous.

When the clutches subsided, my thighs grew heavy. I rested my head against the slope of the bath, panting and confused. The sick taint of shame stole over me as it used to when I was a teenager. Ralph's weird cries echoed in my ears and I lay in the cringing regret of my post-orgasmic stupor.

I didn't know why I felt so bad when it had just felt

so good. I simply knew I couldn't stay in that space any longer. I needed to distance myself from whatever had just happened. Quickly, I wrapped myself in a towel, bundled my hair in a turban and pulled the plug, leaving the scene of the crime with steam billowing around me like dry ice. Jack, our lodger, sat opposite the bathroom door, slumped, cool and rebellious. His knees were raised and open, his back to the wall, a cigarette in one hand, a saucer of ash on the floor.

I pulled up short, heat rising in my already-hot cheeks. Jack stood but it was more like he bloomed in fast motion, a surly, stubborn bud unfurling and swelling to become a glorious tropical flower whose nectar was poison. Tribal tattoos swirled on one big bicep and his short hair wasn't merely red. It was a tantalizingly decadent russet reminiscent of ruthless Tudor kings, forest hunts and witchcraft. He smelled of beer and cigarettes.

I gripped my towel. "We don't allow smoking in the house."

Jack swaggered past me into the bathroom and tossed the butt into the toilet. A small hiss extinguished the cigarette. "I forgot," he said flatly. He stood before the toilet, looking at me as he unzipped.

I wrapped my towel tighter, hurrying away.

I didn't get chance to investigate the attic until Saturday morning when Ralph was holding his weekly whittling workshop at the community center in town. I hadn't asked about the repair. Something told me not to. The closest I came to mentioning anything was when I complained Jack had been smoking in the house while Ralph had been busy upstairs. I tried to make the word "busy" sound as loaded as possible.

Ralph shrugged. "Ah, he'd probably been down at the pub, that's all."

"Well, aren't you going to call him on it?" I said. "He's more your friend than mine."

"It'll be a one-off, don't fret."

But I wasn't convinced and I did fret. I was disappointed, too, that Ralph had sided with Jack. We didn't even know him very well. He was a friend of a friend of Ralph's, in need of somewhere to stay, so we'd offered him our spare room for a nominal rent. The deal was supposed to last a couple of weeks but he'd already been with us a month. Some people, you give them an inch and they take a mile. Sure, the extra money was useful, but we should have been charging more for a long-term let. However, we aim to be good and kind, and Jack was out of work. Mind you, he always managed to find beer money, didn't he? But on the plus side, he slept late and, since Ralph and I have our morning routines, I was grateful for that.

And if I'm being honest, I rather liked how Jack's presence disrupted the normality of me and Ralph. The mild threat, while often irritating, was secretly welcome.

It was a bright autumn day of low temperatures and crisp sunshine. I heaped the fireplace in the living room with dried newspaper bricks and pinecones while Ralph stirred porridge in the kitchen. I gazed into the leaping blood-orange flames, entranced. At the fire's heart, the pinecones were charred, malevolent flowers. When Ralph left for his class, he pecked me on the forehead, and even though he'd recently showered, I caught a hint of the smell that had been hanging around him for days. It wasn't his smell. This was feral and musky, on the edge of repellant. To my shame, I found its nastiness arousing.

Ralph hadn't cleaned the pan he'd used for the porridge, nor had he returned the milk to the fridge. This was unusual. He's a tidy man. Jack was in bed. This wasn't unusual. He rarely emerged before noon on a weekend. I made for the attic, intrigued but also drawn by an inexplicable pull. It seemed to me discovering what was up there would satisfy my mind and a whole lot more.

Crazy, I know, but ever since Ralph had brought his Victorian curiosity home, I'd been twisted up with vast, unfathomable cravings. It was a yearning for nicotine, sugar, sex and heroin; for ecstasy, annihilation and for flinging myself off a cliff and embracing airy, exhilarating transcendence. It was all those things and none of them.

The door was ajar and that smell seeped out as I pushed, an ancient, earthy scent riding the regular aromatic wave of fresh wood and leather. My hands were shaking. Sunlight slanted in through two large, sloping windows, pale angles hanging like a ghostly representation of the attic's pine beams. A dusty haze fuzzed the center of the workshop and I switched on a random selection of lights, sending shadows scuttling out of the corners.

Ralph's work surfaces were strewn with chaos, while sawdust, leather, chunks of wood and mess littered the floor. The corrugated tube of a dust extractor snaked among the debris. Saws bared their teeth. Tools and knives dangling from hooks and poking from pots glinted with medieval menace. From a high beam, a wooden African mask gazed down with blank, black eye sockets.

But I was used to the mask's face. It was always there. The face that troubled me was a new one, a dark, burnished face with beady glass eyes and a broad snout pierced by a ring. It belonged to a life-sized, stuffed leather pig, deeply upholstered like a Chesterfield sofa. "Grotesque" is the word that sprang to mind. I stared at the inert beast, my heart quickening. I couldn't say if I was excited or afraid. I knew only that I was reacting strongly to the pig's presence.

Leaving the attic door open so I could listen out for Jack or the phone, I drew hesitantly closer. The pig was unlike anything I'd ever seen. It stood on metal trotters, sunlight glossing its quilted bulk. The leather was a dark oxblood, its pouches and pits so taut the skin gleamed with the hard polish of wood. On the pig's back was a brown wooden saddle, a fine crack running vertically down its center.

I might have guessed at the pig being a plaything from a nineteenth-century nursery if it hadn't been for the huge, ruddy phallus protruding below its hindquarters. The penis wasn't corkscrew-shaped as on a living, breathing pig, but realism obviously wasn't the aim here. If I'd been looking for confirmation the Victorians were an odd bunch, it was jutting out in front of me, larger than life, and then some.

I glanced around the attic, wondering what Ralph made of this bizarre artifact. I recalled hearing him jerk off on the night he'd supposedly been working on the repair. Christ, our problems were bigger than I feared if my love rival was a leather pig, hung like a horse.

But no, this was something else. The attic possessed an unsettling atmosphere, a brooding eroticism hanging in the air, oppressive and enticing. Objectively speaking, the pig wasn't attractive, I could see that. But somehow, it created an attraction, almost as if it had charisma. I know this sounds loopy, but I sensed an intangible danger lying in wait for me. In my head, one voice urged me to leave and get a breath of air, while another voice begged me to stay. The latter was not the voice of reason; it was fueled by lust, and even though I've been a committed atheist since the age of fifteen, I felt as if the devil himself had a hand in it. And I couldn't turn away.

On one of Ralph's workbenches, a number of carved miniature pigs, all with spread wings, were scattered about the surface. Flying pigs, I mused as I rolled one in my hand. It was unvarnished, still slightly rough in its execution and, at a guess, made from beech. Other pigs were well shaped and finely crafted, while some had been abandoned at an early stage. I set the pig down, feeling as if I no longer knew or understood Ralph. *Is this*, I wondered, *how marriages disintegrate? You find flying pigs in your attic and can't discuss it with your husband?*

The attic was warm although it shouldn't have been. I wondered if Jack had surfaced yet. I hoped when he did, he would add more bricks to the fire to keep the living room heated. I imagined he wouldn't; too much of a layabout to care. *He'll start to care when it gets colder*, I thought. I slung my cardigan over a chair, comfortable enough in one of Ralph's old shirts and a pair of stripy leg warmers I'd knitted for myself two winters ago.

I knew what I wanted to do. I wanted to sit astride the pig. I'd wanted to do so ever since I'd first entered the attic. And I might have done that, might have kept it nice and simple if, on approaching the pig, I hadn't been struck by an overwhelming urge to handle its big, shiny phallus. I suddenly wanted to feel it in my fingers, hard, polished and lewd. My hunger to touch the pig was also, inexplicably, driven by a desire to give pleasure to a lover. I had to remind myself this was an unpleasant object whose heart was sawdust, whose cock was wood.

I dropped to the floor alongside the pig, reaching below to fondle its phallus like some sick milkmaid. My fingers couldn't encircle the pig's girth, so I ran my hand, cupped like a C, up and down its length. The

wood was as smooth as glass and marble! That irresistible tactility practically powered my caress. I stroked
greedily, slipping along the swinish shaft, then molding
my palm to its blunt, rounded end. My groin tingled as
I imagined a thick, hard cock sliding inside me, and I
remembered, with a tug of nostalgia, the wooden dildo
Ralph had once carved for me. It was curved to hit
my G-spot. We'd named it Nessie after the Loch Ness
Monster. I didn't know where it was anymore. I needed
to rectify that.

An over enthusiastic caress on my part caused the
pig's stout member to creak and shift. For one terrible
moment, I thought the beast was alive, its porcine
arousal swelling in my hand. I tested again, eliciting
another grunt from the wood. Then, terrifyingly, the
shaft dipped a fraction as if it were coming loose in
my hand.

Oh hell. I held my breath, fearing I might have
broken the monster. How on earth would I explain that
to Ralph? But no, not broken. This cock, I realized, was
much more than a cock. I repeated the action, pulling
the shaft backward. The entire pig shuddered and
squeaked. With a groan, the wooden saddle split open
down the center and began to rise and separate. I pulled
harder on the phallus, now understanding it functioned
as a lever. I leaned backward as the saddle separated
further, a compartment emerging from the pig's center,
three tiers of drawers opening out beneath each saddle
half, staggered like those of a cantilever sewing box.

I shuffled backward on my knees, gawping in astonishment. The drawers resembled wings. Ralph's miniature flying-pig carvings immediately made sense. Or at least, I saw a connection between them and this. There was no sense anywhere in the attic. It was a madman's playroom.

I couldn't deny my excitement. My heart was thumping, my stomach fluttering. Our attic had the weirdest treasure. I was about to peer forward to inspect the contents of the drawers when I glimpsed a figure in the corner of my eye. I shrieked. I had company. My heart stalled. I felt woozy, hot.

Standing in the attic doorway was Jack, wearing nothing but a pair of faded, black jogging bottoms, ragged at the hem. He was propped against the doorjamb, arms folded, smirking. His biceps curved into the broad bulk of his shoulders, black tattoos licking at his contours. The hair on his creamily pale chest glinted red-gold in the mellow, autumn light and further down, a neat coppery line ran from his navel, down his flat belly, and disappeared into the waistband of his joggers.

I pressed my hand to my chest as if to keep my heart from leaping out. "How long have you been there?"

"Long enough," he replied smoothly.

I blushed, saying nothing. There was no point.

"Stunning, isn't it?" Jack strode into the room, hands in his baggy pockets. His outline smudged when he walked through a wedge of dusty sunlight. He looked mythic, otherworldly. Sensation pulsed in my groin, and I quickly grew tender and wet.

"You shouldn't smoke in the house," I said.

"I'm not smoking."

"But sometimes you do. Ralph and I don't smoke and we don't want people smoking in our house either. You have to go outside. I can smell it from your room too. It's not on, I don't like it, this is our house, mine and Ralph's. You can't just—"

"Okay, okay. I've got the message."

"What are you doing up here?"

"Same as you," he said. He stood a few feet from me, looking down and smiling. His cock was lifting inside his joggers, pushing obscenely at the fabric. I wished I wasn't on my knees, wished my cunt wasn't tingling so insistently.

"No, this is my house," I said, sounding bolder than I felt. "This is my husband's workshop. I have every right to be here. You don't. You've overstepped the mark, Jack. You're arrogant and presumptuous. And nosy. You have no damn—"

"Quit with the attack!" He jerked his chin at me, eyes flinty with anger. "I saw you. I stood here and watched you work that shiny pig-dick. Saw how you loved it." He took a step closer, deliberately intimidating. "And you know what? I did exactly the same thing when you and Ralph were sleeping. Yeah, that's right. Crept up here one night and wound up making out with...with that." He flipped a dismissive hand toward the pig. "Because I had no choice, see? I had no fucking choice."

He gave me a long, hard stare as if, with the force of his eyes, he could make his words sink in.

I looked at the ground. "I know. I'm sorry."

"And Ralph had no choice. None of us do."

I nodded. "It's the smell."

"I don't know what it is," he replied. "But it's here, that crazy, fucked-up...bondage pig. And it's got to us. We have no choice."

I nodded again.

"Take a look." His voice was gentler, but his words still felt like an order. "It's worth exploring."

I have to confess, at first I thought he was referring to his cock. His directness thrilled me and I imagined dipping a hand into his joggers to free him. One tug of the drawstring and he'd be mine. An urge to betray Ralph swept over me. I wanted to be reckless and greedy, wanted to have another man all over me, inside me, everywhere. When I caught Jack's intended meaning, I mentally backtracked and kneeled up to examine the contents of the pig's trays as politely as I could. Jack moved to stand behind me, his bare feet astride my legs. He swept my hair back over my shoulders, his gesture tenderly proprietorial. My cunt throbbed with need.

Spread before me, the six shallow drawers were cluttered with bondage gear and strange-looking implements. Tentatively, I rummaged among the tangle of brown leather and brass, growing more confident and curious by the second. Jack continued to lightly stroke and lift my hair, making me nervous although I liked it. I selected a slim wooden paddle, unvarnished and crudely fashioned, and ran a thumb along its chipped, rough edges. I was glad Jack couldn't see my face.

"Spanking," he said as I set the piece on the ground. He wasn't informing me. He knew I wasn't naïve. He was itemizing the things we would do together. Or at any rate, that's how it sounded to me. We hear what we want to hear.

When I set aside another paddle, this one in dark, brittle leather and patterned with a grid of holes, Jack said, "More spanking."

I swallowed and noted my hand was trembling when I reached into the trays again. Arousal swam between my thighs. *Stop this*, I told myself, *stop this!* Another voice said, *Hey, you're doing nothing wrong, just inspecting a freaky antique with your lodger. Yeah, right, Simone. A lodger with a boner who's stroking your hair while your husband's at work.*

My fingertips skimmed over rough and smooth, soft and hard. Objects clinked together, some pieces too entangled to budge. I took care to choose something interesting.

"Pinwheel," said Jack.

I held a small brass roller, its wide, leather-coated wheel spiked with four rows of metal spines.

"What's it for?" I asked.

Jack reached out a hand from behind me. I passed back the roller. With one hand, he unfastened the top buttons of my shirt. He slipped my clothes down from my shoulders and swept my hair aside, baring my neck and back. I clutched my shirt by my breasts, covering myself because I was naked beneath, not yet dressed for the day. I caught a waft of Jack's sweat as he leaned close. His murmured words were warm against my ear.

"Say again?" he taunted.

My voice creaked with lust. "What's it for?"

A pause. "It's for punishing sluts who ask stupid fucking questions."

The spikes stabbed my skin and he rolled the wheel across my shoulders, slow and hard. I groaned loudly, his insults and the pain sparking a surge of fierce, dark lust. "Again," I whispered. I seemed to speak the words before I'd even thought them. I dipped my head like a supplicant, offering him my naked back. "Again."

"Like this?" He rolled another track across my shoulders, then stopped.

"More! Please."

He gave a soft, satisfied laugh, then rolled the barbed wheel up and down, round and round, fast and slow until I couldn't tell one track from another. I felt as if a thousand hot, tiny spears were raining down on my skin, a monsoon of cruel sensation. I writhed, swayed, hunched and gasped, and whenever Ralph popped into my head, I told myself I couldn't help it, none of us could, we weren't to blame. We were in the grip of a power that defied comprehension. This wasn't me asking for it, nor was Jack doling it out. This was the bondage pig who'd come to corrupt us, to drag us down a path of chaos and depravity. We weren't to blame.

"Please!" My heart and hands racing, I tugged open several more buttons and shucked off my shirt, arching my back to present him with my breasts, my nipples hard and high. Jack rolled the wheel over one shoulder, down between the valley of my breasts, below the underswell, up, around, down, and oh, oh, fire stabbed my nipple and I was dizzy with longing, crying out for something and not knowing if I wanted more of this or less.

Then a voice cut into my consciousness, cold as ice.

"We should use the collar on her. You can attach wrist cuffs to it, front or back. Take away her hands, then we can use her how we want."

"Ralph!"

From behind, Jack cupped my chin firmly in his hand, tipping my head back against his crotch. His erection pressed against me. "Sounds like a plan."

He held me fast, and I felt so deeply ashamed, sluttish, aroused. This near stranger had me in his hands, fixing me on my knees so my bared, adulterous body was being offered to my husband. I closed my eyes, the afterimage of Ralph in the attic doorway stamped on my mind. Wide-shouldered and athletically lean, he stood much as Jack had done earlier, arms folded and coolly observing. Where Jack was red-haired, Ralph was fair, but both men scared me: Jack because he was trouble; Ralph because he'd caught me *in flagrante* with Trouble and I feared he might be angry. He had every right to be.

Ralph strolled toward us. My heart thumped, and when Ralph passed through the dusty shaft of sunlight, something peculiar happened. He was transformed to me. Briefly, he appeared to be a magnificent, celestial vision, but the real change must have been in my perception. My earnest, reliable and slightly dull husband became the man I fell in love with all those years ago: passionate, idealistic, driven; a man determined to get what he wants. And I knew that what Ralph wanted right then was me, and for me, him and Jack to surrender to wild, primal lust and destroy all limits of seemliness and order.

Quick and efficient, Ralph selected a couple of brown leather items from the pig's deepest drawers and tossed a handful of brass clips in his palm. Jack stepped aside with a chuckle of approval.

"Hands behind your back," said Ralph. "Not like that. Higher."

Deftly, he cuffed and buckled my wrists between my shoulder blades, his bossiness making my horniness soar.

"And just so we know who you belong to..." With those words, he fastened a matching leather collar around my neck, slipping his long fingers inside to check it wasn't too tight. Metal clinked as he linked my cuffed wrists to my collar. When I let the collar take the strain of my arms, it pulled against my throat so I had to keep my hands high. I found the position uncomfortable but, in spite of that or perhaps because of it, intensely arousing.

Jack bobbed down in front of me and lifted my breasts in turn as if testing their weight. He grinned at me, looking me dead in the eye. I glanced away, ashamed, because I didn't want to like this but couldn't hide how much it was turning me on. Jack tapped harder, slapping upward, his hand skimming off me as I bounced. I groaned and Ralph dropped to his knees at my other side, wrapping an arm around my waist. Jack stepped back as Ralph tilted me forward to deliver a series of hard, merciless blows to my ass. "You like that, do you, Sim?" he hissed. Slap. Slap. Slap. "Like it when some other guy plays with your tits."

I yelped and squealed, heat blossoming under my husband's hand. "Yes," I gasped. "Yes, I like it." Ralph was rough, messy and energetic in the way he spanked me, his breath huffing fast, his arm clasping me tight. I flinched and jerked, writhing to escape and wobbling awkwardly in his grip.

"Put your dick in her mouth," Ralph urged Jack, but Jack was about to do precisely that, so the request was redundant. I figured it wasn't actually a request, more a granting of permission, not that Jack was asking. His joggers were off, his cock was hard, and he was aiming himself at my mouth. Ralph pinched my jaw, raising my head to Jack's level. I opened to take him, spluttering crudely around his length as I drew back and forth, still unsteady on my knees.

"Go on, Simone," encouraged Ralph, his voice by my ear. "Show him what you can do."

Jack held my head still, fists in my hair, and moved according to his pace, hips rolling with languid ease. My breathing steadied and I lashed my tongue around his shaft. When he let me, I slurped hard on his end, making little popping noises because that's how Ralph likes it. Jack seemed to like it too. Pleasure rumbled in his throat and he clutched my hair tighter, my scalp stinging.

"That's my girl," said Ralph, hooking his arm around my back. Keeping me upright and balanced, he reached his free hand between my thighs and plunged his fingers into me, hard and fast. "Let's see what we have here."

He curled his fingers into me, pressing and shunting until my head was spinning and I had to break off from Jack to gasp and whimper.

"She's so wet," Ralph said to Jack. "Go on, try her."

Jack fell to one knee and did what Ralph had just done, his thrusts equally vigorous. Ralph stood behind me, tucked his hand into my armpits and eased me backward. At that angle, with my knees spread for Jack, my hands locked in cuffs, I felt defenseless and exposed, a thing to be used by these two eager men.

Jack's hand pumped between my thighs and as my cries hurried to a peak, he ducked down to taste me. With his tongue flat and generous, he rubbed at my clit. I felt so loose, so wet, and then, in the dizzying midst of that, Jack's tongue began darting over my bud in sharp, intentional patterns. Ralph propped me against his chest and massaged my breasts, his calloused fingers scuffing my nipples. My pleasure tightened, I panted with nearness, and Jack's tongue was pure, unadulterated magic.

"She's going to come," Ralph said. "Just a little more. Keep going."

I focused on the bondage pig, on its cantilever trays and stout, buttoned haunches. The color of the leather seeped into my mind. Such a beautiful color, red-black, like blood and ink. Jack slid a bunch of fingers into me, screwing left-right-left when my swollen tightness resisted him. I wailed to feel the fullness of him. His tongue skittered on my point and then, oh, I was gone, lost, tumbling though crimson skies as my orgasm pulsed and clenched. Over and over I fell, six distinct waves of pleasure coursing through my body.

"Good girl," said Ralph.

Jack knelt up, his mouth shining with my juices. "Fuck," he breathed. "I felt that." I stared at him through my post-orgasmic daze. He wiped the back of his hand across his mouth. His lips still gleamed and his eyes were heavy and serious, altered by lust.

Ralph unclipped me. I let my hands fall, each wrist still wrapped in a tatty brown cuff, my neck still collared. I wondered about all the people who'd worn these cuffs, all the scenes the pig had witnessed. I was weak, as floppy as a rag doll, and when Ralph indicated I should kneel on all fours, I tipped forward onto my elbows, unable to bear my weight on my arms.

I hardly knew what was happening to me. And then I knew Jack was fucking me because Ralph said, "Be my guest," and a cock was pushing into me and it wasn't

Ralph's. Inside, I was pink and sensitive. Jack's hard, fat shaft prized me open until I was snug and pulpy around him, the contact so hot I fancied I must be melting.

"Oh, jeez, that's good," he sighed. "Such a sweet little pussy."

He was slow to start, every lunge and retreat making me moan for more. I was hazily aware of Ralph undressing and then I was acutely aware of him lifting my shoulders. His cock reared up before me, his head glossy and blood-flushed, his length surging high, a network of blue veins spread beneath his velvet-smooth skin. I found strength in my arms and took him in my mouth, clamping my lips below the rim of his tip and fondling his warm, weighty balls. As I bobbed on Ralph's end, Jack began to fuck with more urgency, his fingers digging into my hips. I slid to the root of Ralph and he gave a low, appreciative growl, holding my head to keep me there.

When I withdrew and swallowed him down again, he said, "We've got you skewered, Sim."

"Spit-roasting you," gasped Jack.

I moaned around Ralph's cock as Jack powered with increasing savagery, his fingertips on my hips creating dents of pain. Exhausted and half-delirious, I was being buffeted between the two men, unable to do anything much except take them. Then, with a harsh, rasping cry, Jack pulled out of me, and seconds later, his climax pattered on my back in several hot splashes.

Ralph cried out in response, sounding agonized and

shocked. I knew that sound so well. So close, so close. Moments before he came, I felt him swell to a peak of rigidity in my mouth. He held still, thighs shuddering as his liquid jetted at my throat and I was drinking him down, fresh, thin and salty. When I released him, he was quick to kiss me, seeking out his own taste as he held my face, light, affectionate and almost proud.

After catching his breath, he said, "You're amazing."

I could hardly speak. "So are you," I managed. "Both of you." I reached for Jack. "Dirty bastards. But amazing with it."

Jack flopped onto the wooden floor, an arm flung above his head, copper hair glinting like filaments in his armpit. "I blame the pig," he said.

"Likewise," I said. "Don't you dare get rid of it, Ralph."

We laughed tiredly, united in post-coital coziness.

"Man, I need a cigarette," said Jack, idly strumming his chest.

"Smoke away," I said. "I don't care."

Jack turned to Ralph who shrugged, saying, "I don't give a fuck either. Don't give a fuck about anything right now. I hope the house isn't on fire. Don't think I could move."

Jack grunted in amusement. I thought about the fire I'd made that morning. It seemed silly now to think how concerned I'd been about Jack keeping it alight. Nothing mattered. We could stay in the attic all day if we wanted, pausing to fetch food and fucking till we ran out of energy. Yes, I thought, we could do that quite easily. To hell with responsibility. And so that's what we did, as if the hands on the clock had stopped and the world had fallen away, leaving only the three of us.

Jack moved out after five weeks, saying, "Three's a crowd." We were sad to see him go, but our parting was entirely amicable. He tempered our disappointment with a promise to stop by occasionally for some "attic time"—as we'd begun to refer to sex, even when it didn't take place in the attic.

A week later, Ralph got rid of the pig. By that point, we were practically stupefied with horniness and fatigue, yet the impulse to continue never wavered. We'd tried every kinky object stored inside the beast several times over, and our house was a disaster zone, domestic duties falling by the wayside as the hunger to fuck took over. We tested friendships and family relationships by neglecting social events, emails and phone calls, preferring sex to anything else. We were insatiable. And sore too, especially in the first week with Jack.

The pig's original owner no longer wanted his possession back, claiming life was more manageable without "that thing" to feed. I could understand. Ralph sold the pig at auction for a tidy sum and we dusted ourselves down, still happily horny but not crazily so. Now, every day on a chain around my neck, I wear one of Ralph's tiny flying pigs, a hand-carved reminder of the glorious times we shared. I often wonder where the bondage pig is, and whether others see its influence as a blessing or a curse.

Sometimes, I swear pockets of that weird, feral scent are still lingering in the attic. When I catch a hint of the aroma, I breathe in its darkness, convinced the spirit of the beast is still with us, keeping our fires burning bright.

CURRY, EXTRA HOT

N.T. Morley

Kendra was at the counter in the kitchen peeling and cutting up ginger for Thai green curry—extra hot—when she heard Arturo's footsteps behind her.

"Don't make this easy for me," he said, his voice heavy in her ears.

"Don't make *what* easy for you?" she asked, distracted, but by then Arturo had gotten his arms around her—and when she yelped, he shoved the gag in her mouth.

Arturo pushed the gag home, pulling its strap tight around her head and buckling it easily at the back. Kendra realized all of a sudden that it wasn't his usual ball gag. This was something weird—it had a strange shape, elongated with a swelling, sort of arrow-shaped tip to it....

Holy crap, she realized: the gag was the shape of a dick! Arturo had silenced her with a short, fat dildo. *Shit*, she thought. *That's perverted.* She'd never encountered the toy before, though she'd seen them in porn and in kink shops. *He must have stopped at Mr. Leather on his way home from work. Whatever he bought, I hope he didn't put it on the WestBank card, we're almost overdrawn....*

Arturo wrapped his big hard hand around Kendra's slender wrist, pulled her arm up behind her and spanked her.

Kendra yelled into the gag and began to flail a little; he spanked her again and took something out of his pocket or off his belt. Like a surgeon working fast to save a life, Arturo held her against the counter and put the blindfold on her with one hand. He could do it easily because she wasn't really struggling yet—because she was simply so surprised and because she was used to letting Arturo blindfold her. She all but forgot she was supposed to be unwilling or something.

Don't make this easy for me, she thought. *What is that supposed to mean? Struggle*, she guessed.

So she struggled, squirming against Arturo's greater bulk and strength. But by that time, he had pulled her away from the table and was frog-marching her, gagged and blindfolded, into the bedroom.

He bent her over the edge of the big four-poster bed and pinned her there.

Arturo was lean and muscled. He swam, he pumped

iron, he bicycled everywhere. He had eight-plus inches on Kendra—her five-four to his just-over-six—and even if he hadn't outweighed her by a hundred pounds, the simple fact of his muscle mass made her helpless.

She couldn't get away. Arturo wouldn't *let* her get away. So she struggled, feeling the power of his weight and his muscles and, more importantly, his determination to ravish her.

He held her effortlessly with one hand, holding her wrist up behind her and his weight holding her down. Her other hand flailed helplessly. She tried to squirm. All she did was tire herself out—and that happened quickly, not just because she hadn't been doing her cardio lately but because her pulse raced faster and faster as her excitement rose.

She was wet within seconds.

She could still smell the ginger on her hands as Arturo held her down and stretched his long arm out so he could seize the ropes he'd stashed on the side of the bed. He got her wrists encircled in moments, looped them over the bed frame tie-downs she was always whacking her knee on and secured her wrists to the sides of the bed.

Then he forced her legs open and started working on those.

She struggled, all right—but she felt weak inside, weak and gooey. The scent of ginger was powerful; it overwhelmed her senses.

Kendra had spent the afternoon around the house doing chores and relaxing, so she wasn't wearing much—in fact, she might just as likely have been nude, if she hadn't been cooking. She was barefoot and her hair was back in a ponytail. Her snug red gym shorts were T-shirt thin, and of course she didn't wear a bra under the old, worn wifebeater she'd liberated from Arturo's underwear drawer. She could already feel her nipples, stiff with arousal, rubbing against the silken cover of the bed.

And that was *before* Arturo, having secured her ankles to the bedposts, dug his teeth into her tank top and *ripped*.

Kendra felt the pull of the fabric at her tits, the wrench of his teeth at the shoulder straps, and suddenly the thing was gone. She hoped he wouldn't give her shorts the same treatment—she liked this pair *lots*. But the hope was forlorn; the gym shorts were old and tight and already halfway coming apart down the center seam. Besides, wasn't it she who'd given Arturo an open invitation? "I don't own a single item of clothing I wouldn't trade for a good fuck," she'd purred in his ear by way of telling him that he could pull this shit on her anytime he wanted.

How many times had he taken her at her word? Half a dozen in a year, at most. Yet, every time was unpredictable—just like this—and every time got her so fucking wet—like now...so wet she fucking saw stars. Like now.

Arturo knelt behind her, dug his teeth not into the waistband of her threadbare gym shorts—but into the *crotch*. He started a rip with perplexing ease—and then Kendra gave out a muffled yelp through the gag as Arturo pulled and twisted and ripped.

In a second, she was naked, bent over and exposed. Her ass in the air and her legs spread very far apart and bound to the sturdy bed frame, Kendra was helpless and wholly open; Arturo could do anything he wanted to her.

The bed was perfect for this kind of scene. They had bought the bedroom ensemble with a careful eye toward its height compared to Kendra's height. The four-poster frame was high to begin with. Add that particular box spring and that particular mattress and the particular mattress pad and this particular comforter, and the bed was exactly the right height to bend over and bind a barefoot girl of exactly Kendra's body shape in exactly this position. If she was wearing heels, it got awkward, but as long as the scene didn't last too long all the heels really did was make her lift her ass in the air, which was, yeah, kinda uncomfortable after a while—but she'd seen the digital photos; it looked *hot*. As long as the scene didn't last more than ten or fifteen minutes, six-inch heels turned her ass from that of a tied-up and helpless girlfriend into the ass of a fucking sex goddess.

Either way, this position was her favorite because of Arturo's propensity for doing nasty things to parts of her that were particularly exposed when she was bent over like this.

There was her ass, of course—her buttocks. Arturo loved them. He took a long lush minute to spank the shit out of them, reddening Kendra's bottom severely. She squirmed; she struggled; she squealed into the gag. After twenty spanks on each round cheek, when he felt her up, she was *dripping*.

He fingered her easily, smoothly, giving her two fingers up inside her and insistently thumbing her clit until her eyes rolled back in her head and she started pumping her hips, half-involuntarily.

That inspired Arturo to drop to his knees behind her and bury his tongue in her ass. Kendra moaned as Arturo's tongue swirled around her snug rear entrance. Her pleasure mounted as he licked deeper—and then his finger was in her, just one, at first. It always felt so dirty when the sick little pervert went right to her ass. Kendra had learned to like it. But she'd never learned to expect it.

She realized she could still smell ginger—stronger than ever. It couldn't be her fingers, could it?

It wasn't. It was the peeled ginger root, she realized—Arturo must have snatched it from the kitchen and stuck it in his pocket.

When a peeled ginger root is thrust inside the human anus, it causes a powerful tingling sensation. It's deeply erotic if you're into that sort of thing—at least, that's what Kendra had read. "Tingling" was one way to put it. It was a little like getting a spearmint-oil enema or something. Heat and cold swirled together, making her head spin and her pussy go all funny. Confused sensations rolled through her naked body. She would have been *pissed* if it was anybody other than Arturo. But he always knew just how far he could push her.

But still, Kendra couldn't help thinking bitterly, *does that son of a bitch realize that ginger root doesn't have a flange?*

Then the sensation rocketed to new levels as the full impact of the ginger root hit her. It didn't just tingle; it *stung*. But it still did things to her inside—gooey things, making waves of cascading pain and pleasure get all tangled up in her belly and her throat and her clit.

Kendra still hadn't assimilated the sensation of the ginger root up her ass when she heard the telltale hum of a plug-in vibrator and felt the pressure on her clit. Pleasure blasted through her, conquering any lingering anxiety. Arturo knew from experience that the base of the vibrator wand tucked easily into the bed's railing— especially since he'd installed a strap there to hold it. And in this position, that held the vibe right up against Kendra's clit.

That left his hands free. Arturo mounted her easily at first, getting his head inside her—and then he encountered an inexplicable tightness. Kendra felt his cock stretching her almost painfully—*almost*. Her eyes popped open wide behind the blindfold and she howled into the gag. Arturo slowed his thrust momentarily—but he knew the timbre of Kendra's moans even better than she knew them herself. They were moans of pleasure.

However tight she felt, it was fucking infuckingfucking-*credible*. She didn't know why she was so fucking tight. She sure as hell wasn't *dry* inside—far from it. So it had to be the ginger.

Of course. Her ass was assaulted by all sorts of unfamiliar sensations. Her pussy responded. It was a kind of sympathetic magic.

Arturo had to work to enter her fully, and Kendra had to work to take it. He reached down and steadied the vibe against her clit, which only made Kendra's muffled howls of pleasure rise in volume as the soft round head of the vibe connected more firmly with her clit. By then he was deep inside her, his cock working hard to get in and out of a channel made tight by the fullness in her ass and her pussy's reaction to the sensation assault on her body. Her tongue worked fervently against the dick-shaped gag as she moaned. Her eyes roved wildly behind the leather blindfold.

She cried out more loudly, until even the gag couldn't really silence her. Sometimes she cared if the neighbors heard. This wouldn't have been one of them…except she realized she was really being a screamer tonight. Well, she thought, what the hell? Six o'clock on a Friday, anyway—right? What the hell. Half of them wouldn't be home, right?

Who was she kidding? Half of her neighbors were state workers. They'd left at four to beat the rush hour. They were relaxing on their couches—above, below and to either side of her. They could probably hear everything—and even with the gag, Kendra was giving them plenty to hear.

She decided she didn't care. She just moaned louder, practically spitting out the gag. She was getting closer and closer, her ass still tingling wildly, sensation flooding through her naked, tied-up body. She fought against the ropes, trying to fuck herself on Arturo's cock. She was getting close…very close.

Arturo pinned her tight, not allowing her hips to pivot. He fucked her rhythmically, tormenting her, matching his strokes to the sounds of her squeals and always giving it to her just a little slower and softer than she wanted.

Until the end, that is. Then it seemed like he could tell, somehow (was the fucker psychic?) exactly how close Kendra was to exploding in pleasure.

He kept on holding the vibe against her, but he went to work with his hips and his cock and his weight, letting the combined power of gravity and his gym-toned muscles do the work.

Arturo gave it to Kendra fast and deep, pounding her with what felt like a grudgefuck—except it was exceedingly shallow. Arturo knew, from vast experience, that the way to make Kendra cum was to fuck her fast and shallow.

He did that, long enough to drive her right to the brink.

Then he seized the ginger root and pulled it out.

The sudden vacancy in her ass was what drove her

over the edge—not least because it let air in. The ginger root was big enough that it left her gaped for a second, and the icy sensation of air on her ginger-tortured asshole was enough to make Kendra go rigid and practically scream behind the gag. The sudden rigidity of her hips and her legs gave Arturo the necessary leverage he needed to bring her over the edge with those short, sharp thrusts just barely inside her that she so adored.

Kendra came harder than she'd come in *months*—maybe all year, and that was saying something with a horndog, sex-expert pervert boyfriend like hers. She came so hard it made her plowing by the borrowed fucking machine last month seem like a French kiss.

Her whole body was suddenly suffused with sensation. Deep in her core, she spasmed—feeling the pulses from her cunt to her throat to her nipples to her belly and all the way up into her ass. With the sizzling, tingling sensation still pouring through her, Kendra was left in a daze.

She felt Arturo fucking her faster, deeper, harder—far more smoothly, with exactly the rhythm he used when she watched him beat off. She felt a rush of pride and excitement and submissive tension; she was his fuck-hole. Knowing Kendra was well and truly finished, he decided it was his turn.

It didn't take him long; he must have been really turned on. That brought Kendra a warm glow of pride... although who was she kidding? All she'd done was bend over and—

The flood of his seed deep inside her obliterated all conscious thought for Kendra as she felt a wave of deep affection and receptive pleasure.

Arturo's hands started working again, undoing the knots and unbuckling the gag. The penis-shaped gag came free, and Kendra sighed in pleasure, smiling. As Arturo freed her, Kendra felt the lingering sting in her ass.

She decided two things.

One, Arturo was buying her another pair of gym shorts tomorrow.

Two, they were sending out for Thai food. You just can't have homemade curry without ginger root.

BURNED

Alison Tyler

Jenny was the type of girl who stole things. Small things, like the few bucks remaining in your billfold if you inadvertently left your wallet on the counter. Important things, like the carnelian beads your mother had given you for your sixteenth birthday. Irreplaceable things, like your husband. I've known her type of woman before. In fact, I've gotten good at spotting them over the years. Why? Because when you're married to a man like Rick, you have to expect ladies will worm their way out of the holes in the headboard in order to try to steal him away.

What makes Rick so fucking special?

Well, there's the fact that he's handsome. And by handsome, I mean turn-your-head, wolf-whistle, catcall, panties wet when he meets your eyes, dreamboat, movie-star handsome.

How did I hook up with a man like that?

Fuck you.

No, really. How many times have I been out to dinner with my husband and had a waitress pull me aside and ask me that insensitive question. "So how did you two land together? What's your secret?" As if a troll like me must have performed a magic trick by the light of the full moon to woo my man. Sacrificed a goat. Bathed in pig blood.

I'm not ugly. Don't set yourself on the wrong path there. But I didn't win the gene pool Olympics the way Rick did. My man's tall—six feet four inches in bare feet. He's the type of hunk I grew up gazing at in posters on my wall. Magnum, P.I. The Six Million Dollar Man. Broad shouldered, barrel-chested, gorgeous from tip to toe, and that tip includes the most beautiful cock I've ever seen.

And me?

I'm barely five feet, and I've got what my grandmother always used to call "character." That means that my lips might be a little fuller than your average runway model. My hair is kinky curly. My nose wrinkles when I smile. My eyes are dark, and I always have those purplish smudges beneath them—part Hungarian bloodline, part insomniac's curse.

Why does Rick love me? Not because I could take on a Victoria's Secret angel. That's for sure. At least, not without playing dirty, sucker punching her when she flapped her white-feathered wings on the catwalk. He loves me because one day two years ago he wandered into my studio while looking for a friend of his who'd just moved out—that was his line, anyway. I was hanging paintings on the wall, organizing oils, stretching drop cloths. The door was open and he stepped in, glanced around and said, "I like that one."

I turned to see who was talking. I had my black hair scraped back with a red bandana, battered overalls on over a white wifebeater tee, kick-ass Docs splattered with teal paint. "Which one?" I asked, turning to look where the stranger was pointing.

"The girl on the bed."

"Oh, her," I said. She was my former. Ex. Lover. Capital on the Ex. I should have taken a knife to the canvas based on what Jenny had done to my heart, but I was too proud of the work to destroy the piece. My goal was to sell the painting for a hefty price tag and then splurge on a trip to Paris. I thought that selling her ass would give me pleasure. The painting, you see, was a nude.

Rick walked through the studio as if he had a reason to be there. "I'm Lola," I told him, offering a hand. He actually ignored me as he continued to look at the pictures, but he was so intent, I forgave him the rudeness. "You're good," he said.

"I know."

"Really good."

"I *really* know."

I took the time to look him over. Part of me did so

automatically. As an artist, I'm always assessing the lines and the angles, the way people's features fit. The way I might paint them if I had a shot. The other part of me looked at him in a less clinical way. I hadn't had a cock in a while. I wondered if he was all show, or if he might be able to do the deed in a manner that would work for me.

"My friend used to live here," he said, finally explaining. "I was in the neighborhood and thought I'd see if he was still around."

"By *friend*, you mean drug dealer?" I asked. I'd found remnants that could mean nothing else. And people had come by at odd hours, other needy folk like Rick, searching for their savior in a dime bag.

He looked at me.

"No judgment," I added.

"In that case..."

That's how we found ourselves getting stoned in my studio. I didn't have the bed in yet. We sat on the drop cloth–strewn floor and smoked the little bit of marijuana I had left in my coffee can. Do all druggies keep their stash in Folgers, or is it just me?

He told me he was going through a rough breakup. That he hadn't gotten high in forever. That he'd driven to his dealer's place on a whim. I told him that I had moved in here when my ex and I had flamed out. Told him that I painted more when I was unhappy than when I was happy. Rick proved me wrong on that one, let me tell you. He turned all my used-to-bes into so much nonsense. Back then, we were new. We were raw. We were fucking on the floor like animals before the afternoon had ended. The pot? Maybe marijuana helped—we were relaxed, and there was none of the weirdness about going on a date first, wondering if you'd get a kiss on the cheek or a grope on the ass. He had his knees bent, and he touched my foot with his foot. He put one hand on my leg. We were fondling each other as the late-afternoon sun hit the opposite wall.

There was music in the clink of my overall buckles when he undid each one. There was a gentlemanly quality in the way he helped undo the knots on my Docs, the way he pulled off every scrap of my clothing before spreading me out on the floor. But there was brutality in the way he fucked me, and I thought, *I could get used to this.*

I wonder if it's the fact that I didn't act as if I wasn't good enough that turned him on. I mean, since that afternoon I've witnessed the power of Rick's appearance on other people. He makes them stammer. Stutter. Forget their own goddamn names. But I've been painting pretty people all my life. I am not wired in that way. I mean, I wasn't. Yeah, Rick made my panties wet. But maybe it had something more to do with the way he touched me, the way he seemed to understand how my thoughts clicked together, more than the fact that he could have bench-pressed three of me if he tried.

Okay, so where does Jenny come into all this?

Well, not at the start. There were two years at the

beginning when Rick and I ate and drank and devoured each other. When my man came home for lunch simply to fuck me against the wall, forgoing food in favor of my pussy, or for the flavor of my pussy.

And then one day Jenny showed up. A girl with a black heart. Rick had never been too concerned with the fact that I was bi. He knew I wasn't going to cheat on him or leave him for another woman or another man. We were rock solid like that. He worked at his job all day while I painted. He fucked me every free second he had. He knew I wouldn't leave him just because he didn't have a pussy. "Bi" in my world simply means that I've been with men and I've been with women. Before Rick there was Jenny. Before Jenny was Max. I go with my heart. I don't care what parts you have as long as they connect with mine.

Jenny showed up the way she always showed up. She came slithering under the doorjamb, appearing in a puff of smoke. Fire-breathers have all sorts of tricks like that. When I returned from a run, Jenny was there on my sofa, curled up in the corner as if she'd been there all along, as if she'd never left. Except we hadn't lived here together. She'd had to look long and hard to find me.

"Lola," she said as I unlocked the door, startling me enough so that I dropped the keys. While bending to retrieve them, I tried to make sense of the situation. Jenny had left me for a girl in her entourage. She'd literally run away with her to join the circus. I'd had dreams of her burning up, of her getting too drunk to do her trick correctly and incinerating herself until all that remained were ashes. But she looked solid and whole on my sofa, her skin still that translucent shell, nearly iridescent, her lips parted into a smile, her green eyes wide and filled with hope.

Stray kitten, ma'am, won't you take me in?

"You can't stay," I said.

"Nice fucking greeting." Those big green eyes went dark. Her voice held razor blades and whiskey. That's what Jenny hid right beneath the surface: Metal shards and Kentucky bourbon. She could take you to a faraway place, a dreamscape you'd never been to, build the pleasure until your eyes rolled up and your heart tried to escape from your chest. And then somehow, when you awoke from the bliss, she'd have burned through your credit rating, cremated all your closest relationships and left even the clothes in your closet soot-stained, singed and smelling of smoke.

"My husband will be home soon," I said. It wasn't a lie. "You have to leave."

"No drink for the road? No kiss for old time's sake? No fuck with your hands over your head and your eyes shut tight?" I could remember being fucked by Jenny. I could remember the ways she could make me come, her small hand curled into a fist and working inside me. Pleasure, always tainted with a little bit of pain. That's what you get when you fuck a dragon.

"You can't," I started, "you have to…" but she was up, moving quickly toward me, her hands around my waist, her lips on my lips. I remained frozen. Her heat would not melt me. Not anymore. I had Rick. I had my sanity. I had money in the bank. All sorts of things I'd had none of with Jenny. But her hand was insinuating down the front of my sweats and her fingers were searching out my clit in that rough, gaudy way they always did. Dime-store trick, carny whore.

I pushed hard. She fell back on the sofa. "You've changed," she snarled, top lip raised.

"I got *married*," I told her. I didn't care if she could put her fingers up inside me and make me come like nobody else ever had. I didn't care if Rick and I hadn't gotten to the true kink yet. We were still young. We'd get there.

"Let me meet your man. I'll leave after. I swear. I just need to know that you're truly happy."

"I'm truly happy."

"I saw your work. You only paint like that when something's wrong in your world."

"You'd know," I said softly. "You put me in that state so many times. But it's different now. Rick makes me happy. And I paint better."

"You sound like a fucking Hallmark card."

"I sound like a normal person."

She laughed, but she stood. I was relieved. She wasn't going to hang around. "There's no such thing as normal," she said, and I saw her fan her fingers out, magically showing me five crisp twenties. I knew she'd taken them from my underwear drawer. It's where I always kept a bit of extra. Pot in the coffee can. Cash with the knickers. In case you ever need a quick favor and I'm not there to let you in.

"See ya, Lola," she said as she left. I didn't move until the door clicked shut. Then I went to my bed and masturbated like a fiend.

"I smell smoke," Rick announced when he came home. "Did you light up without me, babe?"

I was still tangled in the white cotton sheets. Since I paint all day, I love surrounding myself in pure whiteness when I dream. Only imaginary colors stain my sheets. "You could say that," I said. "Jenny stopped by."

I hadn't told him everything there was to know about my ex, but I'd spilled as much as I dared. He'd been consumed by her portrait, wanting to own the very last dirty detail of how we'd behaved together. Emotionally, physically, sexually. I knew he was turned on by what I'd told him, but I still hadn't come entirely clean about our bondage-drenched nights. What if he balked? What if he turned away? I loved him, and I didn't want to scare him. So I'd told him most, but not everything there was to know.

"Did you fuck her?"

"Come on, Rick. I'd never cheat on you. You know that."

"But *would* you fuck her?"

That was a different question. Canvases Rick had never seen flickered through my mind. I had never told him about the time she cuffed me to the shower rod and used her leather belt on me. Never told him about the time she splayed me on the kitchen floor and licked my pussy for hours without letting me come, a candle in her hand, drip-dripping wax all over my body whenever I got too close to climax.

"She's dangerous," I said. "You heard what she's like."

"For me?"

I stared at him. What was he asking?

"I mean, if I was there, if I were watching, you wouldn't be cheating. It would be three of us together. I don't care how I participate. I could play with you, or I could sit in a chair across the room and never even move. You could even tie me down."

He was on the mattress. He had my right hand in his. He brought my fingertips to his lips.

"You touched yourself and thought of her," he said.

"I thought of you," I lied.

He started kissing me. My neck. My breasts. He pushed the sheets away and went for the split between my legs. "I can't do for you what she did."

"Thank fucking god," I said, tilting my hips.

"No, I mean, I can't be a girl."

"Ditto to what I just said," I murmured. "I don't want a girl." I was moving on the mattress, reaching for his cock.

"Lola." He threw me back on the bed and held me there. I looked into his eyes. We had not done this yet.

We had fucked like animals fuck. He had taken me against the wall. He had driven his cock hard into my ass, a drizzle of lube making the ride sublime. But we had done no power play. Not the kind where you might need a safeword. The term *bondage* hadn't even rippled between us. Until now. "You stay," he said. He had his fingertips pressed against my clit. He alternated between licking that hard bud and rubbing his thumb directly across the top. Giving me too much pressure, too much pleasure, all at once.

"Let me watch," he whispered, and he let his thumb side into my pussy.

"I don't even know where she went." But as I said the words, I knew I wasn't telling the whole truth. Sure she'd disappeared, as she always did, leaving only a vapor trail behind. But the look on her face as she'd walked out of the house told me that she'd be back.

I was wrong.

Jenny didn't come to our house. She went after Rick, all by himself.

Rick's a used car salesman. Before you make up your mind what that means, you have to know him. In his real life, in the garage, he is the type of brilliant mechanic who can take apart the most complicated engine and put the pieces back together. I believe he could do this blindfolded. He operates on touch and sense. He loves cars, the smooth clean lines, the purr of a good motor, the way I love the smell of my paints, the feel of my favorite brushes in my hands.

Rick spent years under cars, getting paid for doing what he loves. And then he was wooed away by the owner of a car dealership—a high-end retro vintage spot where Rick's good looks and the cars' sleek styles come together in happy harmony. Rick makes you want to drive off the lot in a cherry '55 Chevy, and he makes you almost believe that when you do, the whole world will tip on its axis and you will slide back in time to when the car was new and the world was simpler.

How'd Jenny find him? She has her ways. Thank god, Rick had seen her picture. He recognized her right off, even with all her clothes on. He told me later how she appeared behind him, coming up quick and quiet. She's like that. That whole morning fog on cat's feet, suddenly all around you in a haze of silver. He turned, and she was there, acting as if she had never seen anything prettier than the car on the showroom floor—and yet wanting, he said, wanting him to tell her that the car did not compare with her own fire-brand of beauty.

She chose a car with flames. Of course she did. Scarlet flames licking up from the grille. She wanted a test drive, but she didn't have ID, wouldn't cough up her name. He passed, and she tried harder. I remember Jenny when she used to turn up the heat so the flames licked you from every angle.

What was she thinking? That she'd get Rick in the car, drive him off to the Hollywood Hills and fuck him? And then what? She wasn't into any long haul. Would she come back and gloat to me, or simply move on down the road with another bite mark out of her belt?

Doesn't matter. Rick didn't fall. But he came home that night and told me everything, from the way her red patent leather shoes buckled at the ankles to the way her seamed stockings were perfectly in place.

I sat on the edge of the bed and I looked in his eyes.

"She's going to come here next," I told him. "I know her. She got a whiff of you, a scent of me and she'll be trying her best to get between us."

"She wants you back?"

I shook my head. "She's not wired like that. But if she can't have me, then she wants me to be as miserably unhappy as she is every day of her life."

"I want to see her fuck you," Rick said.

"Even if it means burning up what we've got?"

"It won't," he promised. "I swear."

When she showed up again, it was nothing like I expected. Never is. She was there all in white on the doorstep, bottle of champagne in one hand, scarlet blooms in the other. I smelled rat even above the roses.

"Just a late wedding gift," she said, "since I didn't get an invite."

"You left no forwarding address."

Rick came up behind me and waited for the introductions. I let Jenny in, reluctantly, and she strode forward as if I'd given her the passkey to my soul.

"Lovely place you have here," she said, sneering at

the fact that our pad was clean. There were no piles of ashes anywhere to be seen. Dinner was makeshift, unplanned, awkward. Champagne gave way to whiskey, which gave way to Rick kissing me in front of Jenny and then looking at her straight in the eye. "Do you think you do better than I do?"

"I know it for a fact."

"Show me."

I started to understand this wasn't about Rick getting off on seeing two girls together. He wanted to know what hold Jenny had over me, what she could do that he could not.

Jenny gripped my hair in her hand and pulled me back for a kiss. I grimaced, but I did not flinch. She bit my bottom lip hard, hard enough to leave marks, to draw blood, and then she slapped my face, so that I put a hand up to the sting and stared at her. "You like that?"

I nodded. I couldn't help myself. I refused to look at Rick.

She tightened her fist in my hair and then she led me like that to the bedroom. Rick followed.

"Do you have cuffs?"

Rick shook his head, while I motioned to my bottom drawer. Rick looked surprised as Jenny lifted the sterling handcuffs from amidst the tangle of my stockings. "You sure you have the key?" I pointed to my jewelry box. Jenny had my wrists over my head in seconds, had my clothes cut off me and my body smack in the center of the bed.

"Roll over," she said. "Show me your ass."

I obeyed, on autopilot. Rick had said he wanted this. Be careful what you wish for.

"See how wet she is?" Jenny asked him. "Part her legs and touch for yourself."

Rick's fingers felt my wet, slicked-up pussy lips.

"Now, watch this," Jenny said. I saw her undo his belt buckle and pull the leather free. I saw the look on Rick's face as she snapped the leather in the air and then landed the first stripe on my ass. "She's tough," Jenny said. "She can take more than you think she can. And she likes it rough."

Jenny striped me with the belt. This was my penance for moving on, my punishment for being happy now that she was gone. I accepted every stinging stripe, every fiery blow. What was Rick thinking? I couldn't waste a second on that. But Jenny could. She grabbed his hand again and thrust it into my pussy. "See? She's so fucking wet, isn't she? Taste her."

She pushed on him, and Rick climbed between the V of my legs and pressed his face to the split of my body. His tongue against my clit had me crooning under my breath. I didn't care if Jenny saw this. I didn't care about anything except pain and pleasure—melting together—filling me up.

"Move back," she said, and she started to stripe me again, that belt like fire on my skin. "I like to make her earn the climax. I like to make her cry out, beg for release."

She knew exactly how much I could take, and only

when my ass felt hot and throbbing, swollen from the punishment, did she drop the belt next to me on the mattress.

"You do it like this," she said, and she shoved me over and sealed her face to my pussy, sucking on my clit as if she'd never stop. My hands were cuffed. I couldn't push her away, but Rick could have, and he didn't. He sat next to her and watched—learned everything he could in a few short minutes. When I came, I saw angels, I swear, wings beating in front of me. I saw fire, white-hot plumes of smoke, and then I saw Jenny's face, that sneer, grinning down at me.

"You like it," she said. "You'll always like it like that, won't you, slut?"

Then she kissed Rick—my taste clearly on her lips—and patted him on the cheek.

"You keep her satisfied, won't you, stud? The way she needs. The way she craves. I won't bother you anymore, if you promise me that."

He nodded, but he seemed too shocked to speak. Jenny was up then, in motion, fumbling around in my jewelry drawer, reaching for the key. "I ought to leave you like that," she said with wet steel in her voice, but she tossed the key to Rick. Her hand darted into my dresser drawer, and I knew she was palming the few twenties that remained.

"Don't make me come back," she said, smiling at us as she left the room. I heard her heels, heard the front door close.

Rick looked at me. I didn't know what he'd say, what he'd do. He moved forward, as if he was going to unlock the cuffs, and then he set the key down on the edge of the mattress where I could see it and reached for the belt once more. I felt my stomach tighten as he rolled me over onto my stomach.

"So that's how you like it?" he asked, his voice harsh.

I nodded.

"Why didn't you say?"

"I thought we'd get there...."

"We're there," he said, and he snapped the belt, making it sing just like Jenny had. "Oh, baby, we're there now."

And we were—we are—in that place where pain and pleasure meet, where they war to top each other. Rick takes care of me in all the dirty ways I so desperately crave. He makes sure I go to sleep with my ass hot from his palm or his belt. He collars me, cuffs me, works me the way I need. So I have Jenny to thank for that, I guess. My dragon girlfriend, my lover from hell.

But I'll tell you one thing. I never did sell the painting. I took it out to the backyard the next morning. Rick doused the edges with gasoline. Together we watched the canvas burn.

ABOUT THE AUTHORS

VIDA BAILEY (heatsuffused.blogspot.com) lives in Ireland, where she infrequently writes erotica. You can find her work in *Love at First Sting*, edited by Alison Tyler, *Steamlust* by Kristina Wright and *Bound by Lust* by Shanna Germain.

By day, **JAX BAYNARD** is a financial investment advisor. By night, she makes her own (and her clients') fantasies come true. This part-time dominatrix's short fiction has appeared online, in several literary journals and in *Pleasure Bound*, *Kiss My Ass* and *Torn*.

HEIDI CHAMPA (heidichampa.blogspot.com) has been published in numerous anthologies including *Best Women's Erotica 2010*, *Playing With Fire*, *Frenzy* and

Ultimate Curves. She has also steamed up the pages of *Bust* Magazine. If you prefer your erotica in electronic form, she can be found at *Clean Sheets*, Ravenous Romance, *Oysters and Chocolate* and *The Erotic Woman*.

Called a "legendary erotica heavy-hitter" (by the über-legendary Violet Blue), **ANDREA DALE** (cyvarwydd.com) hopes none of the "golfing" members of her family read her story. Her work has appeared in about 100 anthologies from Harlequin Spice, Avon Red and Cleis Press, and is available online at Soul's Road Press.

KIKI DELOVELY (kikidelovely.wordpress.com) is a queer femme writer/performer whose work has appeared in various publications, including *Best Lesbian Erotica 2011* and *2012*, *Salacious* Magazine, *Take Me There: Transgender and Genderqueer Erotica* and *Say Please: Lesbian BDSM Erotica*. Kiki's passions include magical realism, the Oxford comma and taking on research for her writing.

MADELINE ELAYNE is a bisexual polyamorous leather switch, but if that's too much of a mouthful, she happily suggests the shortened but still entirely accurate "slut." Her biggest bondage fetish is incorporating long hair into precarious rope bondage scenarios, or just lovely and convenient leashes. Mmm...rope.

LUCY FELTHOUSE (lucyfelthouse.co.uk) studied creative writing at university. She has had stories published by Cleis Press, Noble Romance, Ravenous Romance, Resplendence Publishing, Sweetmeats Press, Xcite Books, Constable and Robinson, Decadent Publishing, Ellora's Cave, Evernight Publishing and House of Erotica.

ADR FORTE (www.adrforte.com) is the author of erotic short fiction that appears in numerous anthologies, including *Hurts so Good* and *Pleasure Bound*, also edited by Alison Tyler. Her tales of erotic fantasy can be found in collections from Cleis Press and Circlet Press.

SHANNA GERMAIN (shannagermain.com) has been a writer her whole life; thus, she has never been and never will be rich. Her favorite bondage involves twenty-cent plastic clothespins and a forty-dollar red leather hogtie. Find her erotic work in places like *Alison's Wonderland*, *Best American Erotica*, *Best Bondage Erotica 2*, *Best Lesbian Erotica*, *Playing With Fire* and more.

STELLA HARRIS (stellaharris.net) has been getting off to erotic fiction for as long as she can remember. She's been published by Cleis Press, Storm Moon Press, Naughty Nights Press and others. She loves predicament bondage because it's a stunningly accurate metaphor for life.

D. L. KING's (dlkingerotica.blogspot.com) short stories have appeared in titles such as *Best Women's Erotica, One Night Only, Luscious, Please, Ma'am* and many others. She is also the editor of *Seductress, The Harder She Comes, Spankalicious, Voyeur Eyes Only, Carnal Machines, Spank!, The Sweetest Kiss* and *Where the Girls Are.*

KRISTINA LLOYD (kristinalloyd.co.uk) is the author of three erotic novels, including the controversial *Asking for Trouble.* Her short stories have appeared in numerous anthologies and her work has been translated into German, Dutch and Japanese. She has a master's degree in twentieth-century literature and lives in Brighton, UK.

SOMMER MARSDEN (sommermarsden.blogspot.com) is the wine-swigging, wiener-dog-owning, wannabe runner author responsible for *Learning to Drown, Hard Lessons, Wanderlust* and *Lucky 13.* Her work has cropped up all over the Web.

DEREK MCDANIEL is an experienced S/M player who recently decided to start writing down his outlandish fantasies. He lives in California with, at present, a girlfriend, a slave and a husky.

N.T. MORLEY (ntmorley.com) is the author of more than twenty-five novels of erotic dominance and submission. These include *The Parlor*, *The Limousine*, *The Visitor*, *The Appointment*, *The Addendum*, *The Embezzler*, *Ashley's New Owner* and *Honeymoon in Bondage*, plus the trilogies *The Castle*, *The Library* and *The Office*.

DEVIN PHILLIPS is the pseudonym of a San Franciscan who only started writing naughty stories at a kinky boyfriend's request, and is now addicted. She's still pretty thrilled that other people want to read them! She lives in San Francisco with said kinky boyfriend and occasionally a few other playmates.

GISELLE RENARDE (wix.com/gisellerenarde/erotica) is a queer Canadian, avid volunteer, contributor to more than 50 short story anthologies and author of dozens of electronic and print books, including *Anonymous*, *Audrey & Lawrence*, *The Red Satin Collection*, *Ondine* and 2011 Rainbow Awards Honorable Mention *My Mistress' Thighs: Erotic Transgender Fiction and Poetry*.

TERESA NOELLE ROBERTS heeded that high-school advice to write about what she knows, which means she's been published in *Best Bondage Erotica* 2011 and 2012, *Kinky Girls*, *Pleasure Bound: True Bondage Stories* and dozens of other anthologies with blush-inducing titles. She also writes paranormal erotic romances, but she swears the paranormal part is purely imagination.

THOMAS S. ROCHE's novel *The Panama Laugh* was a finalist for the Horror Writers' Association's Bram Stoker Award. Roche's other books include the Noirotica series of erotic crime-noir, the story collection *Dark Matter* and four collections of fantasy and horror. A prolific blogger, Roche writes regularly for TinyNibbles.com, Boiled-Hard.com, Thomasroche.com and many other blogs.

MARIA SEE is a Brooklyn native living in San Francisco. Her writing can be found in collections including *Visible: A Femmethology*, *Gotta Have It: 69 Stories of Sudden Sex* and *Say Please: Lesbian BDSM Erotica*. You can write Maria at maria@mariasee.com and follow her on Twitter (@aproblemlike).

DONNA GEORGE STOREY (DonnaGeorgeStorey.com) is the author of an erotic novel, *Amorous Woman*, based on her own experiences living in Japan. Her adults-only tales have appeared in numerous places including *Best Women's Erotica*, *Best Erotic Romance*, *Alison's Wonderland* and *Morning, Noon and Night*.

SOPHIA VALENTI (sophiavalenti.blogspot.com) is the author of *Indecent Desires*, an erotic novella of spanking and submission. Her fiction has appeared in the Harlequin Spice anthologies *Alison's Wonderland* and *With This Ring, I Thee Bed*, as well as several Pretty Things Press books, including *Kiss My Ass*, *Skirting the Issue*, *Bad Ass* and *Torn*.

SHARON WACHSLER lives in rural New England, where she blogs, trains dogs and flogs a disability rights agenda. Sharon's erotica appears in several dozen publications, most recently *Dormitory Heat*, *Girl Fever*, *Periphery* and *Best Lesbian Erotica 2012*. She blogs at aftergadget.wordpress.com (@aftergadget) and occupyathome.wordpress.com (@occupy_at_home), and writes for AbilityMaine.org.

RITA WINCHESTER's work has appeared in print anthologies such as *Frenzy*, *Afternoon Delight*, *I is for Indecent*, *Tasting Her* and *Mammoth Lesbian Erotica*. Rita has been tied to the same partner forever. Visit her very, very neglected MySpace page at www.myspace.com/ritawinchester.

ABOUT THE EDITOR

Called "a trollop with a laptop" by *East Bay Express*, "a literary siren" by Good Vibrations and "the mistress of literary erotica" by Violet Blue, **ALISON TYLER** is naughty and she knows it.

Over the past two decades, Ms. Tyler has written more than twenty-five explicit novels, including *Tiffany Twisted*, *Melt with You* and *The ESP Affair.* Her novels and short stories have been translated into Japanese, Dutch, German, Italian, Norwegian, Spanish and Greek. When not writing sultry short stories, she edits erotic anthologies, including *Alison's Wonderland*, *Kiss My Ass*, *Skirting the Issue* and *Torn*.

Ms. Tyler is loyal to coffee (black), lipstick (red) and tequila (straight). She has tattoos, but no piercings; a wicked tongue, but a quick smile; and bittersweet memories, but no regrets. She believes it won't rain if she doesn't bring an umbrella, prefers hot and dry to cold and wet and loves to spout her favorite motto: You can sleep when you're dead. She chooses Led Zeppelin over the Beatles, the Cure over NIN and the Stones over everyone. Yet although she appreciates good rock, she has a pitiful weakness for '80s hair bands.

In all things important, she remains faithful to her partner of seventeen years, but she still can't choose just one perfume.

More from Alison Tyler

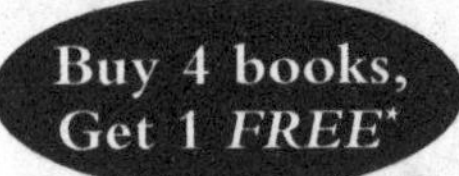

Frenzy
60 Stories of Sudden Sex
Edited by Alison Tyler

"Toss out the roses and box of candies. This isn't a prolonged seduction. This is slammed against the wall in an alleyway sex, and it's all that much hotter for it."
—Erotica Readers & Writers Association
ISBN 978-1-57344-331-9 $14.95

Best Bondage Erotica
Edited by Alison Tyler

Always playful and dangerously explicit, these arresting fantasies grab you, tie you down, and never let you go.
ISBN 978-1-57344-173-5 $15.95

Afternoon Delight
Erotica for Couples
Edited by Alison Tyler

"Alison Tyler evokes a world of heady sensuality where fantasies are fearlessly explored and dreams gloriously realized."
—Barbara Pizio, Executive Editor,
Penthouse Variations
ISBN 978-1-57344-341-8 $14.95

Got a Minute?
60 Second Erotica
Edited by Alison Tyler

"Classy but very, very dirty, this is one of the few very truly indispensable filth anthologies around." —*UK Forum*
ISBN 978-1-57344-404-0 $14.95

Playing with Fire
Taboo Erotica
Edited by Alison Tyler

"Alison Tyler has managed to find the best stories from the best authors, and create a book of fantasies that—if you're lucky enough, or determined enough—just might come true." —Clean Sheets
ISBN 978-1-57344-348-7 $14.95

Read the Very Best in Erotica

Buy 4 books, Get 1 _FREE_

Fairy Tale Lust
Erotic Fantasies for Women
Edited by Kristina Wright
Foreword by Angela Knight

Award-winning novelist and top erotica writer Kristina Wright goes over the river and through the woods to find the sexiest fairy tales ever written.
ISBN 978-1-57344-397-5 $14.95

In Sleeping Beauty's Bed
Erotic Fairy Tales
By Mitzi Szereto

"Classic fairy tale characters like Rapunzel, Little Red Riding Hood, Cinderella, and Sleeping Beauty, just to name a few, are brought back to life in Mitzi Szereto's delightful collection of erotica fairy tales."
—Nancy Madore, author of *Enchanted: Erotic Bedtime Stories for Women*
ISBN 978-1-57344-376-8 $16.95

Frenzy
60 Stories of Sudden Sex
Edited by Alison Tyler

"Toss out the roses and box of candies. This isn't a prolonged seduction. This is slammed against the wall in an alleyway sex, and it's all that much hotter for it."
—Erotica Readers & Writers Association
ISBN 978-1-57344-331-9 $14.95

Fast Girls
Erotica for Women
Edited by Rachel Kramer Bussel

Fast Girls celebrates the girl with a reputation, the girl who goes all the way, and the girl who doesn't know how to say "no."
ISBN 978-1-57344-384-5 $14.95

Can't Help the Way That I Feel
Sultry Stories of African American Love, Lust and Fantasy
Edited by Lori Bryant-Woolridge

Some temptations are just too tantalizing to ignore in this collection of delicious stories edited by Emmy award-winning and *Essence* bestselling author Lori Bryant-Woolridge.
ISBN 978-1-57344-386-9 $14.95

* Free book of equal or lesser value. Shipping and applicable sales tax extra.
Cleis Press • (800) 780-2279 • orders@cleispress.com
www.cleispress.com

Ordering is easy! Call us toll free or fax us to place your MC/VISA order.
You can also mail the order form below with payment to:
Cleis Press, 2246 Sixth St., Berkeley, CA 94710.

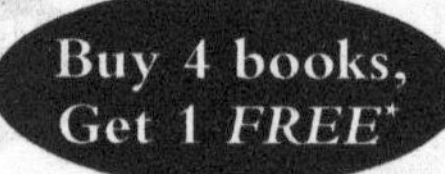

ORDER FORM

QTY	TITLE	PRICE

SUBTOTAL ________

SHIPPING ________

SALES TAX ________

TOTAL ________

Add $3.95 postage/handling for the first book ordered and $1.00 for each additional book. Outside North America, please contact us for shipping rates. California residents add 8.75% sales tax. Payment in U.S. dollars only.

*** Free book of equal or lesser value. Shipping and applicable sales tax extra.**

Cleis Press • Phone: (800) 780-2279 • Fax: (510) 845-8001
orders@cleispress.com • www.cleispress.com
You'll find more great books on our website

Follow us on Twitter @cleispress • Friend/fan us on Facebook

9 781573 449076